BOOTIE AND THE BEAST

BOOTIE AND THE BEAST

FALGUNI KOTHARI

eBook ISBN: 978-1-944048-07-5
Paperback ISBN: 978-1-944048-08-2

Cover design by Ebook Launch
Formatting by Kate Tilton's Author Services, LLC
Editing by Jovana Shirley, Unforeseen Editing

Previously published by Harlequin, India (2014)

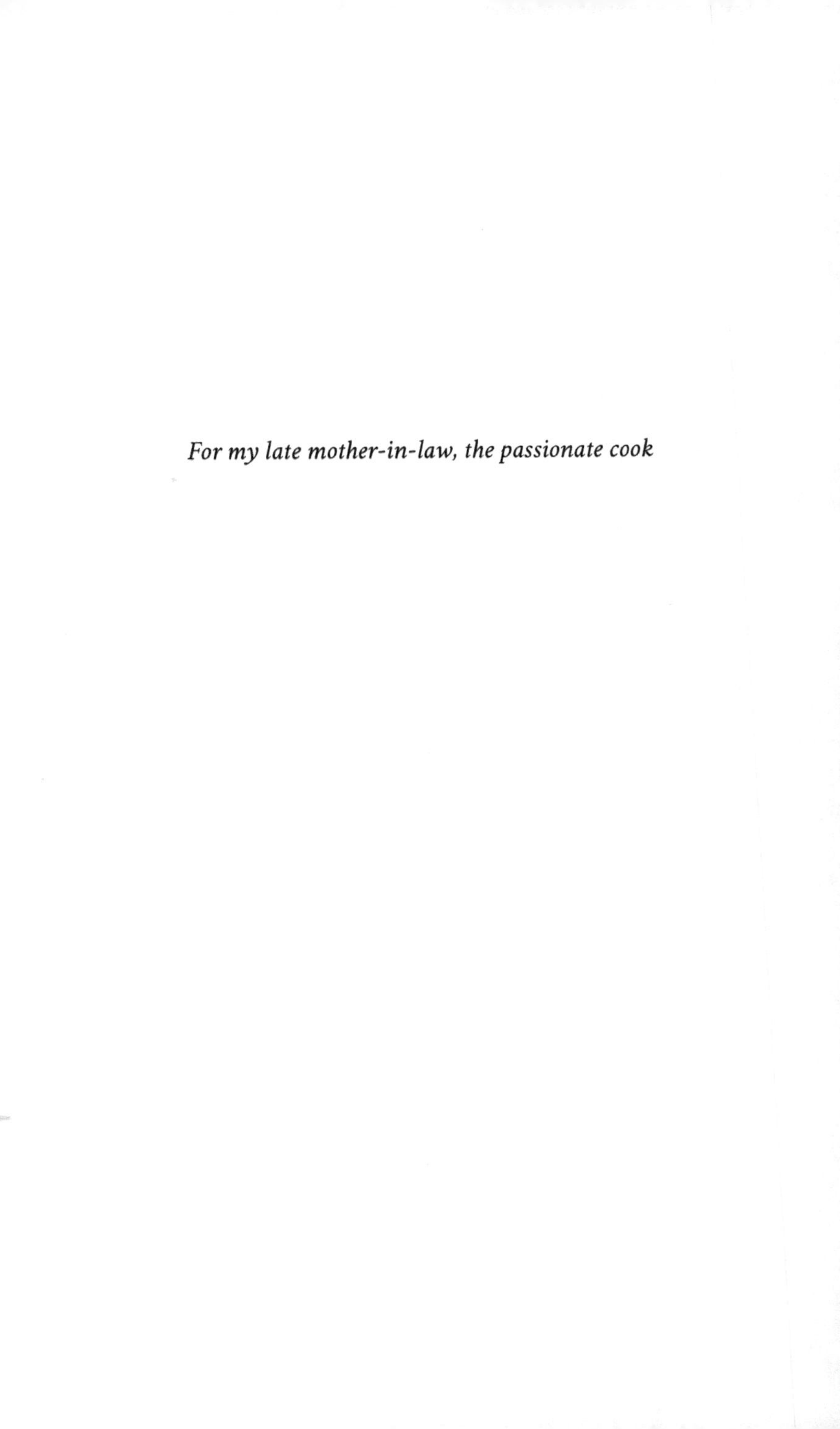

ONCE UPON AN UN-FAIRY TALE ...

Dear Diary,

What a sucky Sunday. Leesha cried and was sad and quiet all day. She's been like that since Savitri Aunty went to Pune to live with her brother after the big fight with Chandra Uncle. My mother says Savitri Aunty will come back soon, but Leesha doesn't believe it. She misses her *amma* like crazy. So much so that she won't even play with me. Not even the Asian Barbie and Ken dolls that Daddy got us from his dentist conference in Singapore tempt her. She said we were too old to play with dolls.

We are eleven! How is that old?

She won't come down to the building playground either. And she won't laugh at my jokes.

Remember the sick little *billi* Krish found under a Maruti in the building parking lot? Leesha looks like that. And Krish won't help her feel better like he helped the kitty cat. I yelled at him to be nice to his sister, but he won't listen to me. He got angry with me and told me to butt out of his life. Vallima and Priya *didi* want me to leave him alone. They think he's sad, too. (I don't believe them. Krish is not sad. If he were sad, he would cry and want hugs from us and not go off with his friends and play cricket all day long and smoke and have beer.)

He made Priya *didi* smoke and drink beer. I saw them do it from my bedroom window. (I was not spying on them!) I told Daddy about it. And, now, my sister is angry with me. She said I was a big mouth with a pea brain.

Remember my wish to marry Krish one day and live in a big house by a huge pond with both our families? I've changed my mind. I do NOT want to marry him anymore. I will marry a real prince, like William or Harry. Someone who has an enormous kingdom and lives in a humungous castle full of pretty white horses with pink bows on their tails. My prince will be very nice to me and his sister and my sister and all of our family, even to grumpy old Dadima. He will give me hundreds of gifts every day. He will not give away the cat to the watchman. That's what made Leesha cry today. Little Kitty had been her *billi*.

And Krish is a BIG FAT MEANIE. I hate him so much. So, note this, dear Diary: he is NOT my prince. He is a BEAST.

Dee

CHAPTER 1

BEAUTY MATHUR: FLIRTING WITH THE
FAIRY TALE

The bold black caption was scrawled across Diya Mathur's burlap-clad hips on the cover of *Pomp Adore*'s latest issue. The tattoo of a budding red rose teased upward over her left hip, inking a path to the flat oval of her belly button that apparently had the power to send men into paroxysms of irrepressible psychosis. A year ago, an online tabloid had made Diya's belly button infamous by citing that world-famous men—movie stars, princes, sheikhs, Fortune 500 list-makers, and the like—fought for the honor to sip champagne out of it.

Krish Menon stared at the glossy image of Diya's navel for a prolonged moment and snorted when it failed to induce any kind of madness in him. Admittedly, he wasn't a movie star or a sheikh or a prince or a tycoon or prone to flights of fancy.

That must be it, he mused.

And the fact that Diya was his buddy and an honorary sister might have something to do with it, too. If he jogged his memory back twenty-nine years, he could almost visualize the red-faced, snotty newborn she had been with the black thread poking out of her belly instead of a navel. The cut umbilical cord had grossed him out but had also fascinated him as he'd watched Lubna Aunty massage Baby Diya one morning. He'd been a fount of questions about it and about infants, he remembered. Diya was the first baby he'd held in his five-year-old arms. Diya's parents, good friends and neighbors to his own parents, had trusted him not to drop her on her perfectly round thirty-three-centimeter head. By the time his own sister, Alisha, was born not two months later, he'd been a veteran baby handler.

Krish drew his eyes up from Diya's belly button, lingering on her toned and religiously worked-out abs for a few seconds before coming to rest on her "perfect handfuls of breasts." A different tabloid had run that headline, and the writer's completely arbitrary form of measuring female anatomy had irritated Krish to no end. It still did. But, as Diya had pointed out too many times to count, his outdated and conservative attitude was his problem and not hers.

Krish pitied the man Diya the Diva would eventually choose to marry and hoped the dude had nerves of steel. He'd need them if he had to see his wife's near-naked torso splashed across billboards and magazines on a daily basis.

In *Pomp Adore*, Diya's "handfuls" were artfully covered in a swatch of burlap and were peeking through an explosion of dark hair that spilled over her shapely shoulders and torso. Her peaches-and-cream skin had been either Photoshopped or spray-painted to a lovely golden hue. Smoky black eyes stared out of a heart-shaped face, and nude-colored, fleshy lips were parted slightly, showcasing the twin rows of white teeth poised to take a bite out of the apple cupped in one hand. The picture was the perfect blend of innocence and sensuality, as if Snow White were superimposed on the biblical Eve.

Krish flipped open the widely read and respected fashion magazine to its dog-eared center where the main article ran. Cinderella laughed out of the page, fortified by a mountain of shoes. On the adjacent page, Belle coyly offered a blood-red rose to a starry-eyed beast. The theme of the spread was bang-on target for its model. Diya's head forever wallowed in the clouds. She skipped through life, dressed in designer clothes, smiling and waving at the world with a pair of rose-tinted sunglasses perched on a slightly stubby nose. Even the cute imperfection of her nose did nothing to skew Diya's fairy-tale take on existence.

Would the rumor that had gone viral across the media this week change the status quo?

He snorted again, underscoring his doubt at the thought. Rolling the magazine closed with a few deft twists of his hands, he stashed the thick scroll into the Range Rover's glove compartment just as a private jet landed on the runway of Dallas Executive Airport. The gray-and-white plane had a capital JES embossed on its tail in red. Or was that pink? He couldn't tell the colors apart. The plane sailed down the airstrip and rolled to a stop barely a dozen feet away from the car.

No, not a mere fairy tale, he amended with a heavy sigh.

Diya's life played like a Cannes Film Festival these days, complete with palatial villas, race cars, jets, yachts, and glam-our-red carpets to strut on. She'd made her mark in the fashion world just as she'd claimed she would. If she only stayed clear of trouble, he might even applaud her achievements to her face.

The door of the midsized aircraft pushed out and dropped open as a staircase. When a bright red carpet didn't spontaneously spill forth, Krish curbed his disappointment. Dallas, it was apparent, wasn't in league with the fashion capitals of the world. But would Beauty Mathur's visit turn it into a contender? Whoa! Now, that would be something. Maybe he should splurge for a warning ad in the *Dallas Observer*: *Run for cover, ye unsuspecting fools! Or be made over!*

While Krish amused himself at Diya's expense, a group of uniformed personnel—the same people who'd met him outside the glass-paneled terminal and escorted him to his parking spot on the airfield—came out of the building again and made their way across the tarmac. They threw an assortment of smiles, nods, and waves his way before boarding the plane where they'd verify passenger IDs, passports, visas, and whatever else needed verification before allowing the passengers to disembark—standard procedure for private planes and VIPs, or so the Immigration and Customs officers had informed him.

It was a whole other level of luxury travel.

As chief financial officer of Armadillo Farms and Foods, he enjoyed many perks and privileges, including flying business or first class across North America and sailing across the Gulf of Mexico in Danny "Dillo" Jones's boat for the annual company holiday. That was as far as his jet-setting experiences went. And even those days were numbered now that the company had been sold.

Armadillo was in its final stages of dissolution and assimilation within the newly expanded Wisco Organic Foods. Dillo was set to retire to his villa in the Florida Keys and spend the rest of his days sunning, sailing, and fishing. But, at thirty-five, Krish wasn't quite ready for beach life yet.

The plan: the offer was for Krish to move to Wisconsin and continue working for Wisco. He'd be the head of finance and a board member, just like he'd been at Armadillo, except with a contract binding him to Wisco for the next five years.

His financial package would more than compensate for the lock-in term. It was a sound opportunity—one he deserved because he had worked damn hard for it. So, why was his gut in a twist over it? Why did pouring all of his resources into a start-up sound so much more appealing? Not to mention, exciting?

Krish took a long, bracing breath, and pushing aside all thoughts of his foggy future, he climbed out of the Rover. Bright sunlight beat down on the tarmac, making him squint through his aviator shades. It was a pleasant Thursday afternoon in February, neither hot nor cold and not a cloud to be seen in the clear blue sky. A lazy winter day he'd intended to spend on the living room couch in his UT Arlington sweatshirt and ratty shorts, flipping channels and brooding about his future, when a phone call from Kamal Mathur had foiled his grand plans. In turn, Kamal Uncle's call had galvanized him to phone Diya, who was in Miami. He'd invited her to Dallas for a visit—insisted she come—and over a few texts, they'd sorted out the how, when, and where they would rendezvous.

He was surprised that Diya had accepted her father's decree to lie low in Dallas for a while instead of traveling to London or Istanbul or wherever she'd been scheduled to go next. Kamal Uncle didn't want her to step foot in Mumbai, not until the fiery rumors about her turned to ash. Krish had anticipated a horrendous phone joust with a fire-breathing virago, an argument about male chauvinism and female independence, and frankly, he felt a bit let down it hadn't come to that. After a pounding hot shower, he'd pulled on a crisp pair of jeans and a newish navy-blue pullover, gotten in the Rover, and driven to the airport to pick her up.

As he waited for Diya to disembark, a trio of spotted-brown chickadees flew in front of the plane. Tweeting, they spun playfully about before settling down on the stair rail like an avian welcome committee. The joyous chirping amplified when Beauty Mathur—brand ambassador of Jabbir Enterprises and Shipping's fashion label, Scheherazade—strolled out of the aircraft. At the exact moment, the sun chose to beam brighter and focus its golden spotlight on her.

The brightness reflected off Diya's white bolero jacket and denim shorts hurt Krish's eyes, as did the bejeweled belt cinching her tiny waist. A wide-brimmed straw hat protected the top half of her face from his view and from the sun. Diya didn't allow her skin to tan ever. The bottom half of her face curved into a stunning smile when she noticed the chickadees, and as he'd taught her when she was eight, she began whistling to them.

Krish's own face split into a grin at the familiar Cinderella phenomenon. But, before he could call out to her or raise his hand to catch her attention, a tall man in white linen pants and a short-sleeved linen shirt joined her on the landing. His overly handsome olive-skinned face creased into laughter at the cooing going on between the woman and the birds. He slid an arm around Diya's waist with ease, and she turned to him, giving him a radiant smile. The man leaned into her, murmuring in her ear, and then he kissed her upturned cheek.

Krish had seen enough media coverage of Diya and Hasaan Jabbir over the last few months to recognize the billionaire Anglo-Saudi shipping mogul and international playboy at first glance. Not only that, the Jabbir family held several diverse business interests all over the world—including their latest fashion venture, the House of Scheherazade—and were frequently in the news.

Hands curling into fists, Krish watched and wondered about the relationship between Diya and her boss. *Is the rumor true then?*

He swallowed the lump of spit that had lodged itself in his

throat. No, it couldn't be. Diya wasn't that stupid. But Kamal Uncle was right. Someone needed to drill some sense into her, and it looked like he'd been drafted for the task.

"Watch your step, Diya." Krish moved, striding toward the plane.

With luck, she'd heed the warning, both literally and figuratively.

Her whole posture went rigid when she finally noticed him, and Krish felt his own jaw tighten in response.

He didn't understand why she reacted to him in that way. *She* had refused his proposal. *She* had rejected him as a suitor. If anyone should be offended, it was him. Not the other way around. But had anything about her made sense to him ever?

"And a nice, polite hello to you, too, Beast," Diya said with a frosty smile. Then, she started down the stairs on a pair of glittery white stilettos, as if she hadn't a care in the world.

She called him Beast whenever he snarled at her in disapproval, which was pretty much constantly in recent years. She had a knack for getting under his skin, sometimes for no apparent reason. Biting back a slew of harsh words that wanted to leap out of his mouth, he kept his focus on the man following Diya down the steps. Krish reached them just as they stepped onto the tarmac.

Diya waved a hand between them. "Krish, meet Hasaan Jabbir, the genie behind Scheherazade. Hasaan, this is Krish Menon, the friend I told you about." She paused for a heartbeat, and then a slow smile melted the haughty expression off her face as they stared at each other. Krish felt an answering grin tug at his lips. "One of my closest childhood friends," she added before throwing her arms around him for a bear hug. Just as abruptly, she unhugged him and stepped back, giggling as she readjusted her hat on her head, which had gone askew.

Krish itched to yank her back into his arms, but he shook hands with the sheikh instead.

"*Merhaba*, Krish," Hasaan greeted in a lilting Arabic accent. "Diya speaks of you highly. Many thanks for your offer to meet us on such short notice. We seem to have a mess on our hands."

Hasaan was too good-looking, way too smooth, too damn much of everything for Krish's peace of mind. But the hell of it was, he sounded absolutely sincere. Krish reined in the urge to punch his smiley face.

"Interesting terminology. Is that what you call a pregnancy in your world? A mess?" If he couldn't punch the man, he'd at least verbally eviscerate his scruples—or the lack of them.

Not that he believed that Diya was foolish enough to get pregnant—even accidentally—and definitely not with a man who was reputed to be so unsteady in his affections. But the world believed she was, and neither Diya nor Scheherazade's publicists were denying the rumors. The question was, why?

"Krish." Diya's eyes narrowed in warning.

She knew him well enough to know he was on the verge of losing his temper. Hasaan, who didn't know him at all but had to know the ways of men, smiled crookedly and braced himself to take a hit by planting his feet a little wider.

Diya stepped between them, skewering each of them with a glare. Krish kept his eyes on Hasaan. Even the reverse progression of the Border Security officers coming out of the plane, four of them carrying three gigantic pink trunks and a pink carry-on, did not distract him.

His eyes dropped to Hasaan's chest where Diya's hand rested. *Are they a couple?*

"You are right to worry, Krish. I apologize for my rudeness for leaving Diya to explain the situation alone. But I must be on my way." Hasaan nodded at the plane, and Diya dropped her hand. "I need to get back before all hell breaks loose."

There is more trouble brewing? Damn it, what has Diya gotten herself into?

In a peculiarly humble move, Hasaan bowed and raised Diya's hand to his lips. "A thousand *shukrans*, my friend. I will not forget your support. *Khuda hafiz* … until we meet again."

Diya hugged Hasaan and kissed his cheeks three times, like they did in Europe. "*Al'afw*. There are no thanks between friends. And please stop worrying. Everything will be fine. Allah will make it so; you'll see. Just keep an open mind, all right? *Khuda hafiz*."

When the thank-yous, you're-welcomes, and god-keep-yous were done and Hasaan disappeared into the plane, Krish finally allowed himself to relax, though the tangle in his head remained. He wanted to bombard Diya with questions, but he'd wait for her explanation first.

"It's cooler here than in Miami," she remarked as they walked to the Rover. Correction: he walked, and Diya sauntered as if she was strolling down a runway, which—ha—she was, wasn't she? "Thank God we didn't have to go through immigration or baggage claim. Hasaan uses his diplomatic passport while traveling in the US … for political reasons … so we get the VIP treatment."

Krish grunted at the unwanted glimpse into the lifestyles of the rich and mighty and hurried forward to help the officers load the luggage into the Rover. He'd flattened the backseat already, and even then, the gigantic pink trunks were a tight fit. Diya would have to sit with the hand baggage on her lap like a plebeian on the drive home.

Baggage. Such a versatile word. It collectively applied to the woman, her luggage, and the situation she was in.

Krish silently berated himself for his uncharitable thoughts, especially when Diya slid into the front passenger seat and settled the carry-on on her lap without being prompted and without a pout. Sighing, he turned to the officers and thanked them, making sure nothing else needed to be done, like tips or fees or signatures of any kind.

There wasn't. Hasaan seemed to have taken care of everything. Krish cast a last glance at the plane as it whaled down the runway and cast off into the sky, taking Hasaan with it.

The chickadees had flown away, too. The baggage had been loaded. It was time to go home.

Krish got behind the wheel. The car's interior was drenched in Scheherazade now—the perfume Diya was being paid a bomb to endorse. Not a bad scent. It was strong, exotic with just a hint of jasmine. Just like its endorser.

Her hat had disappeared, and she was fussing with her hair, gathering it into a ball behind her head. She'd removed her jacket, and the neon pink of her shimmering blouse made Krish want to scratch at his eyeballs.

"Buckle up," he instructed gruffly and twisted the key in the ignition.

KRLD came on, announcing the local weather report. Hailstorm expected tonight and over the weekend. And, because he was still annoyed with her—or rather, annoyed that she could so easily twist his guts into a muddy puddle—he put on his characteristic honorary-older-brother sneer.

"The plastic bags are in the side pocket," he said, making her frown in confusion. "For the morning sickness or afternoon sickness, Dee-Dumbs."

Diya's rosebud lips stretched flat in displeasure. But, instead of socking his smart-aleck mouth with a fist—she'd stopped retaliating in that manner years ago—she fished out a pair of diamond-studded sunglasses from her bag and slid them on. They covered nearly half of her face; the frames were that huge. Then, she pulled out a heart-shaped box of baklava from her bag and tossed it in his lap. He loved baklava. She'd remembered.

"Happy Valentine's Day, Beast," she said tonelessly, making Krish feel about two feet tall.

Mere words of thanks or apology wouldn't do this time, he thought. *Nope, it wouldn't do at all.*

CHAPTER 2

BOOTIE MATHUR: FAIRY TALE OR FLIRTY TALE?

The digitally manipulated picture beneath the pun-riddled headline was hideous. Her pose and the burlap sarong were the only two things true to the *Pomp Adore* cover. In the pic, her hair looked unwashed and unkempt, her eyes wild and scary. Her blood-red lips were peeled apart in a facsimile of vampire fangs that were about to rip into the bow-tied, fungus-ridden bootie in her hand. Her abdomen was no longer defined but distended from an advanced pregnancy. The rose tattoo had been expanded, colored fully black, and its thorns seemed to be digging viciously into the green-veined skin of her stomach.

Diya Mathur swallowed the panic that had been threatening to choke her ever since she'd lost her mind and completely demolished her already-notorious reputation to save a dude in distress. What had she been thinking? Hasaan didn't need her to be his knight in shining armor. He was more than capable of saving his own skin. But no, her quixotic goodwill had reared its pretty little head—all wobbly because of a teensy bit of guilt since she *was* partly to blame for the fiasco—and thrown itself in front of the mega merger about to put a speed bump on Hasaan's carefree bachelor life. But even knowing she'd done the right thing didn't stop Diya's stomach from churning like the giant cement mixer she spotted on a construction site on the road. She prayed she wouldn't really have to use the stupid vomit bags the Beast had referred to as a joke.

"Fairy tales are going to ruin this child." Dadima had predicted Diya's fate in a dour tone and with a dire shake of her unnaturally black head.

Diya had been six years old then and had refused to change out of her glittery-blue Sleeping Beauty costume until Prince Charming arrived at her doorstep, bearing new clothes for their wedding.

Diya hadn't believed her cantankerous old grandmother then, and she wouldn't believe it now, even with the *stone the pregnant infidel to death* threats looming over her head. Fairy tales were her lucky charms, her survival mantras. They could never harm her. In fact, they helped her put life in its proper perspective.

Example: her Sleeping Beauty phase, which she'd pretty much spent in a haze of denial, waiting for Prince Charming —aka the Beast—to grow up. The phase had ended the night of her twenty-first birthday when she realized the magnitude of her self-delusion. Soon after the figurative eye-opening event, she'd announced her ambition to be a fashion model to the world, starting with her best friend, Alisha Menon— sorry, Chawla now that Leesha was married to Mr. Hunk Charming, Aryan Chawla. Anyway, Diya had whispered her plans in Leesha's ear because she was mortally afraid of what her dentist parents, Kamal and Lubna Mathur, and gynecologist sister, Priya Shroff née Mathur, would say about yet another vocation switch—her one hundred and eighth one. Soon-to-be advocate Leesha hadn't laughed at Diya's proclamation or acknowledged it. She'd simply disconnected the phone.

Not at all put off by her BFF's rudeness, Diya had forged full-speed ahead with her new plans and more or less parked her size-two bottom at Mumbai's Lips Inc. modeling agency until they took notice of her. It hadn't taken them long to notice. What was there not to notice about five feet nine inches of sleek limbs, flawless skin, and attractive features? Diya knew what she looked like. She also knew there wasn't a man, woman, child, or animal in the world who overlooked her. Not even the Beast—though the poor knave tried hard to. Anyway, Rocky Currimbhoy, cofounder of Lips Inc. agency, had rocket-launched her career in a matter of weeks, much like Cinderella's fairy godmother swirling a magic wand about and transforming a dowdy cinder-sweeper into the belle of the ballroom. Not that there was any dowdiness in Diya—not even back then. Just a bit of naïveté that had been scrubbed off since.

Fast-forward eight years, and Beauty Mathur honest-to-goodness loved to strike a pose. Any pose. Even ones that made her muscles scream in protest or blood rush to the brain, causing a migraine. Her super-busy model's life suited her perfectly unlike some of the other vocations she'd tried—and failed at—in her many years of adulting. Beauty was her thing. Fashion was her passion. And she was incredibly good at it. If she wasn't, Hasaan Jabbir would never have pursued her for Scheherazade.

For years, she'd been a Rapunzel trapped in the tower of professional ignominy, surrounded by an impossible wall of overachievers—case in point, the Beast on her left. But, unlike the incarcerated, long-haired princess, Diya had quit waiting for a princely rescue. She'd climbed down from the tower herself, waved her tresses about, and changed the course of her life.

It had been either that or agree to enforced domesticity with one of the truly blah men her family had paraded in front of her like a clichéd bachelorette reality show.

An arranged marriage was a fate worse than death. *A fate soon-to-be realized for poor Hasaan*, Diya thought mournfully. For her, too, if her "situation" didn't get sorted out soon and to her family's satisfaction.

Her father had called last night, yelling his head off at her gullibility. When she'd tried to explain her knightly reasons, instead of being pacified and calling her a hero, he'd started up his usual matrimonial threats and parental blackmail. And, this time, her mother and sister had chimed in like a couple of chorus girls, taking his side. The sparkly fairy tale was rapidly losing its glamour. Not for her, but for them.

Dear busy gods in heaven, are any of you listening? Help me out of this. Please!

"Stop browsing all the rubbish, Diya. You'll give yourself an ulcer," Krish said, maneuvering the SUV through a light patch of traffic.

Leesha and Hasaan had said the same thing. *"Haters will hate. Ignore them."*

But she was a people person, a crowd-pleaser, and it was hard to ignore trolls. Hard not to be the darling of the crowd.

With a last pout at the nightmare version of herself, Diya closed the pink leather cover over the tablet and slid the device back into her rose-pink handbag. Then, she forced herself to look at the Beast.

It was both a shock and a relief that he was behaving like a gentleman—mostly. Apart from the couple of mildly sarcastic comments he'd made in front of Hasaan and calling her Dee-Dumbs—which might have started off as a pejorative but had long ago morphed into his special nickname for her—he'd been courteous though broody. But that was Krish. He was a natural-born brooder. He brooded on a daily basis with no provocation whatsoever.

He dropped his hand to the console between them when they stalled at a red light, fiddling with the buttons to change the music station and turn the volume down. He had broad, capable-looking hands, the backs lightly dusted with dark hair. A sexy little vein pushed up from the middle knuckle of his right hand and ran all the way up his arm, which was bare beneath his pushed-up sleeve. Diya dragged her eyes away from the flexed strength of his forearm to his face.

"Talk to me." His laser-beam stare pierced her through the barrier of his prescription sunglasses, making her nerves tingle.

Krish was nearly blind without his glasses. These were aviator-style, and they sat well on his broad-boned face. Even through the dark green glass, she could make out the general shape of his eyes, and her memory filled in the rest. Krish had the Menon eyes, large and brown and soulful with thick but short, no-nonsense eyelashes. She used to nag him to get corrective eye surgery done or get prescription contacts at least. He'd ignored the advice, just like he ignored every fashion tip she gave him. Totally his loss, in her humble opinion. As Diya stared without speaking, his unruly eyebrows rose above the thin metal frames in askance.

Then, the light turned green, and the traffic began to move. With a frustrated sound, Krish turned his attention back to the road, giving Diya a longer opportunity to gather her thoughts and study his profile.

Everything about the Beast was dark and mysterious. His skin tone was just a shade darker than his mother's and sister's and several shades darker than hers and yet, surprisingly, well hydrated and blemish-free. He had a noble-sized nose and a stubborn jawline that she found super sexy. Even so, no one in the fashion world would call Krish Menon good-looking. They would vote him as average or having a face infused with character—which was a polite way of saying he was nothing much to look at. But did that stop the shivers of undiluted attraction from rippling through her whenever he was in close proximity?

Krish had no clue that he affected her this way. Thank heavens he lived thousands of miles away, or her retarded shivering would give her away for sure. No one in either of their families suspected she still hadn't gotten over the crush she'd had on him since forever. If they found out, they would pity her. If Krish found out, it would make things even more awkward between them than it already was. Worse, he'd think it was his duty to see her happily settled in a relationship, and like he'd done once before at her father's behest, he would either propose to her himself or start introducing her to his eligible friends.

It might come to that anyway what with the marriage madness afflicting her father. Daddy was behaving as if turning thirty—which she would in August—without a husband and toddler to tend to was a biological crime fit for the *Record Book of Disgraced Mathurs*. It wasn't her fault she was unlucky in the love and wedded bliss departments. Unlike her parents, her sister, and her BFF, some people like Hasaan and herself . . .

"Diya?" Krish prodded again, oh-so gently squeezing her hand this time.

She suppressed another shiver and sighed. *I have to tell him sometime, right?*

"It started with the purchase of the stupid bootie," she began and quickly related the whole silly story in sequence.

On December 23, she and Hasaan had been spotted, buying a Christmas bootie in the Dubai Mall.

"It was the cutest baby bootie ever. It was hanging in the window display, a miniature Christmas stocking in silver and purple wool, and I just had to go in and buy it for your sister and Aryan. You know they're trying to get pregnant, and I thought the bootie would amuse them. It does. They call it their fertility charm. How was I supposed to know that some crackpot paparazzo stalker would take our photos and use them as evidence of a pregnancy?"

The stupid, incriminating photographs had triggered a collective exultation in the media who had speculated over Hasaan and her being an item ever since she signed on as Scheherazade's brand ambassador in early December. True, Hasaan and she were joined at the hip at this point—in a professional and platonic manner—but did anyone believe it? Of course not. Where was the fun in that?

Apparently, neither did Krish because he quirked a highly skeptical eyebrow at her, which she ignored.

Soon after the inciting incident, Jabbir Enterprises had begun courting Al-Hanna Shipping regarding a possible merger with the intent to consolidate two large shipping kingdoms into one massive empire. Now, that was a news-worthy story. Soon after that, Hasaan and she had begun traveling for Scheherazade's worldwide publicity tour, and the bootie/pregnancy speculation had gathered momentum again despite the PR team's succinct but solid denials of the relationship. The rumors had lost steam again when they both went back to their respective hometowns for a short break toward the end of January.

"That's when Hussein, Hasaan's older half-brother and CEO of JES, decided that the merger would benefit from a more airtight and personal fusion. And, since Hasaan isn't romantically attached to anyone currently, he was offered up as a bridegroom to one of Sheikh Al-Hanna's daughters. Naturally, Hasaan went ballistic. His mother is Italian, and he lives in Istanbul, so he's not at all conservative in his thinking. He expects ... expected to find his own bride at some point in the very distant future. Anyway, he's been rebelling ever since—and who would blame him? He's been throwing wild parties all across Europe so that his imminent fiancée—her name is Saira—and her family will see how totally unsuitable he is as a groom. It's not working." Diya shook her head in bafflement. "The engagement is still on, which is shocking because Sheikh Al-Hanna is super old-fashioned and believes that westernized Muslims are no better than infidels."

"A westernized Middle Eastern man. How quaint," Krish inserted when Diya paused to catch a breath.

She ignored the droll comment. "A few weeks ago, while I was in Mumbai on break, I happened to visit Priya in her clinic. Again, how was I to know I'd meet a fan there and that she'd take my picture and post it on social media? And some stupid media-monger with nothing better to do than prowl the internet, looking for conspiracy theories, would resurrect the bootie/pregnancy gossip, link it to my visit to a gynecologist, and pronounce me 'with child' again—not by Hasaan this time, but by Aryan Rajaram Chawla!—conveniently leaving out the fact that the doctor was my sister?"

Diya fought down the urge to scream in outrage as a fresh bout of panic tried to burn a hole in her stomach. "Just because I went to a party with my best friend's husband without said best friend—who was too busy to come to the party with us, mind you—means I have to be seducing him, right? Mann was right there with us ... along with Millie and Pareena and seven other friends! But, oh no, nothing is ever written about them. None of them are stuck with labels like the 'Bimbo Who Stole Her BFF's Husband.'"

Krish snorted, doubtless at the bimbo comment. "You

want things to be written about you. You love being outrageous. So, don't complain when it happens."

"Yes. Fine! I do like to generate oodles of press. Good press though. Not this pregnancy stuff. But I suppose I can't pick and choose what will be written about me and what won't." Diya pouted.

Again, the Diya-Aryan linkage had unlinked as soon as she resumed the Scheherazade tour, and the Diya-Hasaan baby rumor had rekindled even though she flashed her flat belly at every opportunity and guzzled bubbly at every party. The media hadn't relented, even when Hasaan and Saira's engagement and wedding dates were announced—it was to be in six weeks in Saudi Arabia against the poor man's wishes. To drown his sorrows, Hasaan had gotten disgracefully drunk in Miami two nights ago. The smash-hit band, Bedouin D'Araba, had performed at the party. It would've been an epic end to Scheherazade's Arabian-style publicity campaign had Hasaan not misbehaved in front of certain influential people who'd promptly filled Sheikh Al-Hanna's ears about his future son-in-law's outrageous conduct.

Shifting to get more comfortable—though with the carry-on, the baklava box, and her jacket on her lap, it was impossible—Diya turned to face Krish. "Can you imagine how Sheikh Al-Hanna reacted? Do you know how conservative he is?"

"It's the second time you've mentioned it in two minutes, I'd have to be deaf and a moron not to get the message."

"Ha-ha, Krish, you're soooo funny. *Not.* Anyway, the sheikh finally declared he would not tolerate a son-in-law who was an Amreeka kisser."

"What?" Krish's mouth twitched. "Another one of your weird made-up terms?"

Diya sighed. "Not mine. The sheikh's. Anyone who flouts Sharia law is an Amreeka kisser."

Krish shot her a long look, clearly trying to gauge if she was making it up.

Diya shrugged. "He won't allow his daughters to step foot on American soil, not even for a holiday. Not his sons, mind you. They can do as they please. The world is full of sexist double standards. Too bad there isn't a magic wand to restyle people's minds. Anyway, the whole merger thing is up in the air now, and Hasaan is in the doghouse with his family. They've threatened to disown him and pull all investments from Scheherazade."

If Hussein made good on the threat, it would not go down well for the brothers. Scheherazade was Hasaan's baby.

Krish took an exit off Interstate 30 and drove through a picturesque residential neighborhood that meandered uphill and downhill, branching off into by-lanes or private drive-ways at whim. Diya didn't recognize the Dallas suburb from her previous visit with Krish. True, it had been a few years since she last paid him a visit, and his neighborhood might have gotten an upgrade. Still, she was good with roads. Which meant he'd moved.

"Exactly what does this *Twilight* episode have to do with you and the pregnancy rumor?" asked Krish before she could ask him where they were.

Diya suppressed a sigh. The story was proving too complicated for the numbers man.

Also, she was stalling.

"Someone took photos of Hasaan and me at the Arabian Nights party—well, at the after-party—and posted them all over social media, okay?" she confessed. "The pics are kind of blurry, but it's not impossible to guess who's who if you know who you're looking for. My tattoo is distinctive, and Hasaan is ... well, he's Hasaan." Avoiding the Beast's beastly glare, she turned her head to stare out of the window and at the lovely, flowering lawns and the super-cute to gorgeous houses rolling past.

Why didn't anyone tell me he'd moved?

"Again, what does it have to do with the rumor?" Stubborn and obtuse—that was Krish.

Diya huffed out a breath. "It was a smash-hit party, Beast. Most of us were wasted or naked or both."

A long pause and then a growl. "Which category did you fall into?"

She threw him a cheeky look, which only made Krish frown even more ferociously.

"Both. But only semi of both," she added in a rush before puffs of red-hot steam shot out of his eyes, nose, and ears.

And she'd left the party at a reasonable hour because she was exhausted from the traveling and long nights and even longer days of media pandering and mingling and schmoozing. She needed sleep more than a good time right now, but she didn't tell him that. After all, she had her frivolous image to uphold—especially in his eyes.

"Damn it, Diya. What happened then?" He was gripping the steering wheel so tightly that his knuckles had gone white and the sexy vein flat.

"I told you! The pics went viral. Add that to the already-simmering cauldron of baby rumors and interfaith trolls and …" Diya trailed off, feeling horribly helpless again. There really was no way to control wagging tongues or idiots. "So, I told Hasaan to use the hoopla about us to his advantage … if he wanted to get out of the marriage yet save the merger. I can't believe his family is forcing him into marriage in this day and age."

Who was she kidding? Across the world, marriages got arranged as much now as they had fifty years ago and for less glamorous reasons than dynastic mergers. But not in modern-thinking families.

Not in my family!

"I can't believe Daddy thinks I've shamed him on purpose. I can't believe he's turning into an old ogre, just like his mother," Diya burst out as Krish veered the Range Rover off Hemingway Drive and into a private driveway.

READ FURTHER AND DIE!

I'm floating on cloud sixteen! Last night was my birthday party at Olive restaurant. OMG! The Shoe Cake!!! Chocolate and fudge on the inside and pink, blue, and silver butter-cream frosting on the outside—the exact colors of my dress. So totally awesome!

The blight? Ravi. What kind of boyfriend falls ill on the most important day of his girlfriend's life? Well, ex-boyfriend now that he's proven to be a weak, sickly jerk. Obviously, he's not my prince. Imagine my horror that I almost went stag to my own party! (Maybe Leesha is right. Maybe I shouldn't brag about my In a Relationship status so much.)

I did say, almost. The Beast offered to be my birthday knave :O Go figure! (Oh, yeah. Krish's down from Dallas for a mini vacay before he takes up some fancy-schmancy internship.) Tonight, he completely reversed my opinion of him. He was by my side the whole evening and even slow-danced with me at the very end. He addressed me as Princess Diya all night long. My friends are beyond jealous because they think I have a college-age boyfriend. I love it! Who knew the Beast of Malevolence could reform into the Prince of Benevolence, even without true love's kiss?

Oh, he confuses me so. If I marry him, my initials will remain the same—DKM. How cool is that? Also, is that a sign or what?

Happy sweet 16 to me!

CHAPTER 3

*K*rish drove the Rover down a one-lane cobblestone driveway that led to his temporary home. Tall, gracious hardwood trees, lining the narrow lane, waved in usual welcome. Normal, wholesome, natural —that was his life.

He got out of the car as soon as he pulled up in front of the double garage, allowing himself some deep breaths of relief and fresh air that wasn't soaked in Diya's perfume or drama. Could the woman not do anything in an ordinary way? He needed a moment—maybe a dozen—to digest what he'd heard into some kind of logical perspective. Then, he walked to the back of the car and began unloading the three pink trunks.

This was what he was talking about. *Pink!* The color was absurd on luggage. It was absurd anywhere and on anyone who wasn't toddler-sized. A grown woman should not use this much pink. And since when had Diya's narcissism reached the level of monogrammed luggage? Krish stared at the brown and beige curlicued DKMs branded into the pink leather in stupefaction.

"O-M-jeez! You bought a house? When? What happened to the no-fuss, no-muss bachelor pad of yore?" Diya squealed while peering through the windshield at the reddish-gray edifice peeping out of the woodlands.

With a heave-ho, Krish yanked one heavy trunk to the ground and then jerked straight up as if stung by a bee. *Heave-ho?* Twenty minutes in her company, and he'd reverted to fairy-tale speak.

"I sold it. I'm looking for a new place, and until I find one, I'm crashing here." He wondered if his new place would be in Wisconsin. He had until March to make a decision. Where to live? Where to work? What the hell did he want out of life?

"You know I hate living in hotels. The house belongs to my friends—Rayna and Darren Peters. Not sure if you ever met them?" When Diya shook her head, he explained, "They're my college buddies. Rayna is an economics professor at my alma mater, and Darren is a writer. He writes historical fiction. They're both on sabbatical, doing research in Cambodia … which worked out perfectly for me."

"Ooh, you're house-hunting? I love house-hunting. I'm going to help you find your dream house, Beast," Diya declared, grinning at him over her shoulder.

"Absolutely no, thanks. I don't want to end up in some drafty old castle that'll bankrupt me with its first electric bill. Or worse, I refuse to get stuck in some hobbit hole."

"Suit yourself." Shrugging, Diya turned away to face forward again and began stuffing her jacket, hat, and the baklava in her handbag.

Krish wrestled the other trunks out without any heave-ho-ing, each baggage heavier than the last. By the time he accomplished his goal in triplicate, his shoulders ached, and a nice little muscle spasm burned between his shoulder blades.

To his shame, Diya jumped out of the car on high heels while holding her handbag and set it down by the trunks with one hand as if it weighed nothing. Her handbag weighed twenty-five pounds easily, proving that she was in much better shape than he was. She'd always been.

"I'll bring it all in." Krish rotated his shoulders in preparation for more exertion and jerked his head, indicating the house. "Go on. Explore. I can see you're dying to."

Diya gave a little hop on her stilettos, devouring the storybook house with happy eyes. The setting was absolutely delightful and whimsical, from the stone-peppered driveway that wove through the woods to the gray-paneled two-car garage to the red-gray pavers that hopscotched up a dozen steps, leading up to an arched alcove. And, as Krish had brought the hobbit hole to her mind, the dark brown door with its arched top and solid iron door knocker looked as if Frodo Baggins might answer when she knocked. Old-fashioned lanterns swung on both sides of the door, and veils of ivy, intertwined with braided branches, hugged the exterior walls of the house, magically parting away from the windows and doors.

"The Beast of 'Bad Romance' lives in a fairy-tale house. *Lah-lah-lah-lah-lah! Da-da-da-da-da-ah!*" she belted out, shaking her body to Lady Gaga's famous song.

Of course, he snorted at her antics. Besides being a brooder, Krish was a class-A snorter. "It's just a house, Dee-Dumbs. Calm down."

A little wider, a little higher, a moat, a drawbridge, maybe a turret or two, and it would transform into a mini-castle. No, it wasn't *just a house*. It was the house of her dreams. Well, not the house itself, but the setting was quite similar to it. Her dream house was a mud-walled, brightly painted cottage nestled in a vibrant glen in the middle of the woods on the banks of a tinkling brook with a redbrick chimney puffing out clouds shaped like silver hearts. She still had the drawing stashed away in a drawer back home along with her lock-and-key journals.

"Tell me there's a brook tumbling close by." Widening her eyes and clasping her hands to her chest in hopeful prayer, she spun around to face him. She would die if he said no.

"But of course, milady. Would this lowly knave dare to invite you to your dream cottage with no brook in sight?" he said, giving her one of his patented Grim Reaper stares. But his humor got the better of him, and he burst out laughing.

Diya's heart liquefied like it always did when Krish's teasing turned sweet. She wanted to leap into his arms and hug him. She hadn't seen him since Leesha's wedding. Hadn't spoken to him—really spoken to him—in years. She wanted to press her lips to his and slake all of her shivery, unquenchable desires. But, of course, she didn't—she couldn't—knowing and fearing that, instead of melting with her, he'd freeze. He'd stop teasing her. He'd stop smiling altogether, and like he'd done on her twenty-first birthday, he would push her away.

So, Diya locked her kisses away and kept up the light-hearted banter. "Lead on, knave. Take me forth to my bedchamber, which needs must look over the brook." She bent and hefted a rose-pink trunk upright and yanked up its handle.

"Leave it, Diya. I'll come back for it." The growly baritone traveled up her spine, and she nearly groaned.

Stop it! Do not succumb to patheticness, she sternly told herself.

What was wrong with her that she found Krish's grouchy authority so totally shiver-worthy? She knew plenty of bossy-type men. Plenty! She'd even dated a few … and then never had the urge to repeat the mistake.

"Three trunks and one handbag. Two of us, so two each." She counted for the numbers man. When he started shaking his head, she stiffened her spine. "*Equality* is the word of the decade, darling. Unless elves and dwarves are going to crawl out of these woods to help us, there is no need to go all macho on me. Besides, I refuse to give you a reason to bitch about how spoiled and helpless homeland *desis* are in foreign lands. Seriously, Krish, I know how heavy those trunks are. Let me help."

"Why make them so heavy and so many and so pink that they hinder my hospitality and my manliness?" he muttered under his breath, but she heard him.

She shot him a look of abject pity. "Dude, if the mere sight of my pink luggage threatens your manhood—" She broke off, squealing, when he lunged for her and began to run around the car when he tried to grab her again. "Wouldn't have guessed you suffered from pink-o-phobia, Beast. Or is it a fetish?"

I'll show her a phobia and a fetish, thought Krish, shaking his head.

Diya had a mouth on her, and she used it inventively. Never failed to amuse him. She was baiting him to come after her, but instead of regressing to childhood behavior, he climbed back into the car. He wasn't going to help her break her legs by giving chase. He had no idea how she'd managed to bounce about on the cobblestones in mile-high heels without falling on her face.

He ignored her chicken *pluck-pluck-pluck* sounds and steered the SUV into the garage, sliding it in next to his silver Porsche. Hail had been forecasted for the next few hours, so both cars needed to be roofed.

He retraced his steps to the trunks where Diya waited, a sweet smile lighting her gorgeous face. His breath caught in his chest at the sight of her all flushed and happy, and without thought, he pulled her close. Then, he wrapped his arms around her in a tight hug like he should've done at the airport.

"I'm glad you came. I've missed you," he said, swallowing the lump in his throat.

They hadn't seen much of each other in the last few years; work, life, their own hasty actions had gotten in the way of their friendship.

"Krish ..." His name slipped from her mouth no louder than a warm breath, and she pressed her lips against his jaw where his pulse beat.

She seemed breakable all of a sudden, liquid, as if his confession had melted her bones. He tightened his hold. He wanted to wrap her up and shield her from the whole nasty world—himself included. He might not be able to sort out any of her problems, but he swore to himself that he wouldn't add to them. Starting now.

She was trembling against him. The change in the air was apparent, the storm imminent, even though the sun shone bright above them.

"You're cold. Come on. Let's get you in the house. Go in through the garage. It's easier, less of a climb." He briskly rubbed her bare arms, smiling into her face half-hidden by the retro sunglasses. She stepped back, smiling. Yet he got the feeling he'd missed something. Something important. "What is it?"

She shook her head and grabbed the handle of the upright trunk with one hand and her handbag in the other. "Come on, hobbit. Your elf-mistress wishes to get settled in."

He set one trunk in front of him, and the other one behind, ready to roll. "If I'm a full two and a half inches taller than you, who's the hobbit here?"

She looked down her nose at him. "Not me when I'm wearing pointy shoes. And, in case you've failed to notice, oh sight-challenged Beast, I'm prettier than you are, and I have less body hair."

And amen to that, Krish thought.

TOGETHER, they rolled, pulled, pushed, dragged, and eventually kicked the luggage up the steps of the garage, through the kitchen, up another short flight of stairs, and down the hallway to the bedrooms. Krish was set up in the guest room next to the hall bath. As the second spare bedroom was too small to accommodate Diya's luggage, it was decided that she should use the master bedroom.

Diya looked about the spacious, charmingly cluttered bedroom once her pretty-pink trunks had been divided as per need and had been stacked either inside the walk-in closet or against its outside wall. "Are you sure your friends will be okay with me using their room?"

Krish nodded. "It's the only room with an en suite bathroom. I knew you'd prefer that."

"Much appreciated," she replied. Not having an attached bathroom would've seriously sucked. And sharing the hall one with the Beast would've ended in murder or a suicide.

She recalled a few family vacations when the M Brigade —made up of the awesome Menon and Mathur kids—had shared rooms and bathrooms. As the only guy in the foursome, he'd asserted his manhood by endlessly torturing them. He'd banged on doors while they were inside, or he'd locked himself or them in the bathroom just to annoy the crap out of them. He'd hidden toilet paper rolls and their toiletry bags; he'd squeezed out the toothpaste and dumped their shampoo in the drain. Once, he'd packed a bunch of dead lizard tails in Priya's duffel. Diya would never forget how her sister had screamed when she unpacked it at home.

Priya had not only thrown all her clothes out, but their mother had thrown the bag out, too.

Diya did not trust Krish to behave himself, even now. Besides, a girl needed her own bathroom like she needed form-fitted clothes; while she would make do with ill fits and wrong sizes, she'd be self-conscious in them.

"I want to see the brook," she announced, throwing open the large patio doors opposite the bed. She stepped out onto a cute little brick terrace with dramatic views of a picture-perfect woodland.

The terrace itself was tiny but cleverly outfitted with cushioned wrought-iron furniture where she imagined spending lazy mornings having breakfast and lazier afternoons napping or reading—her main itinerary for the next week or two. On the right was a high brick wall covered in lilac vines. From there, brick-laid steps with wrought-iron rails spiraled downward to a patio on the lower floor, which opened into the woods.

No two rooms in the quaint little house were on the same level; they twisted and wove together via steps going up or down throughout the space. There were skylights and/or floor-to-ceiling windows in all the rooms—all the ones she'd seen so far—to let the light and the outdoors in. Each window framed a different yet equally naturalistic and enthralling vista. The house truly was a part of the woods.

Krish joined her on the terrace. "If you go down the steps and turn right, you'll come to the brook. I can see it from my window," he said, popping a whole baklava into his mouth.

She pouted. "I want the room with the brook view."

He finished chewing with relish before answering, "Your junk will not fit in my room."

Diya narrowed her eyes. "Just what do you have against my things, Beast? They're just things. Stop obsessing."

Krish's eyebrow quirked up in irony. He'd exchanged the

sunglasses for a pair of stylish spectacles with thin metal frames. Through the glass, his brown eyes seemed huge, his lashes long and dense. He was standing way too close to her. She shivered.

"Because I refuse to deal with your sarcastic eyebrow all week, I'm going to explain something to you. As the face and body of Scheherazade, I must be seen wearing and using only Scheherazade products. I cannot promote any other product or advertise any other label for the two years of my contract—unless my contract with the other brand precedes theirs."

His sneer at her supposed obsession with pretty possessions vanished into the woods. "Oh."

"Yes. *Oh.* Scheherazade is an extremely popular brand in Asia and Europe, not so much in the US yet. That's why I'm traveling with everything *and* the kitchen sink in those trunks. It's out of necessity, Beast, not choice."

She braced for a taunt or two, something along the lines of, *If you can't shop in Dallas, Dee-Dumbs, however will you pass your time when I'm off, making gazillions?* To which, she'd reply—

"What do you want to do first? Unpack, eat, or shower?" Krish asked, poking a hole in her fantasy dialogue.

To her shock, Krish didn't make a single snide remark about her explanation or her contractual restrictions.

Diya shook her head, as much to clear it as to say no. She was beyond tired at this point and functioning on sheer force of will, hence the spontaneous daydreaming. It had been a crazy, busy few months, and the last two days had sort of bled her energy levels dry. If she was indeed the vampire the tabloid twerp had portrayed her as, all she wanted to do was gorge on a blood-filled vein and then snore inside a coffin.

"I'll get to the unpacking and showering tomorrow. I'm hungry and sleepy. So, lead me to the kitchen, oh pied piper, and show me where everything is. Then, I'll let you go. You probably need to get back to your office and resume snarling at disobedient figures—of the numerical and human variety."

Krish slanted an undecipherable look her way. "As a matter of fact, I've taken the day off."

"What? Don't be silly. You don't have to babysit me."

Krish was a Menon to the hilt—the hardest of taskmasters. He hated losing billable hours and became intolerably grouchy when he did. It was a testament to his regard for her father that he'd taken the afternoon off to fetch her from the airport himself and not sent a taxi. To be fair, he'd sent a taxi only the once to pick up his family during their visit a few years ago due to some emergency at the office. Leesha and Savitri Aunty hadn't made a big deal about it or complained about his deficient host behavior. Diya wasn't so forgiving. Family should always come first.

But she was fair as well. He had fetched her and settled her in; now, he could go.

She flapped a hand in a shooing motion. "I mean it. Go back to your office. Play with your spreadsheets. Punch some numbers. Do whatever it is you do. I'll be fine."

"I'm not going back to work today," he said in clear exasperation. He seemed serious.

Diya stared at Krish. Then, she checked his forehead, cheek, and throat with the back of her hand.

"Nope, no fever. You could be delirious from low sugar. Or"—she paused for dramatic effect—"you were kidnapped by a UFO and are now an alien in Krish form."

"Smart-ass." He chucked her under her chin and then began walking away. "Come along, elf … or should I say rat since I'm the piper? Let me introduce you to your domain— the kitchen."

She stuck her tongue out at his chauvinist backside but decided not to take umbrage, not when he clearly teased and when it was patently true. It was no secret she loved to cook.

Besides, his previous statement trumped all other concerns for her.

She rushed after him, out the room and into the hallway, her heels clattering against the wooden floor. "I'm confused. Since when do you take days off?"

The Krish Menon she knew did not play hooky. He worked twelve to sixteen hours a day on most days, sometimes even on Sundays. Work was his religion. Numbers were his mantras. Profits, projections, and spreadsheets were his portals to nirvana. He thrived as a beast of burden.

And, as if that confession of sloth wasn't shocking enough, what he mumbled next made Diya trip on the steps leading down to the kitchen and crash into Krish's back. She could not have heard him right.

"What?" she gasped, clutching his arms for support when he spun around to steady her.

Nary a smile or sneer darkened the alien in Krish form. "I said I have dinner plans. You're welcome to join me if you're not tired."

"What?" Diya repeated. "Dinner plans? Like, for Valentine's Day?"

Something flickered in Krish's brown eyes. It was neither a confirmation nor a denial. To Diya's frustration, he changed the topic and that was the end of that.

CHAPTER 4

*M*uffled, rhythmic *meows* lured Diya back into the land of the conscious.

She woke slowly, blinking at the cracked creamy-white ceiling that was bare of all light fixtures but enhanced on all four sides by decorative molding. A table lamp glowed across the room, diffusing the night. She always left a light on because she preferred not to wake in the dark—especially in a new place and on a strange bed—and get spooked.

Outside, thunder and wind whooshed like an angry symphony, rattling the windows and spooking her regardless. The purring grew urgent along with the sound of sharp nails tapping and scratching against glass.

Eyes half-shut, Diya rolled out of bed to rescue the cats. There were three of them: a black one, a reddish-brown one, and a black-and-white one. They leaped inside the room as soon as she pushed the patio door open, and the first splashes of icy rain plopped on the terrace. She quickly closed the doors and locked them again and then drew the thick curtains over the moaning night.

With one eye, Diya checked the time on the cuckoo clock —ten after midnight.

"The witching hour," she croaked to the cats, her voice rusty with sleep.

One well-fed feline—the red one—was stretching in a cat pose on the shag rug, no doubt delighted to be out of the brewing storm. The full hailstorm wouldn't hit for another two hours.

A chill settled on Diya's bare limbs, the room suddenly cold by the brief exposure to the elements. Teeth chattering, she shuffled back to the bed, but the black cat had stolen her spot. After a staring match, the cat coiled into a ball and closed its eyes.

"Fine, you can have the spot," Diya conceded and detoured to the left side of the bed. Like she had a choice. It was their house, wasn't it?

She looked about for the black-and-white cat, hoping it wasn't on the bed, too. Nope. The cat was ensconced on the cushioned armchair in front of the mahogany writing desk.

There were three more cats in residence—the Peters' menagerie consisted of six cats and four parakeets. Krish had told her that those three were old and rarely came out of the den, preferring to spend their time sleeping in front of the fireplace.

The Beast was good with beasts, always had been, and the animals couldn't have asked for a better caretaker—with the exception of tonight. She wondered who would've let the cats in if she wasn't around.

She wondered if he was back from his date. *Probably not,* she thought, sniffling morosely.

Not even Krish, the workaholic fuddy-duddy, would hurry home from a V-Day date because of a bit of thunder and rain. If he'd gone to the extreme trouble of asking a woman out, he'd make it count. Maybe even score.

And good for him if he does, she decided firmly.

A thoroughly unbidden picture of Krish getting a lap dance flashed into her brain.

Diya collapsed on the bed with a moan, squeezing her eyes shut against the visual. She hugged a pillow, pressing her face into the fluffy softness. A cheap substitute for a warm body, but it was all she had. All she'd ever had.

It was absurd to feel betrayed by Krish. Absurd to feel utterly alone and rejected.

She blamed Hasaan for her pathetic mood. His over-the-top parties and weird reading habits—they'd formed a mile-high book club, discussing everything from epic Arabic romances to really smart smut dealing with gender politics, sexuality, bigotry and class—were obviously playing havoc on her wits and emotions, which she always, always kept under tight control whenever the Beast was close.

Okay, enough! Time to take back that control.

Krish's dates and whether they danced on his lap or on his head were none of her business.

Banishing all indecent images from her brain, Diya rolled to her side and tried to go back to sleep.

Easier decided than done. She couldn't help but wonder about the wonder woman who'd scored a date with Krish. Last count, he'd been involved with a corporate headhunter named Aya Ahuja. He'd meant to bring her to his sister's wedding in London last September, but he'd shown up stag at the last minute and not seen fit to enlighten anyone as to why. They'd all assumed he'd broken up; Krish's revolving-door relationships were legendary after all. It was another Menon family trait—to run far, far away from personal entanglements. Which begged the question, who was he entangled with tonight?

Still none of your business …

Maybe, but her pathetic heart wouldn't let it go.

She'd taken her bitter jealousy too far in London, enjoying many a tipsy joke at the absent Aya's expense. The woman's name was absurd—Aya meant *come* in Hindi. It took a better woman than Diya not to make fun of it.

Aya? Nahi aya. Aya gaya!

When Krish had overheard her making fun of his missing girlfriend—*ex-girlfriend?*—at Leesha and Aryan's combined hen and stag party, he'd lambasted Diya in front of everyone. He'd always been a party pooper.

She'd proceeded to demonstrate exactly what the opposite of a pooper looked like with the help of a couple of enthusiastic fun lovers—Mann Singh and Harry Colt, Aryan's friendly and fantastic groomsmen. At some point, she might have asked both Macho Mann and Handsome Harry to marry her—a joke obviously, but Krish had remained unamused. She'd also begged Harry to escort her to her hotel room—more like carry her since she'd been wasted by then. The next thing she remembered was the Beast shaking her awake and snarling at her. They'd proceeded to have the most god-awful fight then.

Diya winced, remembering the shouting clearly. What was not so clear was the kiss. She had a feeling they'd locked lips, but she wasn't a hundred percent sure. And she'd die before she asked Krish if they had or not. Besides, it would prove his point if she did. The point being that she took crazy risks in the name of fun. That she was silly and stupid and a disgrace to her family. She'd definitely slapped him at some point that night. Her palm still tingled in memory and remorse even if he'd deserved it.

And that, dear Diary, was the latest episode in the dramatic lives of Beauty Mathur and the Beast.

Sighing, Diya rolled onto her side and abruptly came up close and personal with a snoring ball of fur. Jealous as a cat —was that an expression? Were cats jealous? They seemed to be as territorial about their possessions as dogs were and meaner to boot. Diya wondered if it was prudent to fall asleep next to a cat. She didn't want to end up with scratches on her face because she'd accidentally poached a pillow.

She'd been scratched by a cat when she was eleven. By Little Kitty, the tiny, motherless kitten Krish had rescued and given to Leesha, only to take his gift back a month later. He'd dumped Little Kitty in the hands of the watchman's son because he'd been angry and hurting about his parents' separation. He'd told Leesha that they were better off alone, without love and family. Diya had tried to steal Little Kitty back for her best friend, but Krish had found out and put a stop to it. After that, he never rescued or brought another animal home. He'd changed overnight.

Krish had assured her that the Peters' felines were friendly—or as friendly as felines could be—and wouldn't mind sharing their room with her. Still, it would be best if she confirmed the living arrangements with the boarders themselves.

"May I share your space?" Diya respectfully asked the cat.

The feline remained curled up like a dead worm for fifteen minutes before Diya relaxed enough to close her eyes.

Ten minutes later, Diya rolled onto her back and flipped the pillow from her chest to her face to block out the light and her blighted thoughts. Maybe she was done. She'd slept deeply for a good six hours; exhaustion and a full belly had done the trick. The full glass of Malbec Krish had poured for her also helped.

He'd made her a sandwich with kale and slices of avocado and tomato, enhancing the flavor with diced jalapeno peppers. He hadn't joined her for the meal since he was going out for dinner. But he'd kept her company, drinking coffee while she ate and interrogated him, and he hadn't been able to resist another piece of the baklava. Mellow from the Argentinian wine and from the sheer freedom of not being under the spotlight or the scrutiny of millions, she had quizzed Krish about his date—not that he'd answered her impertinent questions. Eventually, with one hunger sated and the other one inflamed by a one-sided conversation, she'd made her way back to the bedroom where, too tired to change into her nightshirt, she'd simply stripped off her jacket, jewelry, and pants and flopped into bed.

Diya sat up and reached for the tablet she'd left charging on the nightstand. No point trying to go back to sleep. She was done for the night. She checked her e-mails and messages. She felt a resurgence of panic when she Googled her name and fresh articles popped up. Gossip about the pregnancy had tripled overnight. So had the threats, dire predictions, and moral judgments. Her life was in utter shambles. Again.

Desperate for a pep talk and/or a shoulder to cry on, Diya called her BFF. With the storm messing up the signals, it took several tries before she connected via video chat. As it was half past ten on a working Friday morning in Mumbai, Leesha's sleepy brown eyes and disheveled mass of hair stunned Diya.

"Are you still sleeping?" She gaped at her best friend.

"Would I have answered your call had I been sleeping?" Leesha scowled. Brother and sister had their scowls and growls down pat—added eccentricities of the distinguished but un-fun-loving Menon gene pool. "I'm lounging about."

"In bed?" Diya narrowed her eyes. "Are you sick?"

"Yes, in bed. And, no, I'm not sick. Do I look sick?" Leesha raised two eyebrows.

"If you're not sick … then what the heck is going on with you Menons? Is it the Apocalypse? It must be. The world has to be ending for you and Krish to take a day off and do"— Diya threw her hands up in the air—"nothing!"

"I don't know about Krish, but I've spent the whole of Valentine's Day being *very* productive … if you know what I mean."

Leesha's smug tone and lewd expression finally rang a bell in Diya's jet-lagged brain. She forgot about her heartburn-riddled envy over the phantom Aya. She even overlooked the humbling fact that her unromantic best friend had someone to celebrate V-Day with but not her.

"Ooh!" Diya chortled wickedly. "I hope you tried the positions mentioned in that article I'd sent. The ones that guarantee a baby boy." She crossed her fingers that the bootie charm was working its magic for her BFF.

"Puh-lease. I invented my own amazing moves that guarantee a baby girl." Leesha buffed her nails on what looked like Aryan's shirt.

Diya snorted. The sound put Krish, the snorter, back in her head. His lone form metamorphosed into a tableau of him and Aya performing V-Day porno moves.

O-M-jeez! Delete! Delete! Delete!

This much mental stimulation with nowhere to spew could not be good for her.

"Hey! Did you know the Beast no longer has a lair?" she asked, grasping at random straws to distract her brain.

"What do you mean? Where are you staying then?"

Diya rubbed her hands together and updated Leesha on everything that had transpired since her arrival, including her suspicions of a sinister UFO abduction and the return of alien Krish. By the end of the gossip session, they were both howling and hiccuping in laughter. The cat, thoroughly miffed at the hullabaloo, jumped off the bed and strutted off to a corner with its tail in the air, triggering more hilarity in Diya.

Leesha's humor came under control first. Her eyes moved off-screen and simply lit up with what Diya had labeled the

Love-Lust Look. Aryan had come into the bedroom, Diya deduced, feeling happier than happy for her friend's happily ever after. She would not spoil it by feeling glum for her lack of one.

"What's so funny, sunshine? Oh, sorry. You're on the phone." The microphone picked up Aryan's sexy-as-hell British clip clearly.

That accent! It could derange a girl with functioning ovaries. It had deranged Leesha to the point where she chucked a lifetime's worth of relationship phobias and staunch opinions out the window and married a man several years her junior.

Leesha's answer was to angle the tablet in such a way that all three of them could see each other. Evidently, Aryan had just come out of the shower. His hair was wet, and his scrumptiously ripped torso glistened above the towel wrapped about his hips. Now, there was a shiver-worthy man, and yet not a single atom inside Diya's body shivered in his presence. Such a tragedy.

"Hello, darling!" She blew him a kiss through the screen. "When will you realize you chose the wrong goddess?"

"Well, hello, gorgeous. How are you?" Aryan grinned at her. Then, he mischievously covered Leesha's ears with his hands and mock-whispered, "The minute this wench turns into a pumpkin, we'll sail away into the sunset. Keep your bags packed, love."

"I won't wait forever, you know," said Diya, pouting. But, the minute her words left her mouth, she stiffened.

Wasn't that exactly what she was doing? Waiting for Krish to wake up?

No! It wasn't. She'd rejected his proposal. She'd moved on. She was holding out for a real prince now. Diya closed her eyes. Then, why on earth had she refused Hasaan Jabbir's proposal?

Because his proposal had been nothing but a desperate act of a drowning man. It had been no more real than Krish's martyrdom had been.

"Is something wrong, sweetheart? You have a funny look on your face."

"I'm just tired. Jet lag." Diya forced her lips into a smile.

Aryan was a darling, always worrying about her like his wife did. Like her parents and sister and, yes, even Krish did. They all worried for her. She felt blessed to be so loved.

It was a curse to be so loved.

"Has something else happened, Dee?" Leesha turned the screen back to her and frowned at it.

Diya shook her head. What else could she do? She could hardly confess that she'd been fooling everyone for nine years about her true feelings. That her foolish heart hurt today because the Beast had left her all alone on a stormy night in a stranger's house and gone off on a stupid date. To his credit, he'd asked her to join him. Of course, she'd refused! What sane woman would agree to be a third wheel on a V-Day date with a guy she wanted for herself?

"Did you speak to my parents and Pree? Are they over being mad?" she asked, refusing to feel any sorrier than she already felt.

Such feelings of desolation and desperation were common in any sob story of unrequited love—correction: unrequited romantic love. That Krish loved her was indisputable. But he loved her the way he loved his sister, not the way Diya wanted him to love her.

"Not yet. The *well-wishers* aren't helping matters. Dee, you know how brutal and judgmental Indian society can get, and it's not just your reputation you're playing with; it's theirs, too. You realize that, don't you?" Leesha said softly.

How had it come to this? A good turn was supposed to win her brownie points, not rotten tomatoes.

Diya dug into her soul for some optimism. Hasaan had asked for a week, and she'd give him the week. Her family would have to understand. Burying their heads in the ground like ostriches wouldn't hurt either. Better yet, her parents should get out of Mumbai for a few days. She'd make sure they did.

"Do you want us to come there?" Aryan offered.

"What? Come where? Are you insane? I can't fly off to Dallas right now. I have mountains of work—"

Aryan clamped his hand over his wife's mouth to shut her up. He'd learned amazingly fast that the only way he'd have any say around Leesha was to physically restrain her.

Diya heaved a sigh. "Thanks, you guys. But there's no need. Krish and I can entertain each other."

In a way, Krish was easier to deal with than his sister, who wouldn't be fooled by Diya's false bravado. Plus, it had been way too long since she tormented the Beast. She enjoyed every little vindictive moment between them in which she exacted penance for sins he had no clue he'd committed.

"Are you sure you don't want Leesha to come?" Aryan asked again, so utterly sweetly.

"One hundred percent sure. Go back to your porno moves, darlings. I'm going to try to get some sleep." She burst out laughing when Aryan turned an endearing shade of a ripe tomato and disappeared beyond the screen, calling his wife a braggart as he went.

"You just had to tease him, didn't you?" Leesha shook a finger at the screen. "Bye. Talk to you soon. And behave. Don't tease Krish too much. You know his temper," she warned and clicked off before Diya could protest that she did no such thing.

Her laughter faded as she lay back down on the bed. Oh, she knew the Beast's temper intimately. More like distemper, it meant pain and death to the animal not vaccinated against it. But she could handle it—handle him for a week or two. No sweat. She was fully inoculated against him, shiver or no shiver. She closed her eyes as the storm raged against the house.

Alone. He'd left her all alone.

An hour later, when Krish peeked into her room, Diya pretended to be asleep, so she wouldn't have to invite him in. She didn't want to chat when she felt so vulnerable. She didn't want to know whether he'd scored or what his current score was, not when she still batted zero because of him.

He came in anyway. She heard him move toward the bed. She felt the comforter being pulled up to her chin and gentle hands tucking her in. She heard him move around the room, checking the locks on the terrace door and the windows.

Tears stung her eyelids at his thoughtfulness, protectiveness, but she didn't dare open them until he left the room.

He'd do the same for Leesha and Priya and for both our mothers, Diya assured her heart as tears leaked from her eyes and rolled down the sides of her face. He'd do the same for a stray cat. It meant nothing more. It was just who he was.

Tomorrow, when his attraction waned in the light of day and she went back to being a diva, she'd face the Beast again.

When a person was as beautiful as Diya Mathur, it was only natural she'd attract both admiration and scorn.

In Krish's opinion, humans were happiest when they smeared shit on a thing of beauty. For that matter, on brilliance, too. No one liked a person who was smarter, better-looking, or just plain luckier than they were, and they derived an ugly pleasure from toppling that individual off his or her pedestal. He'd seen it happen in the world of finance. Men and women sacrificed their friends, their families, their peace of minds, maybe even their souls for a few seconds of fame and a truckload of money.

He'd been fortunate in that regard. He'd never had to make such a decision or choose between right and wrong. He'd never had to take a sorry step to move ahead in life, never had to compromise his principles. It didn't mean he was gutless. His reputation for giving no quarter wasn't unjust or an exaggeration. He was a ruthless businessman. He liked to win far too much to be anything else. And success drove him as much as his work ethic.

He'd had a good run so far. He'd moved quickly and steadily up the corporate ladder, driving forward at a punishing tempo, snatching up opportunities as they came his way. If he'd had a thing to prove to himself and the world, he'd proved it in spades. He'd graduated with honors with double degrees in economics and finance from the University of Texas and been recruited right off the bat by the McGraw and Steele group—an independent asset management company with offices in Dallas, New York, London, and Hong Kong—to be part of their New York City team. He hadn't even gone looking for a job. They'd offered it to him because he'd interned with them through both his junior and senior year summers and he must have made an impression.

It was sobering to think how different his life would've been if Kamal Mathur hadn't pushed him toward a college degree.

"This is not an investment in your education, son. This is my investment in you. I know you will not let me down." Kamal Uncle's words and faith had changed Krish's life.

After a year in New York, Krish had started handling Dillo Jones's account exclusively. They'd taken to each other like a house on fire from their very first consultation. Their forty-year age difference notwithstanding, under Krish's guidance, Dillo's three-farm start-up had grown and expanded, and when the time seemed right, it had branched into a chain of grocery stores and restaurants. When Dillo had offered Krish the position of CFO of Armadillo Farms and Foods, Krish had been ready for a new challenge. So, he'd grabbed the bull by its horns and leaped. He'd grown to like and respect Armadillo's lazy Texas pace, and while it hadn't been a smooth glide across calm waters, it hadn't quite had the pitch and heave of a stormy corporate ocean either.

Smooth or stormy, his career was a far cry from Diya's. Diya's career, much like the woman herself, floated jauntily across a sea of endless adventures. The woman didn't know the meaning of tame, much less how to spell it.

She'd been horrified when he left New York.

"Are you insane? Who in their right mind prefers Dallas to the bright lights of Manhattan?" She'd clucked her tongue at him over the phone. "I forgot who I'm talking to. I don't know why I thought New York would finally get rid of the fuddy-duddy inside you."

It was the first time she'd spoken to him since breaking off their brief engagement the year prior. Then, she'd started calling him Bronco Krish for the next year or so. How would she react when he told her about the choices he vacillated between now? Move to Wisconsin and the safety of a job he knew and excelled at or dive into the shifty currents of cyber entrepreneurship?

He'd bet she'd have plenty to say. But he wasn't going to tell her. Not until he was sure of his move or desperate enough to listen to the Diva brand of unsolicited advice. To tell her would mean his sister and mother would come to know immediately. They wouldn't be as vocal as her, they wouldn't ask questions, but they'd worry, silently, on another continent. He didn't want his family to stress over him. He'd stressed them out enough for a lifetime as a teenager.

Krish took a swig of his coffee, staring at the misty gray prospect outside the great room windows. It had stopped raining, but the canopy of clouds that had taken over the sky declared the rain gods weren't done yet.

Neither was Diya. He glanced up at the thumping ceiling. She'd been at it for an hour now, the thumps growing louder as time elapsed. She seemed to be marching, running, or jumping about the room in her daily test of stamina. One of the things he most admired about her was her dedication to her body, to her health. Whatever else was going on in Diya's life, she never slacked off on exercise.

His thoughts circled back to Diya's latest problems and the miracle Kamal Uncle expected would happen on Sunday.

Feeling the caffeine kicking in, Krish walked across the living room and climbed the two steps to the open kitchen where two coffee machines sat side by side on a black granite countertop—his own simple Keurig coffeemaker and the Peters' fancy Jura Capresso. A cereal bowl and spoon lay upside down on the drying rack by the sink, suggesting Diya had come down and had breakfast already.

After refilling his mug, Krish made his way to the master suite, gave a perfunctory knock, and twisted the door open. Expecting a garment and accessory war zone, he was pleasantly surprised by neat piles of clothes, shoes, handbags, and girlie stuff stacked on one trunk.

"Divas should not be tidy or so careful with her things. You're ruining your image," he drawled in lieu of a good morning. When she didn't respond to his greeting and continued to face the open terrace, he noticed the pink earbuds plugged into her ears. Leaning his shoulder against the doorjamb, he allowed himself to stare at all the pink radiance with impunity.

Pink yoga mat. Pink ankle socks lining black sneakers with neon-pink laces. Pink sports top and skimpy gray gym shorts that rode low over her hips. The rest of her was all sweaty pink skin and lean muscle. Her hair was in a braid, and a sturdy pink band soaked the sweat off her forehead. He raked his gaze down her body, lingering over the dip in her lower back and the globes of muscle on her world-renowned butt. They quivered as she sprang up high and then squatted for five counts.

He should look away. He wanted to before she slapped his face, yet he couldn't seem to tear his eyes off of her.

Suddenly, she whirled about and caught him staring. Her face was flushed and scrubbed clean of makeup. He felt his own face heat up when he realized just how much of her midriff was on display—from her pretty navel to her solar plexus. The rosebud tattoo on her hip was cut in half by the band of her shorts. Thoroughly disconcerted by her body, he shot his gaze up to her face and was about to apologize for staring when he noticed her red, desolate eyes.

She'd been crying.

"What's the matter? Were you googling again?" He pushed off the door and walked into the room.

"What?" She unplugged the pods from her ears.

"You have to stop tracking the gossip and interacting with trolls, Dee. It'll get you nowhere."

"It's not that," she said, stretching her right leg and quad like a stork. "I can handle bad publicity." She switched legs. "It's Daddy. Why is he being so bullheaded about this? Why now? What's changed?"

Ah, Diya was her daddy's little girl. She would be upset if her father was upset with her. Heck, even Krish hated disappointing Diya's father.

Taking pity on her, he offered her his energy drink.

Without even looking into the mug, she started making gagging sounds. "Ugh. I can smell it from here. How can you drink that mud?"

Offended on behalf of the mud, Krish rescinded his offer and took a long sip of the life-giving beverage.

"*Tcha, tcha, tcha.*" She clucked her tongue just like his old nanny, Vallima, who was against all caffeinated beverages. "You will ruin your complexion by drinking black coffee. Do you want mud for skin, Krishu *aann*? Wait! I forgot. You already have mud for skin."

Krish bared his teeth in an evil smile. Had he actually felt sorry for the cheeky chit?

"I remember Vallima saying the same thing to you when you overdosed on masala chai and Coke, Diya *penn.*"

Penn was girl in Malayalam, his mother tongue, while *aann* was boy.

"I only drink herbals now. Thus, my fair and lovely complexion is safe, and my blood is free of toxins." Diya ate healthy, drank healthy, and lived healthy. And it showed.

Krish gulped down his coffee and set the mug on the bedside table. He had a number of bad habits he should break, the least of which was his addiction to caffeine.

"The housekeeper isn't coming in today due to the weather. I was counting on Maria to help you with your trunks and treasures, but alas." He took off his glasses and wiped them with his T-shirt.

He'd thought long and hard about a Valentine's Day gift for Diya. He had to give her one, or for the rest of his life, he'd pay dearly for the baklava. He'd come up with the perfect gift. Better than the chocolate she wouldn't eat and the flowers that would make her sad when they wilted and died.

He jerked his head at the two still-closed trunks and slid his glasses back on. "If my lady desires to unpack or have any other chores she needs done, I'll be your knave for the day. My belated Valentine's gift to you."

Diya sashayed toward him, and with the back of her hand, she felt his forehead. "Definitely not feverish … and it's nearly nine o'clock. And yet, the Beast is still in his lair, wearing weird, fuddy-duddy flannel pajamas and spouting the strangest offers." She placed her hands on her hips and shot him a flinty-eyed glare. "What is going on, Krish? Shouldn't you be at work? Won't your company dive into the red if you play hooky two days in a row?"

Without meaning to, he tweaked her nose like his father used to. He couldn't decide who was more surprised by his action—Diya or him.

His father, Chandra Menon, had claimed that pulling on a

stubby nose several times a day would somehow balance the scales and improve its size. As a chartered accountant, his father had been all for balancing scales—except in his drinking.

"I'm taking the day off," Krish said, ignoring the bitter-sweet ache his father's memory had brought to his heart.

"But ... but ... but ... *why?*" Diya asked, blinking comically.

"Why not? I take days off every now and then. Not that you'd know my routine since you haven't visited me in years because of *your* work schedule. You're as big a workaholic as any of us, Diya. You don't fool anyone." He curled his hands into fists, so he wouldn't touch her again.

"Workaholic? Who, me?" She struck a vanity pose. "They don't call me the Party Princess of India for nothing."

Party Princess or not, Diya worked as hard as she partied. It spoke volumes about her boundless energy and zest for life. How did she do it? How did she dance all night and then manage to look bright-eyed and beautiful the next morning for a photo shoot? If he spent even half the night up—not dancing, mind you—he'd look haggard and feel even worse the next day.

Ergo, she is the supermodel and you the CFO, you moron!
Ex-CFO?

Damn it! He really needed to sort out his life's quagmires fast.

"We are not talking about my work ethics here," she rallied on. "We're talking about your anal ones." Her expression turned militant. "Daddy forced you to babysit me, didn't he? You have to hold my hand or twist it if I don't agree to his stupid decree, right? Tell me!" She poked a pointy, pink-nailed finger into his gut.

He winced. Jesus! Were they nails or weapons?

"With these cats as my witnesses, Beast, if you are encouraging Daddy in his asinine scheme ... which he only thought up because I told him what Hasaan's family was up to ... I swear, I will murder you."

Krish stepped back before Diya could poke him again. "There's nothing wrong with meeting the man, testing the potential, is there?"

Diya stared at him in horror. "You *want* me to meet some prospective groom my father's plucked out of a hat?"

Put like that, it did sound awful. But he had promised Kamal Uncle he'd try and smooth the way. "He's a great guy."

"How would you know? Do you know him? Is he one of your best buds?" She gave him the death stare.

"Well, no. I don't know him personally," he admitted, feeling sweat pop up over his neck. It had sounded like a great idea when Kamal Uncle put it forth. "But I've heard—"

"From Daddy," Diya derisively cut him off. "Ha! What an unbiased opinion that is." She shook her head to and fro several times before taking a deep breath. "Fine," she said on an exhalation. "I'll meet this ... *paragon* ... just to get you both off my back. When?"

Krish cleared his throat. "On Sunday. And he's—"

She held up a hand. "Spare me the heavenly songs of praise. I don't want to hear anything about him. I will meet him, and then I will decide if we are suited for one another."

Krish was taken aback by Diya's abnormally mature attitude regarding the arrangement. Where had this pragmatism been nine years ago? Why wasn't she ranting and raving about fairy tales and true love and princes or the charming Hasaan? He couldn't believe how easily she'd said yes.

But, of course, there was a catch.

"If I'm going to be shackled to some stranger by the end of the week, I will go down in glory," cried the drama queen. "And, since you've offered to be my knave, you have to do my bidding. You will take the week off. I don't care how busy you are, Beast. If you disagree, the deal is off."

Her mouth fell open when he agreed to her demand without argument. He'd been working from home since the buyout anyway, as the offices were shutting down and shifting to Wisconsin one department at a time. He almost felt sorry for tricking Diya into thinking she was winning. *Almost.*

A savagely calculating look came into her eyes, belying his quick win. It made his scalp itch with unease. Her eyes swept over him from head to toe, and on their way up, they stopped in the periphery of his navel, which wasn't nearly as pretty as hers.

Krish sucked in a breath, making his T-shirt stretch across his chest and billow over his stomach. While he didn't have what Diya referred to as a god-awful jiggle belly, he didn't have the infamously ripped six-pack she lusted after either.

"When's the last time you pumped iron at the gym?" She patted his cotton-clad gut like a mother patted a child's head before doling out punishment.

He was going to weep for siding with her father.

"A while ago. I haven't had time." Or the inclination to renew his gym membership in two years. Though he did play a mean game of tennis and cricket every weekend.

"First project for the coming week is reacquainting you with your major muscle groups," she declared.

Oh, yeah, paying off the debt to Lady Baklava was going to be brutal.

Diya was bewildered by the bizarre twist in her un-fairy tale.

Krish hadn't balked at her plans to physically torture him and had agreed to babysit her for a week? What the what?

"Since you're not heading off to your office, I vote we get started on your six-pack now." Now was as good a time as any to begin the torture. It was payback time. "Run along, Beast. Go change into your gym clothes."

He frowned. "You want to start now?"

"Why not? Do you have something better to do?" *Like hightail it to the office?*

He either owned up his game or owned up to his promise. Either way, she wasn't showing any mercy.

"But didn't you just finish your exercise routine?" he said.

Diya pointed to the door. "I'll stretch while I coach you."

Krish narrowed his eyes but walked out of the room without another word.

See? Bizarre.

She stalked to the escritoire where she'd left her metallic-pink sports bottle in the middle of a mess of books, papers, writing implements, chargers, wires, and a cordless phone. She screwed open the cap and took a long swallow of lemon-flavored water, sighing as the liquid cooled her pumped-up insides and hydrated her body.

What was her father up to? she wondered for the umpteenth time since he'd forced her to come to Dallas and shack up with Krish. And how had he convinced Krish to take a break from his work to babysit her? He couldn't be trying to fix a match between them again, could he?

Not after the disastrous results of his meddling the last time. No, that wasn't it. There definitely was a show-and-tell groom waiting in the wings. Krish had confirmed it. Besides, Krish's revoltingly solicitous attitude indicated he wasn't the nominee. Were he in the running, he'd be running to the hills for sure and snarling the whole way there.

She took another long sip of water and gave a delicate

little burp while mentally dissecting the conversation she'd had with her father early that morning. It had been clever of her to make the situation work in her favor.

"I'll agree to meet the suitable dude if you take an impromptu holiday in Goa with Mummy. Come on, Daddy. Be good old empty nesters and just take off on another honeymoon."

She wanted her parents out of gossip range for a week.

"Dear child, the very definition of empty nester is, we don't need to seek our honeymoons outside the house. What about our patients? We can't just leave them without advance notice."

Her father hated spontaneity. He was a planner. He had to be as an orthodontist.

In addition to a fairy-tale marriage, Kamal and Lubna Mathur shared a thriving dental practice. They didn't even have to travel for work since their office was located on the mezzanine floor of their residence building. That was why, unlike most dentists, her parents kept longer working hours. They were nothing if not super dedicated to their patients.

"We have responsibilities and a life. I refuse to run off and hide like a thief because you can't keep yourself scandal-free for a month."

Gosh, it was uncanny how similar Daddy and Krish were. Grouchy, not spontaneous, workaholics, disapproving.

In Daddy's defense, it had been close to his bedtime, and sexagenarians needed more than their allotted beauty sleep. What was Krish's excuse?

When pleading had failed, Diya had tried to butter her father up, laying it on thick. *"You've certainly had ample practice being a thief. Stealing Mummy's heart and spiriting her away in the middle of the night."*

Her parents' real-life romance could give Bollywood movies a run for their money. They'd fallen in love at first sight, and despite their families' vociferous objections to their union—her father's folks were Hindus, and her mother's family was devout Muslims—they'd eloped in the middle of the night and made a life together. Both the families had forgiven their children—eventually—but the road traveled had been fraught with recriminations. And yet, never once had her parents faltered in their love and support of each other.

That was the kind of love Diya aspired to have. The kind that made you giddy and shivery and so desperately in love that you braved the wicked world together. Her sister, Priya, had also experienced the same madness as a freshman at Seth GS Medical College when she shared her biology notes with Amol Shroff. Last year, Leesha had caught the lovebug, too, with Aryan. Though, to hear both Pree and Leesha explain it, their ultimate decision to tie the knot had little to do with romance and more to do with fiscal and legal practicalities.

Bah! And humbug. Liars and idiots, both of them.

Her mental grumbling came to a halt when Krish ambled back into the room, outfitted in running shoes, ridiculously loose basketball shorts, and a faded black T-shirt no better than a rag.

Diya recapped the water bottle and drank him in. Broad shoulders. Slight slouch. Decently muscled limbs. A beer belly. He was unconditioned, true, but not terribly. His muscles just needed to be reawakened. She licked her lips in anticipation.

"How do you want to do this? Go for a walk? A run? There's a gym in the basement," he said, waggling his eyebrows above his spectacles while his brown eyes twinkled.

A tingling started deep inside her despite her best effort to the contrary.

For the most part, Diya was reconciled to her loveless fate. She had no hope of experiencing the kind of passion she dreamed of—not while the Beast lived and breathed.

Certainly not when he was such a huge part of her life. There was no room to get away from him or over him, and she didn't have the guts to cut him out completely. She couldn't even imagine such a thing. Not that it would be at all possible or practical to pretend that he was invisible at family gatherings. So, she took pleasure in the small things. Like revenge.

She placed her left hand on her hip and sauntered toward him, coming to a stop close enough until they could feel each other breathe. She raised a hand and trailed her fingertips down his chest, testing, caressing, pointing out the parts that needed work.

He caught her wrist when her fingers dipped under the waistband of his shorts, holding it in a deathly grip. His expression was utterly calm, as if nothing she did affected him. It wasn't fair when everything he did affected her on a molecular level.

It hurt her heart to be around him sometimes.

"Walk?" She twisted free and scoffed, "Walking is for pussies."

CHAPTER 6

*F*riday inched forward in a cloud of comic skepticism and intense flirting.

To Krish's initial and immense amusement, Diya had refused to believe that he, *"Really? Truly?"* meant to remain at home for the duration of her stay in the Dallas–Fort Worth metroplex area.

Every so often, he'd catch her staring at him. Then, her eyes would glance at the watch on her wrist or at an appliance that displayed the time—like the old cuckoo clock dangling from a wall or the TV or the oven she was preheating now—before coming back to rest on his face.

She seemed to expect him to spring up, change into office clothes, and rush out of the house with an, Adios, *baby. No more knave for you.*

Or did she want him to leave? Did she want some privacy to mope and wail and wallow at her predicament?

When her eyes did another one of the time-watching circuits, he finally begged her to stop. "You're stuck with me, whether you like it or not." Then, he distracted her by holding up two avocados to her face. "Which one's ready? I can never tell."

Buying organic food had been the third item on Diya's Friday agenda. The first being the nauseating drill of core exercises she'd put him through to jump-start his muscle growth and metabolism, followed by their daily hygiene routines. His had taken ten minutes flat—enough time for a man to shower and change into jeans and a green polo.

Her feminine routine had lasted for more than an hour, part of which she'd spent in the kitchen, concocting a home-made facial mask made of fresh fruit, yogurt, and ground lentil. She'd carried a big, holistic bowl brimming with the paste into the bathroom—said bowl unearthed from one of the pink trunks by yours truly.

"Nothing like a natural body scrub to gently exfoliate your skin. Try it, Beast," she'd urged earnestly. "Better yet, allow me to demonstrate the correct method of application. Your pores will thank you for allowing them to breathe."

To that sage beauty tip by a woman whose face was avocado-green and caked with segments of half an orange, he'd replied, "Thanks, but no, thanks." Then, he'd executed a swift retreat into the den before she got it in her head to forcibly make his pores happy.

He'd spent the next three-quarters of the hour barking out orders and instructions to his team, most of whom had been effortlessly absorbed into Wisco and were tying up loose odds and ends in Dallas. He should be doing the same, just in case he did decide to bind himself to Wisco. But he didn't want to go into work. And he didn't want to bind himself to anything for five years. He had to come to a decision soon, one way or another. He had to figure out what it was he really wanted out of life.

When Diya had come looking for him after her bath and

asked if she could borrow the car to get some groceries, he'd quit brooding and accompanied her on the errand.

They were back in the kitchen now with Krish propped on a barstool, slurping a berry protein smoothie and half a piece of baklava, while India's version of the *Barefoot Contessa* prepared a healthy and very late lunch for them.

His anticipation knew no bounds, and he wasn't getting started on how excited his taste buds and stomach were. He hadn't had one of Diya's freshly prepared meals in ages. Besides being the Party Princess of India—possibly the whole of Asia—Beauty Mathur was also the crowned Queen of House and Kitchen.

She could cook. Like *really cook* and not just throw things in a bowl and call it a meal. In fact, she was a master at an incredible number of domestic crafts: sewing—she could make her own clothes from scratch (not that she needed to), knitting, crocheting, quilting. He still had the quilt she'd made for him when he graduated. A patchwork number in the colors of the Indian flag, so he'd remember his roots. She'd personalized each green, saffron, white, and blue patch with a symbol or a story or a picture that held meaning for him. It lay at the bottom of his closet, within reach. He took it out on the nights he felt unreasonably alone and homesick.

Even all those years ago, she'd known what he needed. Diya always knew what people needed, sometimes before they knew themselves.

Was that why she was helping Hasaan Jabbir? Or was she in love with him?

"Do you actually remember everything you learned from the countless classes you've taken?" he asked, suddenly looking at her flibbertigibbet activities in a completely new light.

She knew Reiki healing. She'd even tried her hand at hypnotism in relation to past-life regression. She'd tried to hypnotize him once. He'd never had a better eight hours of sleep.

Diya looked up from the stove, ladle in one hand and spoon in the other. The rising steam from the simmering soup pot had given her face an appealing dewiness. A few tendrils of her hair had escaped her ponytail and were sticking to her neck and cheeks. She'd made him brush them off her face a few times while batting her eyelashes at him. Diya was a natural-born flirt. She lived to tease, to hug, to make people smile and feel good about themselves. She was a tactile person. The way she'd touched his chest that morning. God, she was a tease.

Her rosebud lips bloomed into a smile. "Like the ikebana and sushi-making classes?"

She set down the utensils and wiped her hands on her pink apron. Below the apron, she was still very much a diva in a frilly yellow top and skinny jeans.

He nodded and took another slurp of his smoothie. Who knew raw vegetables and fruit tasted this good? "How many different types of classes have you taken again?"

Diya was julienning a cupful of baby carrots on the chopping board. The lunch menu was *tom yum* soup, papaya salad, and steamed dim sums. Krish's mouth watered just from the tangy smells swirling about the kitchen.

"Lost count after I crossed one hundred," she replied with a shrug. She tilted her head toward him as if posing for a photograph without slowing down the slicing. "If you sneer at my diverse ADHD non-education again ... if you so much as twitch a sarcastic eyelid, you can kiss this lunch good-bye. I'll feed your share of this age-defying meal to the cats."

"I doubt cats like Thai. Plus, they aren't much bothered by aging—nine lives and all, you know," he drawled.

But her words triggered a rush of bittersweet memories. Had he actually sneered at her back then? Had he really been such a pompous, stick-in-the-mud academic who looked down on the unique way she educated herself?

Suddenly feeling awful and awkward, he slid off the barstool and walked around the kitchen island. The least he could do was rinse his glass and apologize.

"No, seriously, I was a jerk," he said a dozen years too late. "And stupid and ignorant and … just wrong."

"My, my. Who knew exercise could strike your conscience like this?" Her smile grew amused. "You were right though. You all were. If I had pursued that law degree instead of dropping out, I might be a master of one thing and not a brat of all."

Diya's parents had hoped their second daughter would also follow the family tradition and become a doctor. But Diya had never been interested in studies. She'd enrolled in law only because Alisha had.

"Brat of all. I like it. It suits you, being a brat of all. I can't imagine you as a lawyer or a doctor. I can't imagine you at a desk with a nine-to-five job. I don't think I ever did." Krish couldn't remember the last time Diya and he had had a conversation that didn't deteriorate into a fight. He doubted the amity would last.

To hell with not annoying her, he thought and tweaked her nose.

She batted his hand away. "I can't either. I only ever wanted—" She abruptly pressed her lips together and made a strange gurgling sound in her throat.

"What is it? Did you cut yourself?" He reached for her hands, but they were fine, one still holding the knife. When he looked at her face, her cheeks had gone pink, and she refused to meet his eyes.

He froze as it struck him what she'd said—rather what she had been about to say perhaps and hadn't. Diya had only ever wanted a fairy tale.

For as long as he could remember, she'd been obsessed with finding her prince, falling in love, getting married, making a home in a castle surrounded by horses and a dozen children. The M Brigade would often ponder over life, as children did when they had a vast future ahead of them. Diya's lofty domestic goals had been the butt of many a joke.

However, if the thought of her chained to a desk was laughable, he couldn't imagine her cooking and keeping house all day either. He couldn't imagine her as a wife.

No, he'd refused to imagine her as his wife. He'd asked her to marry him, and then he'd tried his damnedest not to think about marriage at all.

He couldn't blame her for walking away.

"You were … probably still are, so good at drawing, painting. Storytelling. You were forever scribbling in those books … your secret diaries. I remember your stories. Did you never want to write? Take up art seriously, as a vocation?" he asked, wondering if his crimes against her could ever be forgiven.

"Just doodles, Beast. No, I never had any goals or ambitions. Not until the modeling, that is. I've finally stumbled on to my thing … my *raison d'être*. My beauty finally has a purpose."

"You thought you didn't have one before?" He was puzzled by her cynical tone. Another thing he couldn't imagine—a cynical Beauty Mathur.

She shrugged again. "You know me. Parties, clothes, shoes, bags, adulation … that's all I want. That's all I need to be happy. And I intend to enjoy every decadence life has to offer indefinitely or until my beauty fades. By then, I hope to be happily married to a really super-duper rich guy who will adore me enough to pay a plastic surgeon to keep me young forever." She exchanged the knife for a ladle. She stirred the soup a few times, and then she shut off the gas. "I hope the dude Daddy's picked for me is super rich," she added with a wicked smile.

It was all such bullshit. Krish was tired of hearing her claim she was nothing but a party girl. She seemed to forget that he knew her better than the idiots she roamed the world with—idiots who couldn't see past the dazzling exterior to the loyal, generous, and compassionate woman inside.

Beauty fades. She had that right. Skin-deep beauty did fade. But he doubted Diya's beauty would ever fade. In his eyes, she grew more and more beautiful every day. Like a rose unfurling in slow motion, petal by petal and every stage a masterpiece.

She'd make some man—maybe even this Neil she was meeting on Sunday—a very good wife. And that man had better be a prince, better treasure her, or he'd have to answer to Krish.

"Beauty Mathur, no part of you is ever going to need plastic surgery. Trust me," he said and gave in to his desire to kiss her cheek.

She shivered as he did so despite that it was very warm in the kitchen.

He frowned, worrying. "Are you coming down with something? You've been shivering off and on all afternoon."

"Just the change in weather. Here, taste this," she said and thrust a spoonful of soup into his mouth.

He swallowed in reflex. "*Tom yum* is named appropriately. It's yum."

His cell phone buzzed just then, the caller ID alerting him that it was Lovey Onden trying to reach him. *At last.* His friendly neighborhood real estate agent, who'd just bid on a property for him, had better be calling with good news.

"I have to take this. I won't be long," he said, walking out of the kitchen.

· · ·

DIYA RELEASED the breath she'd been holding the second Krish left the kitchen. Oxygen hand-springing through her bloodstream again, she took a shuddery sigh and focused on dicing the baby portabella mushrooms for the dim sums.

What in heaven's name was the matter with her? Why had the icy control she'd developed around Krish deserted her since yesterday? She'd honed the ice-princess persona so brilliantly over the years that, sometimes, she dry-iced even herself. It had to reignite now.

And Krish thought she was coming down with the flu. *Jeez.* She didn't know whether to laugh or cry at the tragic comedy of her life.

She did neither. She had no time or headspace for it. Putting aside the stuffing for the dim sums, she started on the *som tam*, the green papaya salad.

She couldn't believe she'd nearly blurted out her secret life goal when they spoke about aspirations. What would he have said, how would he have reacted had she not bitten her tongue in time?

Oh, by the way, Krish, my life's sole purpose since you danced with me on my sixteenth birthday is to be your wife, the maker of your home and the mother of your children. Oh! And please, please, please allow me to be the keeper of your heart, too.

A hysterical giggle burst out of her.

Was being the operative word, she reminded herself sternly. She was past such goals now.

The embarrassing truth was that, with no romantic encouragement from Krish whatsoever, she'd dreamed up a whole castle full of a future with him. She'd been so sure he returned her feelings and her dreams that she'd poured her energies into learning how to be the perfect wife. When Krish had decided to make his permanent home in the US, she'd learned how to be the perfect nonresident Indian wife —the do-everything-yourself wife. She'd learned how to keep a house and maintain it. She knew how to repair a sink leak, change a faulty flush valve, how to apply wallpaper, change a tap, a lightbulb. She even knew about car upkeep and spark plugs and changing a tire without a car jack or a AAA rescue.

She inhaled and exhaled and tried to balance her chi. It was all right. No knowledge was ever wasted. Hadn't she managed to utilize some of the more unusual skills she'd acquired during her travels? They'd also come in handy during her jaunts into the Indian heartland as a representative or a spokesperson for various non-governmental organizations and charities. Young girls—especially village girls—needed to see grown women be self-sufficient and capable and not helpless.

Believe it or not, she'd stopped feeling sorry for herself long ago. She was Beauty Mathur, for couture's sake. She was Scheherazade. At the end of her two-year contract with JES, she'd have enough money in her bank account to buy a small kingdom and rule it for the rest of her life. She didn't need a prince or his fortune or his adulation; she had her own. And would any of it have been possible had Krish not revealed his true feelings by refusing to kiss her?

No, she no longer blamed the Beast for her botched life plans. Or held it against him. Not entirely. Whatever had happened had happened for the best. It was simply Karma. And she had found the silver lining.

"Is it ready?" the Beast growled right into her left ear.

Diya screamed and dropped the knife, and then she jumped back before the blade skewered her bare foot.

Krish bent down to retrieve it and the onion that had bounced away, but instead of straightening up with both and apologizing for scaring the life out of her, he slid all the way to the floor and began howling with laughter.

"That was such a girlie shriek." He sprawled at her feet, laughing like a loon and imitating her screech.

She poked his chest with her toe. "You're a *gaddha*." A donkey, as in stupid beast.

He caught her foot when she tried to poke him again and playfully yanked it. She shouldn't have lost her balance, but she did and fell hard on her butt next to him, yelping and cursing.

"Girlie-girl," he said obnoxiously.

She pressed the heel of her palm to his forehead and thumped it hard against the cherry-wood kitchen cabinet at his back. "Once a *gaddha*, always a *gaddha*. And I'll show you a girlie-girl."

She tried to subdue him, using Krav Maga self-defense tactics. But, for an out-of-shape guy, he wasn't going down easy. How was that even possible? They wrestled to get the upper hand. At one point, she fisted her hands into his thick, wavy hair and pulled. He cursed, flinching back from her.

This is better, Diya thought. Behaving like children was infinitely better than being stiff and awkward. Fun, flirty, and frivolous—that was the way to deal with her Beast.

Crap. Not *her* Beast, *the* Beast.

"Okay, enough. Get off, you *gaddha*," she said and scrambled to sit up.

"I wondered what had happened to your Hinglish, *desi* girl. You've been sounding much too hoity-toity of late." He sat up, laughing, and threw an affectionate arm around her.

Hinglish was English liberally garnished with words from Hindi and numerous other Indian languages and was popular among the predominantly English-speaking but multilingual urban Indian population. If the mash-up language or dialect wasn't officially hanging from the Indo-Aryan language tree yet, it was only waiting for the World Language Board's approval; Diya was sure of it.

"Boss, I've been abroad … sorry, in *pardes* for two solid months, surrounded by people who get confused when I speak *desi*. Much easier to use the global form of communication than be forced to repeat your words over and over again just to be understood." She nudged his shoulder with hers. "Wasn't that your excuse when you stopped speaking it?"

Krish had lost his Hinglish and most of his Hindi and Marathi, too. He spoke Malayalam very well though. But that was because Vallima refused to speak in any other language with him and Leesha. Vallima considered it her everlasting duty to keep their Keralite culture alive in her fully grown charges' lives. Savitri Aunty didn't stress over languages as long as her headstrong children were communicating with her and each other openly and honestly. She was a wise woman.

"Yesss-ssa!" Krish replied in an exaggerated South Indian accent in a poor attempt at homegrown humor. "My *vonly* reason to stop the *bhankas*."

Bhankas usually meant useless jabber. But its meaning altered, depending on the word's placement or context in a sentence. As with most things in life, reading between the lines was paramount in Hinglish.

Krish rose to his feet and offered his hand to pull Diya up. She only took it because she didn't want her girlie-girl parts to feel neglected.

"Now, get lost. No more *bhankas*. I need ten minutes … fifteen, max … and lunch will be served." She nudged him to move aside, so she could get to work.

But he didn't budge. "I am your knave, aren't I?"

Diya didn't know whether to shiver or sigh at the way Krish was looking at her. So, she did both, and then, she set him to work.

"You're sure you're fine? No body ache, headache, allergies?" he asked while pressing tiny balls of the preprepared and well-risen dim sum dough into flat rounds with the help of a roti maker.

"You're giving me a headache with your questions. I'm fine. It's jet lag and the change in weather," she said not untruthfully.

"If you're sure ... how do you feel about coming for a party tonight?" When she felt obliged to check his body temperature again, he growled, "Cut it out, Diya."

"Partying two straight nights in a row. Playing hooky from work. Living in a storybook house"—she ticked off while brushing each flat round of dough with sesame oil and then spooning mushroom filling into it before gathering the edges together like a moneybag and twisting off the top —"agreeing to be my twenty-four/seven knave. Agreeing to be my father's voice of insanity. And you haven't even scolded me for the pregnancy scandal or my tattered reputation yet. Why are you being so nice, Beast?" She paused, widening her eyes and putting a hand on her chest as a horrible thought struck her. "You have a brain tumor, don't you? It's the only explanation for your drastic personality change."

His answer was to pull her nose and give a sardonic shake of his head.

We celebrated KM's 26th birthday at China Garden. He chose to go there even though there are a million other pan-Asian restaurants in Mumbai now. But CG is still his favorite … our favorite because it holds the most memories of family fun days. (And the gin chicken was yum, like always.)

He says he came down from NY for work, but I think he didn't want to be alone on his birthday. Leesha thinks my imagination has run away again. Maybe. Maybe not.

Who knows what goes on in KM's mind these days? He's become so secretive about everything.

The reason for this post-midnight entry is that Daddy has finally broached the subject of our marriage. O. M. Jeez. It seems like I've waited for this day forever. True, KM should be doing the proposing to me and not Daddy to him. But I'm not going to be picky. I'm going to be as practical as Pree and Leesha. KM hasn't exactly given his answer, and I'm anxious about it. He wants to talk to me alone tomorrow.

Maybe he's planning to propose? What if he's going to do the whole bended-knee-and-ring ritual?

O. M. Jeez!!! What should I wear?

Leesha thinks I should kiss him first before saying yes. Just to check if he's a frog or a prince. I haven't thought of him as a frog or a beast for some time now, and I don't need a kiss to prove our love. I have no doubt about our compatibility—sexual or otherwise. He makes me shiver just by looking at me. Exactly like Mummy shivers when Daddy looks at her ... when they think Pree and I are not looking.

See? I can be practical. I know how these things work.

P.S. The pundit has predicted that I'll be married before the year is out. Before my 21st birthday.

No dancing in Dallas? Is this hell?

Diya sent off the text message to Leesha since she'd been banned from posting on social media until her publicist gave her leave. She couldn't even update her status, forget posting photos.

"Exactly what kind of party does not have dancing? It *is* a party we're attending and not a funeral, right?" she asked, angling her body in the passenger seat to look at Krish.

"The kind plebeians call a dinner party," the Beast replied in his usual beastly way.

They were off to Fort Worth, which was a twenty-minute drive from the storybook house. Suburban Arlington flew by as they zoomed across the I-30 in Krish's silver two-seater Boxster S coupe.

The stupendous Porsche was yet another flag in the Beast's personality malfunction. Diya had heard that a man detoured into the chest-beating zone around year forty and procured himself either a flashy car, a motorbike, a mistress, or something equally alter ego-ish. But Krish was a few years off; he wouldn't turn thirty-five until May. Maybe fuddy-duddies went through a midlife crisis sooner than normal men?

She looked him over as he drove, trying to figure out what was up with him. He was behaving quite strangely, and it had begun to bother her. After a few minutes of staring, she began to admire the way his shoulders filled out the leather jacket he wore over a crisp black shirt and dark jeans—clothes she'd nagged him to put on for the party. He'd been quite set on throwing on a jacket over the same ghastly T-shirt and jeans he'd worn all day.

But she'd said, "No can do," and proceeded to mousse up and muss up his hair until it was all deliciously roguish.

He'd threatened to shower the effect off, but thankfully, a work-related phone call had distracted him.

Diya let out a heartfelt sigh. The characteristic that most needed improvement—mainly his fashion laziness—hadn't budged an iota in this midlife-crisis ordeal.

Well, *she* hadn't been lazy at all. It was Friday night, wasn't it? The night to dress up, have a few drinks, and dance. Or dress up, drink, and *not dance* in this case. Seriously, was she in hell?

She'd taken a second shower to get rid of the chef's cologne from the cooking. She'd also blow-dried her hair, moisturized her skin, brushed on makeup, and repainted her nails—all in a matter of minutes.

Oh, all right! It had taken close to an hour to get ready. *Totally worth it,* she decided, critiquing her hazy reflection in the windshield.

Donning a full-sleeved, extra-short hot-pink sheath and a pair of high-heeled black pumps, she had catwalked out of her room and twirled her wares in front of the Beast's gold-rimmed spectacles as a treat.

His eyes had lingered on her legs for many shivery seconds before he pronounced, "You forgot to wear the bottom half of the dress."

The man had zero fashion sense. Zero.

Anyway, to beat the cold—the temperature had dropped several degrees since the storm—she'd draped a brown-and-pink-plaid woolen poncho over her outfit. All in all, she looked uber chic and warm. He did, too. And they complemented each other, black to hot pink, leather to plaid.

Not that she wanted them to match or anything. There was no matching Beauty and the Beast anymore. It was simply a fashionista's observation. In fact, they were meeting some woman called Lovey tonight. Probably Krish's latest GF. *Ugh—no, no. Oh, what joy!* She was dying to meet this girl.

Her mental soliloquy came to an abrupt stop as fat splotches of crushed ice began to plop down on the windshield. The Beast switched on the wipers.

"Is that ice or rain?"

Perfect. Just the sort of weather to help her maintain a chilly veneer.

"It's sleet," Krish replied slowly as if addressing a toddler.

"Really? It's the first time I'm experiencing sleet. Another bucket list item checked off." Diya clapped her hands like a two-year-old. "So exciting!"

Krish flicked on a blinker and took the exit off the highway. "Congratulations. Now, you can die happy."

Diya refused to let the Grinch Who Killed Christmas put a damper on her good mood. She looked too amazing to pout or frown or feel vexed.

After turning left and right on several uninteresting streets, they started driving down University Drive North, which overflowed with restaurants, glowing shops, and movie theaters. It was a veritable promenade of entertainment. Diya's heart bloomed with hope as she looked at the shiny, lively area with its bright lights and swarms of smiling pedestrians. How fuddy-duddy-ish could the dinner be in this kind of setting?

At the end of the street, Krish drove through the gates of an L-shaped building complex and pulled into a parking spot reserved for visitors. He got out of the car and went around to stand on a cobblestone pathway, close to her door. She finished reapplying her lip gloss, raised the hood of her poncho to protect her hair, and then waited expectantly for a beat or two. When the Beast didn't even glance her way, much less open the door for her, Diya sighed and got out of the car under her own steam.

She sternly reminded herself that it wasn't a date. He didn't need to be solicitous. And how would he know that getting out of a low car, from a bucket seat, in stilettoes was difficult?

Still, she'd gotten used to Hasaan's brand of princely chivalry over the past few months. Hasaan never failed to pull open doors, hold out chairs, or slow his stride, so he was walking alongside the woman on his arm and not ahead of her. He knew how to make a woman feel special.

Krish fell into step beside her as they made their way to the building entrance, making her smile. Maybe he wasn't a total lost cause.

A uniformed doorman let them in through a glass-paneled door. "*Buenas noches,* Mr. Menon," he greeted with a smile.

"*Hola,* Juan. *¿Cómo estás?*" Krish replied, slapping the man on his back.

An exuberant exchange of Spanish flowed between the two *hombres*; after, Krish placed his hand on the small of her back and gallantly guided her into the lobby.

Diya's smile widened. It was the first time she'd noticed

that the public Krish was a whole different animal from the private Beast. *Interesting.*

"Swanky complex," she purred as they clip-clopped across a spacious urban-style lobby that was sectioned off into several seating areas by oversize garden pots. Steel sculptures, colorful artwork, and lots and lots of glass accentuated the merry space. Happy-looking people lolled about here and there; some of them smiled, waved, or exchanged greetings with Krish as they walked past. He seemed to know them.

They stopped in front of a line of elevators. A festive sign stood in one corner, announcing *V-Weekend Party Tonight!* inside a golden heart with Cupid's arrow pointing toward the ceiling.

Diya's insides fluttered. Was he taking her to a real party? Probably not. Krish had said they'd be meeting some friends for dinner and that she'd like the gang and Lovey. He'd separated Lovey from the gang like she was special. Was she special?

"How do you know all these people in the lobby?" she asked. Subtler than, *How often do you visit your girlfriend that her doorman knows you this darn well?*

Krish slid his hands into his pockets. "I lived here for the last two years. Moved out only last month."

Delight and surprise zinged through Diya. Delight because him knowing *hombre* Juan had nothing to do with being familiar with his GF's boudoir and surprise that this cool building used to be the Beast's lair. Still, she wouldn't exchange it for the fairy-tale house.

"Wait! I don't think I can take this in. It's too much." She touched the back of her hand to her forehead like a B-grade movie heroine and pretended to swoon, her other hand clutching her black patent leather Scheherazade clutch to her chest. "You lived *here*? You? This hedonistic dream palace was once your home? Who *are* you, and what have you done to the boring Beast?"

Her theatrics were ignored. Krish's gaze was fixed on the number panel above the elevator door where they glowed green in decreasing order. When the doors opened, he steered her into an elevator cab with mirrored walls.

Perfect.

Diya removed her poncho and did one last check on her face, hair, and clothes and blew herself a kiss. "I approve of your choice in real estate. Very cool."

"Hardly my choice. It was a company flat. The office is only two blocks down," he said, sounding very uncool.

"Sneer all you want, but I have your number. I know the fuddy-duddy inside you is on his way out, and a bolder, better animal has emerged from the chrysalis. Wait till I tell Leesha. She'll want to jump on the next flight here to witness the miracle firsthand."

"Clown," Krish said, tapping her nose.

Diya tried to feel annoyed about the constant nose-pulling and being treated like a toddler, but she couldn't quite muster up the feeling because the action seemed to put a heart-melting smile in Krish's eyes. Pathetic—that was she.

A blast of club music hit her when they landed on the terrace-clubhouse floor. And there was the final proof of the Beast's metamorphosis. It was a full-blown party with lots and lots of people and hearts and flowers and dancing and disco lights *and* a DJ.

"Liar, liar, pants on fire. Just a dinner with some buddies, was it?" She poked him in the chest as he held the elevator doors open for her.

Stupendously happy that he was taking his job as her knave to heart, she *cha-cha-cha*-ed into the clubhouse.

·   ·   ·

KRISH TIPPED the bottle of Heineken to his mouth and watched Miguel Rodrigo, the guy from A1-F, and Diya do the hustle to Enrique Iglesias's latest hit.

By day, Miguel was part-owner and designer of a landscape company. By night, he was apparently a young John Travolta. The party was in full swing, saturated with people and noise. It was all a bit much, in Krish's opinion. Just like the dancing queen.

Diya had picked the perfect spot on the dance floor to dance and pose. Of course she had. She knew exactly what she looked like, awash in the pale red disco lights. Beyond alluring. Enchanting. Those endless legs of hers had been created to drive men stupid.

Krish had stupidly been staring at them, too, until a group of revelers obscured his vision, inadvertently saving his sanity. He could only hope Diya's jet lag would kick in soon, and he could take her home and lock her up. He was sick of having to watch every single man in the room—himself included—pant and drool. If that made him a fuddy-duddy, so be it. At least, she couldn't accuse him of being a sexist fuddy-duddy because he didn't care to watch women turn into fools in front of her either.

Krish rotated his shoulders, trying to alleviate the knots of tension in them. He'd known what would happen as soon as Diya stepped out of the bedroom in her costume—he refused to call what she wore a dress. What had possessed him to think she'd be easier to handle in a crowd than at home alone? He should have known how the evening would play out. How many times had he chaperoned her before? A thousand? A million? He knew such nights always gave him an ulcer by the end.

She wasn't going to leave him alone. She'd make him dance with her. Why did she want to dance with a fuddy-duddy anyway?

Why couldn't women take no for an answer? And why were they not happy with the result when men did exactly as they'd predicted all along?

Krish took another long chug of beer, tore his gaze from the dance floor, and forced it across the clubhouse, hoping to catch the eye of a known face or two. His work hours hadn't left him with much free time, and he'd very rarely attended social events at the complex. Yet he knew enough of the long-term residents not to feel completely out of place. And he knew Lovey Onden, one of the key organizers of such events, who knew everyone and everything about everyone.

Diya and Lovey had hit it off like a house on fire, as Krish had expected and hoped. Both girls were bubbly, chirpy, and fun-loving. Though, for a moment, when he'd first introduced them, he'd thought he'd made a mistake in bringing them together.

All his life, he'd watched women act weird around Diya. He realized it was a kind of envy or a slice of awe, like something a man would feel in the presence of Azeem Premji or Warren Buffet. Diya tried hard to be normal—Krish paused, contemplating the word. Maybe *normal* was stretching it, but Diya hid behind a veneer of affability and goofiness to blend in with the crowd. She wanted to be treated like just another woman. But she wasn't just another woman, was she?

Short, curvy Lovey with her mop of boyish hair and easy clothes had been struck dumb by Beauty Mathur. And Diya in turn had been quite out of character, staring down her nose at Lovey. Had it been his imagination that Diya gave Lovey the same frigid treatment she reserved for him alone? Must've been because, as soon as Lovey had begun to tell him about the bid on the three-bedroom condo in the complex, Diya's mood had flipped three hundred sixty degrees. She'd thrown her arms around a dumbstruck Lovey, begging to be shown the flat, and succeeded in making the shorter woman her fan. She hadn't been kidding about her obsession with house-hunting, had she?

"Stop brooding, Beast. You're at a party." Diya snatched the bottle of Heineken from his hand and guzzled it down. There had only been a few sips left.

He opened his mouth to deny it but closed it without uttering a word because, damn it, it was true. He'd been brooding so hard that he'd missed the vision in pink bouncing toward him. Her mood had done another switcheroo. She was no longer miffed with him. For the life of him, he couldn't recall what he'd done or said to piss her off after the Lovey incident. Whatever it was, he was glad it was gone.

She handed the empty bottle back to him, covered her mouth with the back of her hand, and burped. Alisha had her laughing hiccups, and Diya had her burps.

"Nice." Krish laughed, setting the bottle down on the table covered with tiny red, white, and silver heart confetti.

"Sorry. You know I can't control it." Her heart-shaped face was flushed from dancing, not embarrassment. Like he'd said, not an ordinary woman.

"Do you even try?" he asked.

"Only in polite company," she purred, giving him a slow wink.

His eyebrow kicked up. "I'm not polite company?"

She carefully shook her head as if she was a little tipsy. "You're the Beast with a Y chromosome. You're used to all kinds of obnoxious sounds."

"I'm not the one who was uncouth just now," he pointed out.

But he had been when they were children. He'd once fart-bombed the girls' sleepover and then been hairbrush-attacked by a trio of outraged banshees.

Diya waved a hand in front of his face, bringing him back

to the present. "You're a dolt. Why are you standing around, brooding into a beer? Come dance with me. Unless your girlfriend won't like it. Does she give you grief if you dance with another girl in her absence?"

"I supremely dislike that form of hedonism," he declared, not bothering to correct her false assumption about his mythical girlfriend.

She'd been on his case since his Valentine's date. His fault. But she'd been goading him about it and about taking the day off, as if he'd never done something like that before. She made him sound like Sisyphus, laboring to push a boulder uphill for eternity. He'd deflected his annoyance by keeping silent, not fully grasping until later that he'd aroused her romantic curiosity by his actions.

Diya was a closet matchmaker. Show her two single people giving each other *the look*, and her head would conjure up vials full of love potions that she'd try her dandiest to spritz on the couple. Most of the time, she was way off the mark. Like with him. He'd had dinner with Aya, his ex, on Valentine's Day, true, but it had been a business-cum-good-bye dinner. But, if he owned up to it, Diya would smack him on the head and call him a fuddy-duddy again.

"Krish, do something fun for once. Stand on the dance floor and march if you must, but don't be such a fuddy-duddy."

And he rested his case.

"Yes, milady." Krish gave Diya a mock bow. Then, he grabbed her hand and pulled her to the dance floor.

She was going to dance the night away, with or without him, and he'd rather not have her dance with a stranger in her tipsy state.

Laughing in delight, Diya started bouncing as if she were on a pogo stick instead of pointy shoes that defied gravity, but soon, she settled into her familiar, fancy dance moves.

Krish shuffled his feet and silently cursed the gods of dance. Only a sadist would invent this kind of torture and call it entertainment.

Obviously, he was a masochist for giving in to her. Why had he?

"Spin me." Diya threaded their hands together.

He had danced with her countless times before and knew what she wanted. He spun her out. She spun back in. She twirled and twisted around him, and all he had to do was hold on.

They danced for a long time, through the Macarena and the Chicken Dance. Well, she did that last one while he resumed shuffling his feet. He absolutely refused to flap his arms about. But he enjoyed watching her be silly. She sparkled so brightly under the disco ball that his eyes hurt, but it was hard not to stare at her. Not to feel envious of her unfettered joy.

Then, the music mellowed, and so did their movements. He'd slow-danced with Diya before, too.

He placed his hands on her hips and drew her close. She circled her arms about his neck, and with a sigh, she tucked her face into the crook of his shoulder. It didn't matter if she wore high heels or was barefoot; she somehow managed to make them fit together.

The touch of her lips on his jaw made his chest feel heavy and airless at once.

Diya was a tactile creature, and affectionate gestures were only an extension of her limbs. She touched as often as she used her hands, kissed as much as she talked. For his own sanity, Krish kept his distance. Mostly. And Diya toed the line he'd drawn between them. She'd crossed the line only twice—once on her twenty-first birthday and then at Alisha's wedding. No, that wasn't true. They had both crossed the line. He didn't know what Diya's excuse was, but he'd been rip-roaringly drunk both times.

The kiss they'd shared on her twenty-first birthday could almost be excused. It had been a special day, and they'd both been young and stupid in addition to being under the influence. But he didn't know what beast had gotten into him six months ago on the night of Alisha and Aryan's stag party.

Diya had been hell on heels, as usual. Not at all shocking after the staggering amount of alcohol they'd all consumed. And, while he hadn't approved of her flirting with Mann and Harry—Aryan's closest friends—he'd believed she was in safe hands.

He should have worried more about the boys.

Still, he'd watched her closely, and when Diya had asked Harry to escort her to her room, Krish had told himself to stay out of it, even when he saw them staggering out of the ballroom.

I'm not her father, he'd said to himself. *She is a grown woman—despite all indications to the contrary—and she makes her own decisions.*

That self-talk had lasted about five minutes, and Krish had found himself taking the elevator up to Diya's floor. He'd only wanted to make sure she was okay.

But then he had seen her kiss Harry on the lips outside her door, and then Harry had laughed at something she'd said. Then, he'd swept her up in his arms and carried her inside the room, and Krish's control had snapped.

His rage at her cavalier attitude about herself and her reputation had erupted like a volcano. He'd barely refrained from grabbing Harry by his tuxedo lapels and chucking him out the door. The man had looked more worried than amorous when he left the room, Krish had realized later—much later.

Right then, when everything had looked red and vile, he'd

said nasty things to Diya. Things he shouldn't have said. Things he would never have said had he been sober. Things he could never take back.

He'd remembered feeling jealous all night. He'd wanted her to flirt with *him* and no one else. Dance with *him* and no one else. Kiss only him.

She'd laughed at him instead. Then, she had kissed him—nothing more than a teasing bite of his mouth—and suddenly, he'd found himself kissing her back. When sanity had returned, he'd been horrified and repulsed by himself, by his need of her, and so, he'd called her names.

She'd slapped his face then and shoved him out of her room. Like she should have done right at the beginning.

He'd left her with his father's warning ringing in his ears. *"Don't trust women, son. Don't ever let them get close. They will drive you mad or running to the bottle."*

With Diya, Krish felt perpetually drunk even if he hadn't had a drink.

"Why do you flirt so much, Diya?" he asked in an effort to lift the pressure off his chest.

She went still in his arms. She dropped her arms from his neck and stepped back to stare at him. "What?"

"Your behavior." He indicated the small space between them with a hand. "This easy familiarity you have with people … with men, is what gets you in trouble. Sober down before it's too late, Dee. I feel it's my brotherly duty to point out that having a good time is one thing, but is it worth it when it costs you your reputation?"

She flinched at the question. He wanted to cringe at himself. But he had to protect her from herself, from the nasty world. From him.

"Do you understand what I mean?"

"Perfectly." She wasn't sparkling anymore. "Your brotherly advice is duly noted," she said and walked off the dance floor.

He sighed. At least, this time, there was no engagement to break off.

IF KRISH THOUGHT he'd gotten through to Diya, he was massively mistaken.

The evening regressed even further, and as Diya's spirits rose, his sank. Diya gushed about her Turkish prince to anyone who cared to listen—and plenty did—all within his hearing range. She set his teeth on edge with her poems of praise for the inimitable Hasaan, who it seemed, "Never, ever, ever used sarcasm to make a point."

Hasaan, the cross between a god and a saint, gave Krish indigestion in addition to a bad name.

Conversely, she flirted with every man in sight and made a spectacle of herself on the dance floor, writhing and gyrating and rubbing it in his face. To his shock—and sorely against his will—his body reacted to her blatant sensuality.

If any hot-blooded, straight man on the planet, even Prince Hasaan, could resist the sight of a beautiful woman in the throes of a body-jiggling dance without reacting to it, Krish would eat his boot.

Belle of the ball? he snorted. This avatar of Diya's was as far removed from the demure Cinderella as any woman could be.

When Diya made a beeline for the bathroom, Krish sighed in relief. *Finally.* But his reprieve was short-lived when Lovey scooted onto a barstool next to him.

"You and Miguel seem to be hitting it off," Krish said, grinning at his friend.

Lovey had been flirting up a storm with Miguel, who

seemed just as interested in her. Krish had to admit, they made a good couple.

"Never mind that," Lovey said, tut-tutting at him. "I can't believe you never told me that you know Beauty Mathur. You know my sister is in love with her."

Lovey's older sister was gay. Diya wasn't—as far as he knew.

"Want me to get her autograph? Or set her and your sister up on a blind date?" he asked before stuffing his mouth with a burrito. He wasn't doing himself any favors by imagining Diya with another woman either.

Lovey hooted at his wit. "I'd say sure, but she seems to be taken, pal."

Krish coughed and nearly choked on the morsel in his mouth, his throat suddenly and oddly tight. "She's kidding about Hasaan. They're not together. The media is just sensationalizing their business relationship."

And why was he defending her when she was going out of her way to prove otherwise?

"I got that. I meant you, silly," Lovey said.

Krish's burrito-holding hand froze in mid-flight with his mouth open as big as a plane hangar. For the life of him, he couldn't move or shut his mouth or breathe.

Lovey raised her eyebrows. "What? You think I wouldn't guess? I suppose you guys have to keep it a secret because she's a celebrity. But anyone can tell you're together. You're so possessive of her, and she turns green every time you even glance at another woman."

Except for going red with anger, Krish hadn't noticed any color on Diya's face that evening. Not even a stray green from the disco lights.

Lovey is wrong, he decided. She was a die-hard romantic, just like Diya, and was seeing things that weren't there. He'd known the two women were alike. It was why he'd wanted them to meet, hadn't he?

Besides being a real estate agent, Lovey part-timed as a masseuse at a spa and was enrolled for night classes to get her master's in anthropology at UT Dallas. She was a whirlwind of energy and ambition and a self-proclaimed observer of mankind, and as such, she had been observing the byplays between Diya and him, apparently.

Krish set his half-eaten burrito on the paper plate, his appetite vanishing. For the rest of the evening, he sat alone and stared and brooded. He stopped brooding for the two seconds it took him to say good-bye to the gang and then resumed brooding all the way home. Diya didn't prattle on as usual either.

She wasn't in love with him. No way. He wasn't her Prince Charming. They'd established that nine years ago. She'd said it herself when she broke their engagement.

"I'll never marry a dictatorial, unfashionable, ungallant workaholic," weren't the words of a woman in love.

He'd been relieved by her avowal, even as their families gasped in shock and tried to change her mind. He hadn't wanted to marry her. He didn't want to marry anyone ever, but he hadn't been able to refuse Kamal Uncle's dearest wish. How could he refuse the man he idolized?

Love hadn't entered the equation. Not when he'd proposed and certainly not when she'd broken things off.

But what had Lovey meant about him being possessive of her? He wasn't possessive of Diya. He was protective of her. Someone had to be since she clearly had no sense of self-preservation.

Krish tried to unravel his confusion all the way home. But the giant Gordian knot inside his head kept getting knottier, and he spent the worst night of his life in bed, not sleeping. His thoughts were so tangled up by the night's drama that they rushed headlong in the direction he'd placed roadblocks on years ago. He wasn't even going to bring up the half-mast boner he'd been sporting all night with no relief in sight.

Okay, so he'd brought it up. It was one of the things on his mind, clearly. But he was in no mood to take care of it. Not tonight. Not by himself and definitely not with Diya.

He bolted up in bed, his gut twisting. What the hell kind of idea was that? Taking care of his boner with Diya? Was he mad? He was her protector. Her brother … well, her brother-like protector. That was all.

Krish got out of bed and paced in front of the bed. When that didn't help, he prowled into the den and attacked his work. Eventually, he succeeded in streamlining his thoughts and his life plan back on track again. Bonus: he got a shitload of work done.

At the crack of dawn, when he'd only just made it into the kitchen, a bright-eyed and bushy-tailed Diya bounced in and started doing jumping jacks in front of him. Krish hunched over his coffee mug, unable to meet her eyes.

"I'm still mad at you," she coldly informed him. "But anger should never come in the way of good health."

Krish looked up, bleary-eyed, as two mugs of black coffee swam in his veins.

One thing became crystal clear though. Diya wasn't in love with him. She barely looked fond of him.

Reassured that the line of protocol was in place once more, Krish allowed her to drag him to the gym room. He let her contort his body into positions no sane man—especially a frustrated and fatigued one—should ever contort his body into, no matter how badly his *"chakras* begged for realignment."

Damn his masochistic tongue, but he *had* promised to be her knave through her visit. And he was coming to the hard-to-ignore conclusion that he was being slowly murdered for his many manly sins.

Fine, if that was what it took for them to get to Sunday—when, God willing, she'd fall in love at first sight with the Neil chap and be his problem forevermore—Krish would suffer a slow-cooker death.

He made a mental note to phone his lawyer and update his will. Just in case.

CHAPTER 8

"You can take the Indian out of India, but you can't take the game of cricket out of him."

Diya smiled fondly as Krish explained about the Dallas–Fort Worth cricket leagues that scrimmaged every weekend and the monthly one-days and the yearly test matches they played. Krish was an all-rounder for the Dallas team, which meant he bowled, batted, or wicket-kept as required. Cricket had been his one true passion since childhood.

There still remained a tiny bit of tension between them from last night. But, apropos to her forgiving nature and her mentor, Scarlett O'Hara, the majority of Diya's annoyance had dissolved in the light of a new day. The sprint on the treadmill had helped, too. Considering the volume of endorphins in her bloodstream on a daily basis, she could never stay upset for long.

She'd spent the last hour massaging Krish's scalp; that was how *not* upset she was.

He'd complained of a headache, so she'd offered to massage his head and give him acupressure points. To make the experience relaxing for both of them, she sat cross-legged on the floor, back against the sofa, while Krish was stretched out on the carpet with his head in her lap.

"Are you sure you don't want to come watch? It's turned into a beautiful day," he said with his eyes closed, his expression blissful.

Post-lunch and pre-massage, they'd been lounging in the living room. The Beast was chugging his vile coffee and working on his laptop while she sipped bergamot-flavored Countess Grey tea—her favorite from Fortnum and Mason—her attention divided between a show on Food Network, her phone, and Krish. He had just received a text message from the captain of his cricket team, informing him that the canceled match was on again.

Diya glanced out of the panoramic windows of the living room to the bright and busy green woodland outside. The gloom of the last two days had dried up without warning. But, not a cricket enthusiast to begin with, she had zero interest in channeling a baked potato for three hours under the afternoon sun.

"Quite sure. I'm going to chill in front of the TV ... or wait! Will you drop me off at Lovey's spa? I'll get a detox massage while you go play with your balls," she quipped, pulling a snort-laugh out of him.

"Of course, Dee." He stifled a yawn. "I need to change," he mumbled but made no move to get up.

"Slather on sunblock, okay? And wear a ball cap. A bald, sunburned Beast will not make a charming companion tonight." She ran her fingers through his thick mop of hair with nary a bald spot in sight.

Krish sat up with a sexy groan, his hair sticking up every which way. She instantly went goosefleshy all over.

Stop it, she told herself. *Enough with the shivers. Do you want another lecture? Another rejection?*

He stretched one way and then the other, popping his vertebrae. Then, he ran both his hands through his hair to smooth it out.

Her fingers itched to join his. *Oh Lord, please make him stop!*

"Are you sure you'll be up for an evening out after the game?" Maybe going out tonight was a bad idea. Maybe they needed a break from each other. "What if your headache comes back?" She prayed he'd take the excuse and run with it.

He didn't.

"The headache's gone, thanks to you." His lips slashed upward in a smirk. "You'll give me a bigger one if you're trapped at home on a Saturday night."

Not untrue.

"And you're okay with whatever movie and restaurant I pick?" she asked again, eyes narrowing.

He'd said as much when Lovey called earlier and invited them out with Miguel and her. As guest of honor, it was up to Diya to choose the evening's entertainments.

"Yes, Diya," he growled in exasperation.

She wagged her finger at him. "I'm going to hold you to that when you start snarling and complaining."

"I won't," he said, rising to his feet and pulling her up.

"We'll see."

They parted company at the top of the stairs, Krish making his way down the hall to gather up the cricket gear. Cricket seemed to be serious business in Dallas. Both teams were registered leagues and had sponsors and uniforms and whatnot.

Diya skipped into the master bedroom to change her clothes and grinned at the cat snoozing on the bed.

"It's his way of apologizing, you know. He never says sorry. He simply shows it. And it's charming and sweet and

—stop it!" she scolded herself as she went into the bathroom and began stripping out of her kimono-kaftan. "Do not start crushing on him again. Remember last night? Remember what happened at Leesha's wedding?"

But the devil inside her brain refused to stay silent.

Yes, those incidents were awful, but what he said isn't untrue, is it? You are impulsive. You don't think before acting. Your brashness does land you in trouble. He is harsh with you only out of concern for you and not because he means to be hurtful.

Wasn't her she-devil supposed to be on her side and not the Beast's?

Diya exhaled heavily and walked back into the bedroom. She would not get carried away tonight. She would have a great time with the gang, and that was it. She would treat him like a friend, nothing more. And, if she found herself mooning over him or wishing for impossible things, she would think about the suitor she'd agreed to meet tomorrow.

The thought of the suitor instantly cleared up her confusion. That was right. She was here to meet a potential husband. Krish was helping Daddy set her up. He had absolutely no interest in her.

She shrugged on a long jersey dress appropriate for the spa and slipped her feet into a pair of pink-and-purple rubber platforms. She had a little flashier something in mind for the movie-dinner double date.

She groaned at herself again. "It is not a date. Say it till you believe it."

Repeating the phrase like a mantra, she began to gather spa essentials in a large tote, including her AirPods, her wallet, a Kindle, the change of clothes. Ready, she walked back into the kitchen to hydrate her body by drinking two tall glasses of water in preparation for the sauna.

Krish had forgotten his cell phone on the kitchen counter. She noticed it when it began vibrating with an incoming call. She instinctively glanced at it and saw Aya Ahuja flashing across the screen in bold letters.

Diya spat out a mouthful of water back into her glass and looked about for Krish, expecting him to jump out of the woodwork to pick it up. He didn't. And the phone kept vibrating. Finally, it stilled, making Diya sigh in relief. Almost immediately, it started buzzing again.

Wow. Impatient much?

The she-devil on Diya's shoulder ordered her to pick it up. So, without fully grasping what she'd possibly say to the woman, Diya answered the call.

"Hello? You've reached Krish Menon's phone," she chirped extra cheerfully. *Be cool. Just be ... cool.*

A long pause followed. Then, "Who is this?"

Aya sounded a bit taken aback—naturally—but wholly American. There was no *desi* in her voice at all.

"This is Diya. Krish's friend from India. He's putting on his clothes, *um* ... changing into his cricket gear. Ha-ha. Not ... like putting on clothes as if he was not wearing any. Sooo, can I take a message?" Nice, polite, a bit ditzy but friendly. Diya mentally patted her back for handling it well.

A slightly longer pause this time, punctuated by soft breathing.

"Diya?" Aya asked as if she couldn't quite place the name.

Bitch. There was no way this woman didn't know who Diya was or that she was visiting with Krish for a couple of weeks.

"Krish's childhood friend?" Diya reminded pertly. She wanted to add, *The supermodel,* but that would be tacky.

"Ah! I remember now. The troublemaker. Oh, shoot. I'm so sorry. I shouldn't have said that. I was just trying to place your name. Sorry again. It was impolite of me."

Diya's mouth had fallen open at "troublemaker." She didn't know whether to be shocked or outraged at the woman's temerity. Leesha would tell her she deserved to be called names for stooping so low as to answer Krish's phone like some snoop dog. Even so, the awful woman was snarkiness personified.

This was Krish's girlfriend? *Holy crappola!*

Diya began to see why he didn't want her anywhere near the family.

"Would you tell him I called, please? And that I need to speak to him urgently. And … never mind. I'll send him a message. Can you make sure he reads it immediately? Well, nice talking to you. Good-bye."

Diya nodded and hummed a good-bye, too flabbergasted to respond coherently. Before she even pulled the phone away from her ear, several message notifications popped up on the phone screen in quick succession.

WISCO WON'T NEGOTIATE.

LIKED THE SPEECH FOR DILLO. Have made minor tweaks and comments.

LET'S revisit what we discussed on Thursday night.

THREE SHORT, cryptic messages, but Diya had heard and seen enough to put two and two together and come up with shock.

The Beast and Aya Ahuja were made for each other.

Who could be more perfect for him than a corporate headhunter willing to mix business and pleasure—superduper gag reflex—while on a Valentine's Day date?

"Ready?"

Diya jumped a foot in the air at Krish's question. She whipped around, stifling a shriek. "Stop sneaking up on me like that."

He was standing so close that she could count the individual hairs that had sprouted along his upper lip and jaw in a five o'clock shadow. Amusement flashed in his brown eyes, through his spectacles, before they dropped to the phone she clutched to her bosom as if she'd never let it go.

Embarrassment exploded inside her at being caught red-handed with it. She'd not only invaded his privacy; she now had to confess everything.

She thrust the phone in his hands and blurted out, "Your girlfriend called. She asked you to call back ASAP."

Gah! How did she always manage to put herself in these situations where she was forced to hold weird and uncomfortable conversations with the girlfriends and would-be fiancées of her male friends?

Just this morning, Saira had called her to ask point-blank if there was anything romantic between Hasaan and her. Diya had tried to stay noncommittal and vague and had urged Saira to speak to Hasaan about it. If there was going to be an engagement and *nikaah* between Saira and Hasaan, she didn't want to mess it up.

Diya hoped things were working out between Hasaan and Saira. He hadn't called or e-mailed about anything dire, so it seemed everything was fine, and she crossed her fingers that it remained so. Saira had sounded sweet and sensible over the phone, and her tendency to add *jaan*—darling—after every sentence was adorable. Saira had asked Diya to keep their phone chat a secret from Hasaan.

Wait a minute, Diya thought as something struck her. Saira calling her for assurances was one thing—she and Hasaan were strangers, and the baby rumors would concern a would-be fiancée. But why had Aya asked her to play messenger girl between her and Krish?

"Aren't you going to call your girlfriend back? She said it was urgent," Diya said, watching Krish narrowly.

He rarely spoke about his girlfriends to her even though she always waxed poetic about her boyfriends and lovers—real and invented—to him.

He read Aya's messages with a poker face, and then he stuffed the phone in the back pocket of his white cricket pants. "I'll call her later. If you're ready, let's get going."

That's it? "I'll call her later," and zip?

Diya couldn't believe the Beast hadn't ripped into her for answering his phone. And that he wasn't even texting his girlfriend back. Something was off.

She slung her tote over a shoulder and began walking toward the garage, pondering the mystery. By the time she parked her butt in the Porsche's passenger seat, she was bursting with questions.

"What's Wisco?" The name rang a bell. "Isn't Wisco the food market you took me to? Small-time rival of Armadillo?"

"Wisco Organic Foods has bought out Armadillo Farms and Foods. The takeover is underway," he replied after a beat.

O-kay. "And Wisco won't negotiate what with your company?"

Why was he so calm? Why wasn't he at his office? The old Krish would've been a bundle of energy at such a time, dashing about, crossing all the T's, dotting all the I's.

He flicked her a cool look and sighed. "Not with the company. With me personally."

Gah! Trying to pull information out of him was like stuffing your feet into shoes two sizes smaller—nearly impossible and horribly painful.

"What won't it negotiate?" she persisted.

"Nothing to worry about, Diya. It's not important."

Of course it was important. She realized then that his stillness was just the calm before the storm. He was worried about it. He was … unsure. Krish was never unsure. She also realized that he didn't want to talk about it with her. But he had discussed it with Aya Ahuja.

Oh, that hurt worse than a shoe bite. Worse than how the soles of her feet felt after walking in Jimmy Choo stilettos for twelve straight hours.

Diya clamped her mouth shut and stared at the road. He didn't want to talk? Fine. So be it.

"It's just business, Dee. Can't we talk about something else?" he asked after driving in utter silence for five minutes. Talk about something frivolous, he meant.

Now, she was good and angry. More hurt than angry, but why quibble over semantics?

She remained silent. She couldn't think of a single frivolous thing to say to him.

"Have you decided which movie we're watching?"

She shrugged.

"Something's out of joint." He reached out a hand toward her nose, but she took it out of tweaking range. He grinned. "Come on. You don't want to miss the chance to gush over my uniform."

Diya peeked sideways. The uniform was ghastly—baggy white pants and a jaundice-yellow T-shirt with *DFW Cowboys* scrawled over the left breast in blue. She rolled her tongue back to refrain from commenting. Silence spoke volumes sometimes.

Then, the world turned topsy-turvy. Usually, it was Diya who jabbered through the lags in conversations, but today, Krish took over the task. He talked and talked about everything under the sun, except Wisco. She listened in rapt silence right until he made a very rude observation. One she was sure was meant to poke fun at her.

"Massages creep me out. How can you stand having a pair of strange hands on your body?"

The comment itself wasn't insulting. Lots of people disliked getting a massage. But the way he said it and what he was insinuating were. It was a doubly unfair comment because hadn't he just basked in the pleasure of having her hands on his scalp for an hour?

"Models learn to ditch all inhibitions fast. They are expected to strip at the drop of a hat, and being poked and prodded in any and all places for a photo shoot or tailoring measurements is a given. Strange hands have touched my butt, my shoulders, my breasts, my crotch—just about anywhere reachable. And I've had my hands on other models, too. Not only hands, but also a variety of my body parts have come into intimate contact with a variety of theirs and in various stages of dress and undress. The fashion world is not an easy place, Beast. Only the tough survive there."

Add to that, a celebrity—who she was fast becoming because of Scheherazade—had to get used to their personal space being invaded. Actually, a celeb had no personal space to speak of at all. In fact, no person in the world had any personal space left anymore. Not in this tech-savvy, social-media-crazy world. Diya truly didn't mind the invasion of her privacy so much. Because of the way she looked, people had always watched her in one way or another, and she'd learned to ignore those vibes—both good and bad ones—a long time ago.

"I never said your job was easy, Diya," Krish said quietly.

She flapped her hand. "Just forget it."

She'd proved nothing by her explanation, except that she liked locking antlers with the Beast and that she couldn't keep her mouth shut for more than ten minutes at a stretch. Thankfully, the Porsche pulled up in front of the Spa of Harmony just then, and Diya beat a hasty exit.

. . .

KRISH WAS NO LONGER the chief financial officer of Armadillo Farms and Foods. Soon, there wouldn't even be an Armadillo Farms and Foods.

Diya spent her three hours at the spa, searching the internet. It was useless to think that Krish would allow her to grill him about Wisco like a filleted tilapia or that he'd volunteer any information. Clearly, he wasn't interested in talking about it to her. Not even with his family, Diya surmised. If Leesha or Savitri Aunty knew, they'd have told her.

Daddy probably had an inkling about it because Krish discussed most things with her father—his guru—and vice versa. And, of course, Aya knew—but Diya refused to think about that while trying to relax and detox.

The gauntlet had been thrown, so she raised her smartphone and wielded it. She Google-searched both Armadillo Farms and Foods and Wisco Organic Foods, confirming news of the buyout. It seemed the deal had been going on for six months and was in the last stages of completion.

"Diya, you really must put the phone away. It defeats the purpose of a deep-tissue massage," Lovey implored as they began the first of her body treatments.

"I have to, Lovey. I just have to." She would burst if she didn't dig up everything.

She used to shamelessly cyberstalk CFO Krish Chandra Menon, but she hadn't done it since London and their ... weird fight. His name immediately popped up on the smartphone screen. No earth-shattering articles anywhere, just a profile and some sporadic mentions tracking his stellar career over the years. Instances where he'd triumphed beyond market expectation, likening him to an investment genie, or where he'd exercised unnecessary restraint when he should've gone with his gut. All blah two-liners on blah business web pages. Blah for her, but they were big moustache-twirling moments for the corporate gunfighter types.

Outside the sauna room, Lovey snatched the phone from her hand. "That's enough. You can go without drooling over him for ten minutes. Sheesh!"

So, Diya sat on the heated bamboo bench inside an infrared sauna, wrapped in a white terry-cloth towel until her pores opened up and wept. Being blissfully alone was contrary to her nature, but saunas were a great place to meditate. They were also a great place to indulge her Nancy Drew instincts and ponder over the mystery of Krish's business secrets.

Armadillo had sold for a massive profit. Cool. She'd expected no less, considering its CFO. Presumably, Wisco wanted Krish to work his magic for them, too. Also cool. Did it mean he'd be moving to Wisconsin and keep cows in his backyard? Was that where he was house-hunting? But what had Aya's message meant?

Wisco won't negotiate.

What did Krish want to negotiate with Wisco, and why wouldn't they do it?

Diya frowned at the dew-wet wooden paneling of the sauna, wondering if Krish would talk to her if she brought it up. She made a face. He wouldn't. He was the Beast. He brooded and snorted, and he kept his cards close to his chest. He mulled over his problems and his ideas in secret until they became viable seeds that he could sow. Next, he'd fertilize the soil and water it. Only then, he would stand back and watch everything grow.

Perhaps she could ask Hasaan to check on the trustworthiness of Wisco. Or have him unearth some inside information that might give Krish an upper hand in the negotiation. Hasaan knew people—important people all across the globe. His family could move and shake the world with the snap of a finger. Hasaan would even offer Krish a position in one of his companies—not only because she asked, but also because Krish's credentials spoke for themselves.

Diya buried her face in her hot, sweaty hands. She was worrying needlessly. There was no way super-duper organized Krish Menon didn't have another—*several* other prospects or offers lined up in addition to Wisco. He probably had his own death slotted down on his calendar. *This date is more convenient than this one, Lord Death.*

She didn't like that he didn't trust her with his secrets.

Diya stood up and faced a hard truth. She didn't have to like it or dislike it. She only had to accept that his business affairs were not her business. Just like his personal life.

Still, as she exited the sauna to shower and dress for a night out with the Beast—IT WAS NOT A DATE—her mind conjured up images of cows and pastures and compost.

Krish was possibly moving to Wisconsin. *Good God!*

BAR-9 ROCKED THAT NIGHT. The three-floor club was packed with wriggling bodies on all three levels with a different DJ on each floor, pounding out sheer energy through their music, smearing it across the dance floors in thick waves. There wasn't anything remotely Texan or cowboy-like in the club—it could've been a bar scene in New York or Mumbai in fact—and yet Krish knew deep in his gut that he was in a Texas standoff with the Diva.

Latin music throbbed on their floor. All around them, couples were swaying in a slow, sexy rumba, holding each other, the men spinning and dipping their partners, but Diya wasn't pestering him to do any of that. Every time he tried to take her in his arms, she'd dance away from him; they were together yet separate. She wasn't looking at him or talking to him either—not much—and responded to his attempts at dialogue with short, sharp words or shrugs.

He reached for her again, but she danced away, shimmering in her one-shoulder top and dark skinny jeans.

"What's with the mood?" He sounded like a broken record. "Aren't spas meant to loosen you up?"

"Switch!" she shouted in lieu of an answer and twirled away, nudging Lovey at him.

And, before he knew it, Krish was dancing with Lovey instead, who looked equally startled at the abrupt shift. She swiveled her head from him to Diya and back to him. Then, she shrugged, whooped, and continued to bounce to the music.

Krish wanted to bounce his head against something hard. His headache had returned with a vengeance.

There was no reason for Diya to be pissed off. He'd been on his best behavior all day. No sarcasm, no bullying, no pithy comments. What the hell had he done wrong now? He'd quietly sat through—fine, snoozed through the chick flick she'd picked. Was that it? She'd expected him to stay awake while a bunch of women oohed and aahed at Idris Elba? Not happening. Not even to keep the peace.

She'd picked the restaurant and a cuisine he didn't care for. But he hadn't complained. She'd suggested they go clubbing after dinner, and he'd agreed without a squeak. The whole evening had unfolded as she wanted it. And yet, she was pissed? Un-freaking-believable. He couldn't understand what had ticked her off. She'd been fine until the cricket match. Before Aya's phone call.

Was that it? The phone call? Krish cursed under his breath.

The music changed, and Ed Sheeran's "Shape of You" came on. The crowd on the dance floor burgeoned and went a little crazy. Somehow, in the crush, Miguel and Diya found extra space to put on some fancy moves. He whirled her out and then reeled her in and dipped her back, over his arm, with the flair of a professional dancer. Her hair cascaded down to the floor for a heartbeat before Miguel whipped her up again. He spun her fast, making her laugh. He brought her to a stop, her back pressed against his front, and they gyrated that way for the rest of the song.

Krish couldn't tear his eyes away. A fire sparked low in his belly as he stared at them, slithering and squirming to the music while the lights flashed between fluorescent and strobe. Her teeth, the whites of her eyes, the silver-white of her top glowed neon yellow in the throbbing dark. She looked wild and free.

Diya caught his gaze and finally held it, her smile changing, turning sharp as a blade. Krish's heart began to pound harder than the bass beat.

Lovey tapped him on his shoulder. "What did you do to irritate her?"

"I don't know." But he did know, didn't he? "Switch again?" he asked, hustling Lovey closer to Miguel and Diya.

"Never thought I'd see you bend over backward for a woman," she said into his ear, her amusement clear.

But she readily switched partners. As opposed to Diya and him, Lovey and Miguel actually were on a date.

Krish experienced acute frostbite from Diya again. Gritting his teeth, he focused on the promise he'd made to Kamal Uncle and the endgame with the suitor.

"Look, if you're pissed off because of Aya—*oof*!"

His words were cut off as he was pushed into Diya by the crowd surging around them. He gathered her close. The floor was beyond packed now.

She stiffened in his arms. In fact, she stopped dancing altogether and stood in the middle of the dance floor, glaring at him.

"How dare you tell your girlfriend that I'm a troublemaker!" she shouted, trying to free herself from his embrace.

"What? What are you talking about?" Krish shouted back, shaking his head. "She's not my girlfriend, Dee. Aya and I broke up a while ago, before Alisha's wedding. I thought you knew." The music was impossibly loud, and he didn't know if she could even hear him. He grabbed her hand and tugged. "Let's get out of here, so we can talk without screaming."

Diya stood her ground, unmoving, while her expression changed color with the disco lights. Red, pink, yellow, orange. But, eventually, she shrugged. "Okay. I'm parched anyway. I need water."

He held her hand tightly as they meandered their way through the pulsing darkness and the undulating throngs, coming to a stop behind a thick wall of people laying siege on the massive wet bar in front of them.

"Stay here. I'll get us some bottles," he said, relieved he didn't have to shout that out.

He waited for her nod, and then he thrust into the crowd, trying to catch the eye of any one of the dozen bartenders hard at work behind the bar.

As he waited his turn, Krish wondered what the hell Aya had been playing at by saying that to Diya. Aya was a sensible, confident woman. She had no reason to be intimidated by Diya or be rude to her. She didn't even know Diya. He certainly had never discussed Diya with her.

She couldn't still be mad about their breakup, not after six months. No, she wasn't mad at him. Weren't they working together on the Wisco takeover? She was fine at the office meetings. Their business dinner on Thursday had been cordial. Enjoyable even. Was it all a show?

No, it couldn't be. He refused to believe Aya would let their personal differences spill over into work.

Krish rubbed his throbbing head. He was sick of women;

he really was. Couldn't be honest with them. Couldn't be nice. Definitely couldn't be beastly. What was a man supposed to do then? What choices were left? And what did women want? Someone who always agreed and never opposed? Someone who nodded when asked to and smiled when commanded to?

To hell with that, Krish thought. He was no one's puppet. Had never been. Would never be.

By the time he got to the front of the bar, he was tempted to break his self-imposed limit of one alcoholic beverage a day. A second beer or maybe something a bit stronger wouldn't go amiss. And that was exactly why he needed to stay away from women and the unasked-for complications they brought into his life. His life was complicated enough as it was. He ordered four bottles of water and nothing else, much to the bartender's annoyance.

Alcoholism wasn't hereditary, medically speaking. But statistics showed that family members of alcoholics had a greater predisposition toward addiction than others. Drinking had destroyed his father; Appa's very nature had changed from glass to glass, bottle to bottle. As a family, they had never recovered from it.

Krish would not put his mother and sister through that. He battled every day not to turn into Chandra Menon. Not in that. Not to give in to temptation. He kept a tight leash on his temper, his expectations, and his stress levels.

He jostled his way back to Diya with the water. She faced away from him as she leaned against a railing that over-looked the dance floor in a classic bored-supermodel pose. Close to a dozen men had arranged themselves in front of her, vying for her attention in a variety of ways.

With Diya in town, how was he supposed to manage his stress levels? The damn woman was supposed to lie low and not encourage a flirt-fest.

He cut his lips up in a smile he hoped was scary enough to discourage the Romeos as he walked up to her. That was when he realized Diya was busy typing into her smartphone. She wasn't even looking at the fools in front of her.

Well, what was good for a gander was good for a goose.

The girls had twisted the idiom, back when they were children, when Krish refused to take an at-home arts and crafts class with them. He'd been thirteen, much too energized and manly to sit around the house, painting fruit bowls. It was one of the last times Appa had come to his rescue. One of the last times Chandra Menon had been lucid enough to voice how he wanted his son raised.

With only the barest twinge of conscience, Krish angled his head over Diya's shoulder and began to read her texts. She was chatting with someone called Sheikh-Shake. It had to be the incomparable Hasaan.

SHEIKH-SHAKE: Hussein is an ass. Kill me now.

WITH PLEASURE, Krish thought, mentally rolling up his sleeves.

BEAUTY LANGUISHING IN DALLAS: Get in line. Must psycho-kill the Beast first.

KRISH FROWNED. Why was she mad at him? And why was it okay for her to call him the Beast in front of Hasaan but not for him to call her a troublemaker when the shoe fit?

Not that he had. But getting back to his point about what was good for the goose was good for the gander.

· · ·

SHEIKH-SHAKE: Life's a bitch, chérie. I propose we elope to Fiji. Imagine it. Just you and me. The sun, the sand, and coconut mojitos.

BEAUTY LANGUISHING IN DALLAS: Sounds utterly divine. But what about Scheherazade? And Saira?

SHEIKH-SHAKE: Ah. Her. I am allowed four wives. ;)

DIYA GIGGLED, and Krish decided to save her from herself. He plucked the phone from her hands, typed Got 2 go in the message bubble, and sent it off to Hasaan.

"You vile, uncivilized donkey," Diya shrieked.

Then, she went a little mad, stomping on his foot with a heel and shoving him back with both hands. As he wore boots, it didn't hurt so much as trip him. He stumbled back, swearing and flailing. She shoved him again, harder, and this time, he crashed into the wall of people against the bar.

Glasses clinked and fell on the tiled floor, shattering like his temper. Chaos rose in the air along with the scent of alcohol. An elbow hit his face, dislodging his specs, and for a moment, everything was a blur of dark colors and movement.

"He did it!" he heard Diya yell as he tried to extricate himself from the tangle of angry bodies. "Will someone with a gun do me a huge favor and shoot his beastly heart?"

Jesus, this was Texas. Someone always had a gun.

He shoved his glasses back on his nose, swearing and apologizing alternatively, while Diya tried her best to insti-gate a riot. Krish had never experienced the kind of relief he felt when Miguel and Lovey materialized by his side.

Lovey grabbed Diya's arm and steered her away. "Come on. We're taking a restroom break."

The madness seemed to settle as soon as Diya left.

"What the hell happened?" Miguel asked, looking shocked.

Krish shook his head. What always happened when Diya was around. She was a troublemaker.

Fuck.

"Lovers' tiff, was it?" someone asked.

He didn't bother to correct the man.

He bent and picked up the bottles of Perrier that had fallen from his hands. "Take these to her, will you? I need to clean up." The front of his shirt was doused in some fruity cocktail by the smell of it, and he was pretty sure someone had flung ice cubes and whiskey at his back. He smelled like a brewery or like a shit-faced drunk. "Then, I'm leaving. Tell her I'm waiting outside."

In the restroom, he cleaned up as best as he could. He wrapped an iron fist around his temper and walked out of Bar-9, grabbing his leather coat and Diya's pink suede jacket from the coat check as he went.

Outside the club, Krish sucked in huge mouthfuls of cool air until he felt sane again. Then, he noticed that the rest of the party was already outside. Diya was at the edge of the pavement, bent over a gutter in the road, retching, while Lovey held up her hair. Miguel stood close by, holding out a bottle of Perrier for her.

Krish's first thought was that she was drunk. But that couldn't be right. She'd only had one beer and half a glass of wine tonight. She'd barely eaten at dinner though. But that wasn't unusual. Diya didn't have big dinners to maintain her weight.

A queen's breakfast, a rich woman's lunch, and a pauper's dinner, was her mantra.

The vomiting had nothing to do with an eating disorder either.

Krish's blood spiked hot as a third option occurred to him.

"Are you fucking kidding me?" he snarled, advancing on her. "Are you actually fucking pregnant?"

"Krish! What is wrong with you?" Lovey stared at him as if he'd just grown a pair of horns on his forehead and a thick red tail on his backside.

He knew he'd gone too far—he did not actually believe she was pregnant either—but he couldn't take back his words. Sometimes, the beast lived inside oneself and not in a bottle.

This was why he stayed away from Diya. She made him think awful things, say nasty things, *feel* things he could not control.

"You hateful, odious man. Oh, how I loathe you!" With those words, Diya launched herself at him before he could begin to express his remorse. He was too shocked by his own reaction and hers to do anything but break their fall with his body, so she wouldn't get hurt.

Small mercy since he'd already hurt her beyond measure.

~~I am twenty-one years old and officially an adult. KM and L have planned an evening of revelry in my honor, and I'm super excited. My fairy tale has come true. Prince Charming and I are getting married in December. It's unbelievable. Like a dream. Oh, I hope I never wake up from it. I don't want the realities of being married to fog my rose-colored glasses.~~

~~I feel so much for him. Sometimes, when I look at him, I can't breathe. My heart flutters, and my limbs ache. I feel as heavy and languid as the monsoon rains. And, the next second, I feel as light and fluffy as a cloud floating in the summer breeze. I'd float away but for KM who tethers me to him so completely.~~

~~I want to kiss him so badly. I want us to make love, but he hasn't made a move at all despite my hints. He's so chivalrous. Or maybe he's afraid of Daddy.~~

~~I'm not going to give him a choice today. I'm going to kiss him myself. Properly. No more pecks on the cheek or forehead. No more excuses about how young I am. No more waiting until we are married. I won't take no for an answer. Not on my birthday.~~

It's over. He doesn't love me or desire me. I'll always be a child in his eyes. A troublemaker. A fool. An obligation. And that's unacceptable.

The dream, the fairy tale—I'm done with it all.

I will survive this.

I'll show him.

CHAPTER 9

By Sunday morning, Diya's wrath had cooled down to room temperature again. What remained was a tepid embarrassment at her spectacular loss of control outside Bar-9. But that was the Beast's specialty—pushing her to the point of no return.

She'd broken Krish's spectacles—well, bent them out of shape—when she tried to gouge his eyes out. Miguel had had a difficult time with plucking her off Krish. Not trusting Beauty and the Beast alone in the closed confines of the Porsche, Lovey had ridden home with them and lectured them for the whole drive like a miniature jungle warden. She wanted them to take control of their prehistoric instincts and allow their inner Homo sapiens or "wise man" to shine. Last night, the anthropology lesson hadn't sounded half as witty as it did this morning.

Giving in to her prehistoric urge of purring like her feline roommates, Diya sat up in bed and stretched. Two of the cats prowled toward her, their golden-green eyes shining curiously. One cat butted her arm with its head, rubbing it up and down. The other cat crawled into her lap and started licking her hand. They were comforting her. They'd sensed her hurt.

"Which one are you, kitty cat? Nora, Sam, or Europa?" She couldn't tell them apart yet. Not even with their distinct coloring.

The housebound three were named Asia, Gobi, and Susan, but she hadn't seen them yet.

After cuddling with the cats for a bit, Diya scooted off the bed and padded into the bathroom where she began her morning routine. She'd forgotten to floss last night and rectified the slip ASAP. Her mother would have a fit if she went home with a cavity or a gum infection on top of everything else.

The urge to see her mother—to see both her parents—welled up inside her. She missed them so much. This publicity tour had been the longest she'd stayed out of Mumbai and away from home.

Diya gargled with mouthwash and took stock of herself. Her face was swollen from crying, her eyes bloodshot and puffy—but nothing a cold gel couldn't cure.

No pity party, she decided, strengthening her resolve.

Still, she couldn't face the Beast yet. Last night had been … ugly.

Back in the bedroom, she changed into her running gear, pulling her hair into a high ponytail. A crisp morning jog should keep her out of his way and improve her mood.

After checking the time in Mumbai—it was early evening there—she called her parents. When they didn't answer, she tried calling on their home phone and cell phones several times. Had Daddy actually listened to her and was even now honeymooning with his beloved wife in Goa? She called her sister to confirm her theory.

"Can't talk. Sid is throwing a fit," Priya blurted out and disconnected the phone before Diya could even say hello.

Since Sid was Pree's three-year-old son, Diya forgave her sister's rudeness. What with a thriving medical practice and expanding family, Dr. Priya Shroff had less and less time to spare for Diya.

She wondered if Leesha would also become too busy for phone gossip once she and Aryan had kids? The thought was depressing.

Diya called her BFF and got her voice mail. Thrice. Apparently, Leesha was already too busy for gossip. Diya tried Aryan's cell next. No luck there either.

She stood up, frowning at her phone. Was there a global ban on her phone now? Was she not allowed any regular Homo sapiens contact?

She tucked her smartphone into a pink-and-black armband and strapped it about her bicep. *Chin up, shoulders back, abs in, butt tight, and attitude.* Then, she took a deep breath and finally came out of hiding.

Krish was at the six-burner stove, dressed in cargo shorts and a plain white shirt, preparing pancakes. He must have eyes at the back of his head because, the minute she catwalked into the kitchen, he turned around.

He had a new pair of glasses perched on his nose. He looked so darn cute, all sleep-rumpled and grumpy.

Gulp, why is life so complicated?

They stared at each other for long moments. She felt a pang of regret when she spotted the angry red scratches on his throat. From her nails.

This was stupid.

"I'm sorry," she whispered. For the scratches. For fighting. For not being able to let go of the hurt inside her heart.

At the same time, Krish held out his hand to her. "Truce?"

They froze together for several heartbeats, and then they burst out laughing. Together.

And, just like that, they were friends again.

· · ·

DIYA'S PINK-AND-BLACK sneakers pounded down Hemingway Drive, keeping pace with the beats of her all-time favorite Bollywood remix playlist. Being Sunday and early enough that even the birds weren't looking for worms yet, there were zero cars about, and Diya ran freely along the looping path created by the double yellow lines in the middle of the smooth graphite road.

The air was fresh enough to sparkle. It was a tad chilly, but the sun had broken past the horizon of roofs and trees and thawed her epidermis while her workout heated her blood. She'd set off at a moderate jogging pace of three and a half miles per hour as a warm-up. In ten minutes, she was up to five-point-five.

She hadn't asked Krish to join her, nor had he volunteered. The truce was too fresh to prod the Beast's belly when he clearly wasn't a morning person. But the day was yet young, and prod she would. She'd drag him to the gym. Or they could hike to the woods and around the lake behind the house. Consuming the Eiffel Tower of pancakes he'd made for breakfast was bound to make him horrendously guilty of gluttony and therefore desperate to burn off the calories.

The curved road straightened ahead with a slight incline, and Diya kicked up her pace.

She couldn't get the mountain of pancakes out of her mind. Who on earth had he made so many pancakes for? He didn't expect her to consume even one, surely. He knew her special diet. That meant someone was coming over for breakfast. Someone other than Mr. Suitable from Houston, who wasn't due until that evening.

Neil Upadhyay was Daddy's patient, Prakash Upadhyay's grandson. He had a PhD in biomedical engineering and a job as a researcher in some government-funded institution. The man was visibly brilliant, well settled, and smart-looking, according to her father, who had not met the man in person, mind you, but had only heard of him from none other than the proud grandfather himself. The blah-sounding Neil was scheduled to make an appearance sometime that evening.

Diya would meet him—she had to, as she had no other option—ply him with food—leftover pancakes maybe?—and encourage him out the door with a couple of Scheherazade shirts as compensation for a futile trip. The shirts were for Krish, but he'd balked at their color—electric blue, pistachio green, and royal purple—and refused to accept them.

An image popped into her head. Of a faceless man with flat hair with his cheeks stuffed with pancakes and the buttons of his pistachio-green shirt exploding everywhere.

Diya didn't know whether to laugh or cry. Her life had become a Shakespearean comedy. Or was it a tragedy?

Heroine loves hero but has to settle for a friendship. Hero has a closet full of issues he's nurturing instead of the pets he so obviously should. Hero's love interest is a shrew from hell.

Hmm. That was the twist in the story.

Krish had admitted that Aya was no longer his GF. And yet, he'd gone on a V-Day date with her ... which made no sense.

What else?

Oh, yeah, the hero was about to become neighbors with a herd of cattle.

Then, there was the backup hero, Sheikh Hasaan, with his own set of problems and frantic proposals. Diya had half a mind of calling Hasaan's bluff just to shut him up. And last but not least in the roster of men starring in the Comedy of Grooms was Mr. Suitable Man himself, who was most assuredly nerdy, possibly rotund, and probably tongue-tied around women, making him totally unsuitable for her.

What else? Dear Lord, wasn't that enough?

Ah, no, there was more. Last night, as Diya had lain awake, seesawing between mortification and despair, she'd conceded a couple of hard truths to herself. Primarily, she was nothing but a tall, thin wimp, hiding behind her love-hate friendship with Krish.

She loved a man who didn't love her. She was hung up on a man who did not desire her. And she was doing nothing —*not one thing*—to change her situation.

India's press corps—the real news media and not the tabloids—often wrote about Diya Mathur in terms of being a role model for Indian women. In those articles, she was a powerful, modern female who fearlessly tore down societal stigmas and male-dominated mores. She was a rule-breaker, a rule-maker.

So, where was that Wonder Woman now? Where was her boldness, her *Embrace the Change* attitude when it came to Krish Menon?

The bitter truth was that Diya Mathur was a fraud.

Embrace the Change had been the debut ad campaign of her career. Lili Jaanu, one of India's iconic fashion designers and a mother to an openly gay daughter, designed unique unisex couture. Her campaigns touted slogans like *Embrace the Change, Out of the Closet, Love Strips All* and were as much about fashion as about LGBTQ propaganda. Nine years ago, freshly rejected by the Beast and with a brand-new career goal to tweak, Diya had jumped at the chance to work with Lili Jaanu and her then-controversial cause. Fashion magazines had alliterated about Diya, calling her the "flamboyant, freethinking fashionista" and "the ideal New Age woman."

After that, modeling assignments had inundated her. She'd become the Gay Straight Woman and Beauty Mathur and so on. She hadn't sought out the labels—personal or professional. She didn't want to be anyone's role model. It was an outrageous responsibility. She had only ever wanted to be Krish's wife. All those things she'd done—was doing— was to prove to him that she was a capable, functioning adult. Someone he could be proud of and not have to constantly bail out of trouble. And, yes, to show him what he was missing. What exactly he'd rejected all those years ago. That she had broken their engagement was of no consequence. She'd only done what he hadn't had the courage to do himself.

The road narrowed and forked into two lanes around a triangular picketed garden wet with morning sunlight. Diya took the right path, wondering if she'd done the right thing by breaking the engagement.

Right from the beginning, she'd handled Krish the wrong way, aggressive when they were at odds and hero-worshipping him when not. One harsh refusal to kiss her on her birthday, and she'd leaped back from him like a scalded cat. Too afraid to expose her heart to hurt and ridicule, she'd taken the higher buddy road with him. The drama of the last few nights and this morning's truce had shown her that her heart might forever ache and bruise, but it wouldn't fall apart like a rusted old car on the first speed bump. She was made of sterner stuff than that.

Now, all she had to do was figure out how to permanently switch lanes on their relationship. Krish would not make it easy. He would fight dirty to keep things as they were. He'd bring up the past and throw their polar opposite personalities in her face. He would play on her fears, the works, as he'd done the first time around. Jeez, was she ready for that triathlon?

Hopefully, alien Krish wouldn't be difficult to handle. Still, Diya begged for divine intervention. *Oh, benevolent beings in heaven, bless the Beast with compassion and a new brain. Please.*

The Menon and Mathur families would be surprised, even exasperated, when she told them she'd changed her mind again. But she could handle them.

Diya flat-out sprinted for the final stretch, her pulse fast and strong.

She hoped both families would stand behind the spectator lines this time—especially her father—and cheer the triathletes on. If they wanted to hand out bottles of water and glucose biscuits, she was fine with it. What she didn't want them to do was pick sides.

The giant hardwoods protecting the storybook house from the road were the marker. Diya slowed to a jog and then a walk. At the mailbox, she removed her headphones and let her brain empty of everything. She began a series of cool-down stretches, after which she scooped up the water bottle she'd left on the mailbox and began to slowly drain it while making her way to the house. She passed two sedans, two minivans, and a Volkswagen that had miraculously appeared along the cobblestone driveway.

The pancake-eating guests have arrived, she surmised.

Diya took her last unhurried gulp of her lemon-flavored water and mentally shook her head at Krish. He could've told her he'd invited people over for breakfast. She'd have helped him make something tastier, definitely more nutritious than out-of-a-box pancakes.

Another Menon quirk: a mile-wide streak of independence. The Menons never asked for help, not even if they fell into an open manhole and had no way of crawling out of the sludge. And, if help was forced upon them, they held themselves in the person's debt forever.

Diya flipped open the door alarm riveted into the wall by the garage and keyed in the code Krish had made her memorize.

"Khul ja sim sim," she rumbled in a low voice like Alibaba as the garage door shuddered open.

Alibaba and the Forty Thieves had been one of her favorite bedtime stories because it had been one of Krish's favorites.

She smiled, thinking of the many lovely memories they shared. She wanted to make so many more with him.

Her smile grew into a surprised grin as she strolled into the house and took in the ruckus going on in the living room. About twenty high school kids were spread out over the sofas, the floor, and the steps of the family room. She'd majorly miscalculated about the guests. But the Eiffel Tower of pancakes made eminently more sense now and was nowhere in sight. Naturally not. The teenagers would've devoured the food the instant they entered the house.

Krish stood at the head of the class, in front of a whiteboard propped on an easel that already had blue, black, and red numbers and words scribbled on it. That Krish was teaching kids algebra did not surprise Diya at all. The fluttering excitement she felt from watching him be masterful also didn't.

"Hello, everyone," Diya purred, her delight expanding.

A pin-drop silence descended in the room when the kids noticed her.

Krish flicked her a silent *behave yourself* look before introducing her to the kids.

Shooting a pointed look at the whiteboard, Diya shuddered dramatically. "The bane of my existence—mathematics. Math is not a subject; it is a form of torture."

The declaration earned her twenty immediate and heartfelt agreements and one sardonic eyebrow raise that made her shiver deliciously. Oh, Diya remembered that Menon look.

Of course, when Savitri Aunty had raised her eyebrow, it had inspired shivers of a different sort. Savitri Aunty had been a schoolteacher then; now, she was the principal of an all-girls boarding school in Pune. Every evening, the M Brigade would march into the Menon house, sit on the dining table, and do their homework under her supervision. Diya hadn't appreciated or taken advantage of the free, personalized tutelage at all—and didn't regret it a bit.

"You guys are in excellent hands," Diya said. "Krish is a whiz at algebra."

He'd been so good at mathematics that he'd taken over tutoring the M Brigade when his mother temporarily moved to Pune to take care of her health—or that was the story they'd been fed instead of the truth—and before Krish's downward spiral into sulky teenage bad boy. Diya had preferred his teaching methods to his mother's, admittedly because she'd had a huge crush on him and appreciated any excuse that would allow her to sit as close to him as possible. He'd stoically tolerated her for longer than he should have.

"Well, I don't want to disturb you." She waved again at the motley crew and began to walk away.

Right on cue, her spine tingled as several dozen pairs of eyes followed the sway of her hips across the great room and up a shallow flight of stairs.

The Beast cleared his throat behind her. Whether he was warning the kids not to stare at her behind or warning her to behave herself was anyone's guess. Suppressing the urge to add a little foxtrot to her sashay, Diya continued down the passage and into her room.

As she was about to close the door, she heard one of the boys say, "Mr. Menon, your girlfriend is *mucho chiquitita.*"

Plastered to the door like a limpet, Diya strained to hear Krish's reply. Whatever he rumbled out made some of the kids laugh and the others groan.

She pushed away from the door in affront. He'd better not be making fun of her!

"*Ay-yay-yay.* I'm disappointed in you, Mr. Menon. You have a *chiquitita* like that living in your house, and she's *not* your girlfriend? I think it is you who needs lessons from me, *ya*?" said a budding Don Juan a little loudly, making the group crack with laughter, followed by shushing noises.

Laughing softly, she shut the door and leaned against it. She couldn't help melting at the thought of Krish getting ragged by school kids.

Who needs lessons from whom indeed?

Her heart full to bursting, she knelt in front of the one trunk she hadn't yet unpacked. She opened it, rummaging inside until she found the small, square box wrapped in gold and bow-tied with silver curly ribbons with a sprig of holly sticking out. She lifted it out of the trunk and carefully unwrapped it. A Christmas-themed baby bootie in red and green trim, laced with tiny golden bells on its hem, sat inside a beautiful glass case etched all over with dainty little snowflakes. It was the twin of the bootie she'd bought for Leesha but in a different color. The little booties had pulled on her heartstrings and her womb-strings from the shop's window display, and she hadn't been able to resist buying them both—one for Leesha and the other for herself.

She didn't need a fertility charm like Leesha. Not yet. But she could use a good-luck talisman to find the perfect father for her future baby.

CHAPTER 10

*D*iya placed the good-luck bootie on the nightstand and began to stage-manage Operation Skin and Bones—pun intended—to bring down the Beast. She would give their relationship one last try. She had to, or she'd live with regret forever.

However, for her plan to work, she needed to understand a couple of variables. A: How quickly would Krish catch on and start defending his virtue? And B: Would he—could he—sue her for sexual harassment and/or indecent exposure?

She knew Krish liked to laze about his lair on Sundays. He spent pretty much the entire day abed when he wasn't working or on a La-Z-Boy, watching TV. The Peters did not own a La-Z-Boy but had a very nice, super comfortable couch in their family room Krish was partial to.

After her bath, Diya put on a virtually transparent T-shirt with matching boy shorts and nothing else. It came to mid-thigh and cut in a deep V around the neck, and its color was a cross between peanut and gold. It did lovely things to her complexion. She clipped on a thin gold anklet around her right foot, completing the beach-bunny look. Had it been

April or even the end of March, she could've pestered the Beast to take her to the beach where she could've pranced around in a teeny-tiny bikini and asked him to apply sunblock all over her.

Cheesy? Too obvious? Moot point since it wasn't an option. She'd make do with a foot rub. Or better yet, convince him that he needed a full-body massage. Let's see how long he resisted her reflexology moves.

Show skin. Touch skin. Stimulate nerve endings. Take control. Drive him mad. This was war, according to an online article about how to keep your man interested. How to *get* a man interested couldn't be that vastly different, could it?

Diya brushed out her hair till it fell in glossy, perky waves down her back. She applied a touch of lip gloss and a subtle layer of eyeliner. Subtle and stealthy—that was the plan.

Of course, the plan could backfire.

Diya glanced at the pretty bootie sitting on the nightstand and hardened her resolve. No, she was doing this. She would get a verbal answer out of him this time. She was moving forward with her life, and that was that.

But, before she embarked on her quest, she tucked the baby bootie under her pillow. No point in prematurely freaking him out by leaving evidence of voodoo around.

"WATCH IT!" Krish wrapped his hand around Diya's wrist and gently but firmly pulled it away from his upper thighs.

She'd grazed his balls with her knuckles for the second time in ten minutes. This time, he wasn't fool enough to think of it as an accident.

Post a vigorous kickboxing workout, he'd collapsed on the gym room floor, groaning like a man on death row, and she'd offered to stretch his glutes and quads, so they'd hurt less over the next few days. Diya knew her muscle groups and what to do with them. No doubt about it. Spread-eagled, he'd nearly dozed off during the massage but jerked awake the moment she slid her hands up, up, up his thighs until the back of one hand rested in the crease of his groin.

Krish sat up and pinned Diya with a hard stare. She sat back on her haunches, blinking at him in concern.

"Sore? Can't be helped. Your muscles are lumpy, possibly atrophied. I suggest you soak in a hot mineral bath. I have some Dead Sea salts in my luggage if you need them," she said coyly, as if his butt and thighs were the only problem.

She wasn't wrong; his muscles had been screaming abuse ever since he volunteered for her boot camp. She was trying to geld him for siding with her father. It was the only explanation. Man, he seriously needed to update his will. What the hell was he doing, working up a sweat *and* a boner, and on a Sunday of all days? Sundays were meant to be days of rest, emulating a couch potato with TV marathons.

"Just keep your hands away from my balls," he said baldly and then wondered if he was crossing a line.

But she'd crossed it first by invading his personal space. Besides, it wasn't anything they hadn't discussed or joked over before.

Diya's rosebud mouth fell open. "*Ew!* You wish I wanted my hands anywhere near your hairy balls. Disgusting." She shot to her feet as regally as an angry queen rising from her throne.

She'd changed into gym shorts and a sports bra for the kickboxing session. Thank God for that. Her previous outfit had left nothing to the imagination and was the reason Krish had agreed to sweating it up on a Sunday. He would've agreed to swallowing hot coals for breakfast to get her to change out of the barely there piece of gauze, which had unfortunately triggered his stiff state of affairs. Childhood friend or honorary brother, Krish didn't think there was a man alive in the universe who wouldn't be affected by the sight of Diya's centerfold body.

And she knew the effect she had on men.

"Come to think of it"—he paused, recalling the last six hours—"you've been rubbing up against me like a cat all morning."

She was playing him. *Again.* Christ! Hadn't she had enough?

"Keep dreaming, Beast," she scoffed and began to stretch her torso like a swan's, gracefully arching her back and then bending over to touch her toes.

Whoa! She could actually touch her forehead to the part just above her ankles. She stayed bent over for a while with her un-atrophied gluteus maximus flashing him in the face.

Something was definitely cooking with her.

He remained sprawled on the floor because he didn't think his jellylike muscles could support his upright weight just yet and allowed himself to observe the motions of Diya's pink gym-shorts-clad butt with considerable interest.

"Do you know, for most heterosexual male mammals, the round red bottom of a female is her most attractive feature? The wider and redder, the better. I suppose you have an inkling since you wear so much pink around the area."

She took her time to stretch before straightening up and looked down on him, her lashes fluttering like little hummingbirds against her flushed cheeks. "Are you saying my ass is attractive or too big?"

He ran his tongue over his teeth. "I did say *most* male mammals."

"You're claiming that you're in the minority?"

She splayed a hand over a bladed hip bone, right below her tattoo, and thrust her boobs out just a little, and he knew then beyond the shadow of a doubt that she was toying with him.

He itched to smack her round ass, so he dug his fingers into the yoga mat.

"Don't you need to get ready? The dude will be here in"—he looked at his watch—"less than two hours." He needed to remind himself—remind them both—why she was in Dallas. It was not to flirt with him.

"I'm sure you'll entertain him if I'm tardy. Isn't it part of your knave duties? And your obligation to Daddy? He must have asked you to interrogate the dude. Take notes while testing his mettle with archaic torture techniques and then report back?" Her eyebrows rose in challenge.

"Try to be on time—American time and not Indian time. It makes a better impression," he said gruffly.

He wanted her to be impressed, too. Once she was … if she liked the dude … then Krish would be free.

Suddenly, his throat felt parched. He staggered to his feet, grabbed a bottle of lemon-flavored water, and took a deep, deep gulp.

"I always make an impression, Krish. In any time zone and on *all* male beasts," Diya said and sauntered away before he could respond.

Dr. Neil Upadhyay was an unusual lab rat. He was tall, well dressed, buff, and safety conscious. He had roared in from Houston on a massive Harley-Davidson, thoughtfully bringing along a borrowed pink helmet for his date. When alerted to the mode of transportation for the evening, Diya had squealed and shimmied and bounced back into her room to change into Sandy from *Grease*—dark jeans, a shirt, and a pink leather jacket. But she'd left her nude-colored pencil heels on her feet.

The Beast hadn't liked the idea of her riding about town on a motorcycle and had offered the use of his Porsche. Neil —good man—had politely but firmly refused.

"You are so not a nerd." Diya grinned at the biker dude grinning at her from across the table at Wolfgang Puck's Five Sixty. Crowning Dallas's Reunion Tower, the Asian restaurant boasted a panoramic view of the city and a superb menu.

It was a classy choice for a first date, and Diya was rapidly moving past impressed.

"But I am … among other things. I was this close to canceling today." Neil pinched his thumb and forefinger together as their server set his Asian beer and her pot of sake on the table. "When my grandfather called and said he'd set me up with a gal, my first thought was, *No way, Jose!* I mean, I love my dadu, but the whole idea of being set up sounded morbidly sad."

"I completely agree." Diya nodded.

"But then …" He flicked her a sheepish look while pouring hot sake into her cup. His arm flexed under his black muscle tee with the movement. It was tan like his face, thick and capable-looking like Tarzan's.

"But then … what?" she asked, nudging him to continue the story.

She liked Neil. A lot. She was already comfortable with him. He gave off a nice-boy vibe despite his alpha-male body. His Texas twang was a tad thicker than Krish's. In fact, the two men were like fraternal peas in a pod; both had been born and raised in Mumbai, they were roughly the same age, they had migrated to Texas to study in the same year, and both of them were brilliant in their work fields.

Neil's eyelids dropped to half-mast—either in amusement or embarrassment, she couldn't tell. "Promise you won't be offended?"

She was more than a little intrigued, so she pinched her throat and vowed solemnly, "I promise."

"I didn't know who you were. Dadu said you were his dentist's daughter and that your family are good people. That was it besides your name." He paused, his nose suddenly the color of salmon. "Your name didn't exactly ring any bells for me. It was my eight-year-old niece—she's a huge fan—who updated me about you. She's over the moon about this setup, and I have orders to propose to you before the night's done and not take no for an answer."

They were both laughing by the end of his tale, all awkwardness forgotten.

It wouldn't be awful, she thought absently, *to spend a lifetime with a nice man who made me laugh. Right?*

"Still, I wasn't convinced. Supermodel sounded pretentious enough. Super-successful supermodel was kind of daunting. I decided you'd have airs—a snob at the least and a bitch at most—and have an IQ that matched your dress size."

"*You* thought that? The buff biker dude with a doctorate in biomedical engineering?" Diya raised a sardonic brow.

Neil fake coughed to cover his grin. "Terrible gaffe on my part. My apologies," he said, not looking contrite in the least. "I don't stereotype as a rule, but I confess, I did it with you. Anyway, once I agreed to meet you, Maya sent me a list of instructions. What you like. What you don't. Where I should take you … et cetera. But, if all of that fails and you refuse my proposal"—he paused again, his eyes glittering with laughter—"be grateful she gave you a choice. I don't have any. Anyway, in case I fail to impress you, then I have to prostrate myself at your feet and beg you for an autograph. She wants pictures, too, which I have to keep sending all night long or face execution."

Diya was beyond charmed by Uncle Neil. "Your niece lives in Mumbai?"

He shook his head. "Dubai."

"Tell her I'm going to be in Dubai in two weeks and that I'd love to take her out for lunch. If your sister is okay with it, that is." She always tried to do special things for her fans.

"Are you kidding? You'll make Maya's year. And, if I know my sister, she'll join you. And don't be shocked if her husband tags along, too. You have some serious champions in my family."

Diya flapped her hand to dismiss the boons of her fame. "We'll make it a family affair."

"How sweet of you to think of my family as yours already, sweetheart," Neil drawled. "You'll make an excellent wife."

Diya jolted in surprise before she realized he was joking. "You're a tease, Dr. Genius," she said, rolling her eyes.

Then, once it was established that he was no more interested in being set up than she was, they were free to enjoy the date.

What was there not to enjoy? Good conversation, great food—lobster for him and sashimi for her. They had a number of things in common—they discovered that through dinner. They both adored their families—hadn't Neil agreed to meet her, only to appease his grandfather? Just like she had. They loved to travel—but who didn't? They preferred audiobooks to reading. They both loved to cook. It was shocking to Diya that her father had accidentally/on purpose plucked a rather suitable suitor out of his marriage hat.

On the ride back home, Diya was consumed by thoughts of an arranged marriage. Could it truly work between Neil and her?

Jeez! What was she thinking? Hadn't she decided to pursue Krish? Give that relationship a last hurrah?

Diya made a frustrated sound in her throat. Exactly the point. It would be a LAST TRY. One she was sure to fail. Krish would be horrified at her forwardness and would double up his Beast quotient. Look what had happened last night or how he'd reacted just that morning. Wouldn't putting her eggs in different baskets be the smart thing to do?

In spite of their similarities, Neil was everything Krish was not. He was blasé and fun—at least, on the surface. Life would be a joyride with him. Less complicated, less fraught. Less bittersweet.

She weighed her choices: prickly numbers man or a happy-go-lucky lab rat? A smart woman, a practical person would choose Neil.

Diya scooted forward on the bike and wrapped her arms around Neil, pressing her cheek into his back, testing, waiting, wishing desperately for a shiver to course through her veins. For lightning to flash through her heart. For something … anything magical to occur. She wasn't surprised when she remained unmoved, even with the chilly wind whipping past them.

The floodlights came on over the garage as Neil parked the motorcycle in front of the storybook house. He gave her a moment to disentangle herself from him before he hopped off. He removed his helmet and then removed hers because, suddenly, her fingers were frozen solid. She was a mannequin of uncertainty.

She stared at him as he carefully slung the helmets across the curvy T-bar of the Harley.

He is undeniably handsome, she thought, carefully appraising him. A dorky Indian sex god with a perfect stubble dotting his taut cheeks and jawline. His hair was military short, so the helmet hadn't flattened it up against his skull. He had a body frame that told her he was a health nut like her; she was pretty sure he had an eight-pack. She'd felt the rolls of his pecs flex as she'd hugged him on the ride. His nose was aristocratic, and any children they had would have a fifty percent chance of not being disappointed in their noses. Oh, Neil and she would make gorgeous babies.

Neil shot her a quizzical smile when she continued to sit on the bike and paint imaginary portraits of their children.

"Kiss me," Diya said abruptly.

Even his reaction to her insane demand was perfect. He wasn't shocked. He didn't recoil. He didn't judge her. Didn't look at her funnily or lewdly or laugh at her. And thank heavens he didn't make any jokes. He simply looked at her for a long, intermittent moment, during which her heart tried to explode out of her chest, and made his decision with a quick nod.

Neil bent his head and took her mouth, and her first thought was, *It is such a shame I can't shiver with him.*

Her lips opened under his, over his, as they played with each other. Tongues, licks, nips. His arms came around her, and she clutched his head in her hands, a little forcefully, a lot desperately.

Come on. Just once. Please let me feel something for someone else, just once.

When it ended, they both froze as they were—his hands on her shoulders, hers clutching his head.

"It was … bad, wasn't it?" Neil whispered as if he couldn't quite believe it. "It felt like I was kissing my sister."

"I sincerely hope that conclusion did not come from personal experience." Diya tugged a tuft of his hair, and he winced, more from her taunt than her hair-pulling.

"I'm into empirical knowledge, yes, but not in those kinds of data."

"Well, our experiment failed spectacularly. Too bad we dashed our folks' hopes." Diya slid off the motorcycle. Really, really too bad and too sad that he wasn't her prince.

"I can't speak for them, but I am disappointed. I like you, Diya. I didn't expect to," he said, his face open and gentle.

Then, Neil Upadhyay got back on his Harley and kick-started it. Only it didn't start. He kicked it a second time, and it roared to life. For another long moment, they both stared at the helmet in his hands.

He looked up, his dark eyes full of uncertainty. "Maybe we should try again? Sometimes, repeating an experiment can bring you a different result."

A thick layer of regret wrapped around her heart. There was no point in beating a dead horse. She had her result. Zero shivers. Diya shook her head.

"Will you call me if you change your mind?" he asked softly.

She nodded and watched another prince among men ride out of her life.

With a heavy sigh, she started her trek to the Beast's lair. How many gods were there in the world? How many had she appealed to over the years? And not a single one thought she deserved a break.

Long ago, Vallima had told her that no one had everything in life, and one should appreciate what they had and not lament over what they didn't.

Why was it so hard to accept rejection and failure? Why did she want it all?

What had Neil said? That sometimes, repeating experiments gave one different results? Did that mean—

Diya stopped short halfway up the brick steps. Her blood turned to ice when she noticed the wide open door and the Beast looming in the shadows on the stoop. He had a glass of whiskey in his hand.

Crap! What had he seen? What did he hear?

What new hell was he going to put her through tonight?

"Goodness me, Krish. You look like one of those gargoyles

one finds on top of castles in Transylvania," Diya said, sauntering past Krish with a patently fake smile plastered on her face.

Though he wanted to growl at her—and do other things much worse—Krish clenched his jaw tight and methodically locked the door for the night, the resounding clicks adding to the deafening chaos in his head. He punched in the night alarm, breathing in and out with slow, deliberate care.

He followed Diya into the kitchen, where she was concocting her overnight mask. He watched as she took out a bottle of chilled cucumber juice from the fridge and squeezed some into a bowl. A dollop of aloe vera gel, fresh lemon juice, olive oil, and some crushed ice followed, and she began to whip it all up with a fork.

Being insulted and then rudely dismissed sparked his already-simmering temper.

"What the hell did you mean by kissing him? You've known him for less than half a second, and you let him plant one on you? Christ, Diya. When will you learn some restraint? How much do you want to bet that he's messaging his friends as we speak and gloating about kissing Beauty Mathur? Do you even know what he's thinking right now?"

All evening, he'd been in agony. Seeing her ride away on the Harley with that man, imagining, wondering about things he had no business thinking about. God. What was wrong with him?

"I do not. What is he thinking, Krish?" Her eyes flashed, and the crushed ice in the bowl had transferred into her voice. She set the bowl aside on the kitchen counter and crossed her arms across her chest, making the soft pink leather of her jacket stretch over her girlie biceps and shapely shoulders. "What do *you* think Neil is thinking? Tell me, Krish, what would *you* think if you'd been in his shoes tonight?"

That I wouldn't have stopped at one kiss. I would have bent you over the bike and—

Appalled, Krish cut off the thought but couldn't delete the image it had spawned in his head. It spread through him like fire. His hands, his whole body itched to fulfill the promise of that picture.

He took a gulp of the whiskey, holding the glass like a lifeline with both hands. He would not lose control, not in any aspect of his life. He could not allow it.

"Tell me, Krish. Tell me what *you* think of me."

Why wasn't she calling him Beast? He positively felt like one now.

"You know what I think," he rasped out. God, he sounded hard, harsh … insane. He cleared his throat.

She shook her head. "No, I don't know. What do you think of me, Krish? What do you think *about* me? Who am I to you? *What* am I to you? Tell me."

He took another gulp and felt his lungs burn as wildly as his blood. Her wide, smoky eyes went wider at his actions. Did he remind her of his father? He was on his second glass today, past his self-imposed limit. One beer for weeknights and three fingers of scotch for weekends—he'd followed that regime for years. When he slipped, nothing good transpired on those nights.

"I think you should worry less about what I think and more about what Neil thinks. I trust you both had a good time. When are you meeting him next?" *Stick to Kamal Uncle's plan. Focus on the reality, not on a fairy tale.* "Let's hope he's open-minded enough about the kiss—"

"He is," she cut him off. "But *you* think I shouldn't have kissed him. *You* think I went too far for a first meeting, don't you?" She pushed away from the kitchen counter and got in his face. Her eyes glittered like shards of broken moonlight.

"Indian culture is conservative," he tried again, swallowing the bitter taste in his mouth.

She snorted in disgust. "Indian or American, every culture is hypocritical, as you well know. Different rules for men and women, for the privileged and the underdogs, as you have pointed out on numerous occasions before. But forget about general societal defects. Let's talk about me specifically. You don't think I should've kissed Neil?"

Krish wanted to run far away from this conversation, but his legs had turned to lead. "Not on the first meeting."

"Why not? Isn't it expected on a date? I know you've kissed women on first dates. You spent a large part of your college life dating, kissing, having one-night-stands with complete strangers. Or was it all lies and boasts? Tell me, Krish. Tell me why you can do all of that, and yet, when I kiss a man—someone my father approves of, someone I might marry—it's somehow wrong? Shouldn't I know what kissing him feels like before I agree to marry him?"

Logic. The last thing he'd expected from Diya was logic.

"Are … you?" His heart thundered inside his chest. He was finding it impossible to breathe, much less compute a full sentence.

The frosty sheen on her face cracked. Some emotion he was too stupid to recognize flashed on her face. Then, it was gone.

She stepped even closer; in her heels, she was taller than him. She leaned in, and for a microsecond, he thought she was going to kiss him. For a microsecond, he imagined grabbing her and kissing her.

She sniffed at his mouth and slapped him with the truth instead. "Are you drunk?"

"Not yet." But he was buzzed, and it sickened him that he wanted to blame his lack of control on the liquor or on her. He was no better than his father.

She frowned at the glass in his hand. "How much have you had to drink tonight?"

Not nearly enough.

"Enough," he said in a tone as bitter as his tongue.

Her mouth opened to maybe scold him but pressed closed again without uttering a word. Some of her anger melted from her eyes.

God. She was so beautiful that even looking at her hurt his heart. Her lips formed a perfect bow shape and seemed perpetually on the verge of laughter. They were unsmiling now and rosy and shiny. From her lipstick? From licking her own lips the way she did with a quick swipe of her pink tongue? Or were they like that from kissing Neil Upadhyay?

He could still see them in his head. See her hold another man, smile at him, lean into him. Allow his hands on her.

A rage he hadn't known he could feel, that he hadn't allowed himself to feel, rose up and choked him. And suddenly, he had to kiss Diya. He snaked an arm around her waist and pulled her tight against him. The leather of her jacket was cold, her hands were cold, and all he wanted to do was warm her up.

Liar! He wanted to wipe that man's kiss from her lips.

He gave her moment to read the intent on his face. A moment to make up her mind whether to stay in his arms or push him away. To flee. When she didn't move, he gave in to absolute madness.

Only once, he thought, nipping greedily on her luscious mouth. He skimmed his tongue across the seal of her lips, asking, begging to be let into the light.

Only once, he told himself, his mouth opening over hers, his teeth grazing over her fleshy bottom lip.

"Open up, sweetheart." He was grateful beyond belief that he couldn't taste anyone else on her lips. Just Diya. Only Diya. Sweet, passionate Diya.

"Krish?" she mumbled against his lips, her voice shaky. Dreamy. Bemused.

Her body trembled in his arms, and he felt vindicated, both powerful and powerless at the same time.

Christ. He wasn't drunk. He knew what drunk felt like. This wasn't that. This was madness, pure and simple.

"Come on, babe. Let me in." He nibbled on her lips, licking them like candy. "Just once. One kiss before you …"

She went taut as a mannequin in his arms. The next second, she shoved at his chest with both hands. He let her go at once, amber liquid sloshing over his hand.

"Before I *what?*" Her face, which had been flushed with wonder moments ago, bloomed with hurt.

She shoved at him again, harder. He stumbled back a step.

A nasty feeling of déjà vu settled over him when his hip rammed against the granite countertop. They'd been here before. Done this before.

Why can't I have just one kiss?

The Violent Femmes song roared inside his head like a foghorn. Yes, they'd done this before on Diya's twenty-first birthday, right here in Dallas. Only, back then, she'd begged for the kiss, and he'd refused to give her one. He'd wanted to erase the hearts he'd seen forming in her eyes for years. He'd succeeded. He'd destroyed them.

"Before I what, Krish?" Her voice had lost its coolness, its logic. It was sharp enough to cut now. Make him bleed. "Before I marry Neil? Before I go back to Mumbai and my life? Before you go back to pretending there's nothing between us? Nothing, except friendship and family connections?"

She grabbed the glass in his hand, and with a flick of her wrist, she poured its contents down the drain.

That was really good scotch, he wanted to say, but he seemed to have lost his voice.

She rinsed the glass in the sink and left it to dry on a mat. Then, she turned back to beam her hate at him.

He couldn't look away, not even if his life depended on it. She looked magnificent in leather and jeans and righteous anger.

"I love you, you fool," she shouted, fisting her hands in front of her as if she wanted to box him. "I'm in love with you. I've been in love with you since I was six years old. I'm not going to marry Neil, you big buffoon. I'm not going to marry anyone. Not ever. Like you, I've decided marriage is not for me. So, don't worry. And don't go all psychotic, thinking I'm going to trap you because of a kiss or start dreaming about castles and rainbows again. Or run to Daddy and make him impose his will on you. Been there, done that. Never again."

She lost steam then. She wrapped her arms around her stomach, as if to hold herself together. "I'll get over you, Krish. I swear it." Two fat teardrops rolled down her cheeks. She brushed them away with furious hands. "One way or another, I will get over you," she vowed.

She ran then, leaving him rooted to the kitchen floor, stunned and horrified that, with just a handful of words, she'd smashed through all of his convictions, his decisions, and the airtight life he'd built around himself.

CHAPTER 11

For a full minute, Krish stared at the empty space Diya had left behind and prayed his hearing had failed him. Then, before his brain could fully process what his next actions or words should be or would mean, he found himself inside her room.

Moonlight spilled in through the glass panes of the patio doors, giving the otherwise gothic-dark master bedroom some dimension. Diya was on her knees in the middle of the room, sobbing noiselessly. He joined her there.

"Don't." He swallowed hard, undone he'd caused this, that he'd made her cry.

"I can't help it. I'm a cry baby, remember?" she wailed.

Yes, Diya was an impassioned soul, a self-proclaimed drama queen. She bawled twice a week at least, if not more. But these tears seemed real—were real. He'd hurt her. Badly.

He'd sworn an oath to himself at fifteen that he'd never be the cause for someone's disappointment or pain or tears. But, no matter what he did or how he denied himself, he ended up hurting the people he loved.

He loathed to turn into his father. He didn't know how to stop it from happening.

He gently touched her face, wiping the salty streaks with his thumbs. A quiver went through her, and she crumbled further, so he gathered her up in his arms and pressed her face into his shoulder.

She hadn't cried when he disappointed her nine years ago. She'd been brash and caustic then and retaliated by breaking their engagement.

"It's a woman's prerogative to change her mind. You cannot force me to marry him," she'd said to her father when he tried to reason with her.

Krish had listened to it all in silence. What could he have said anyway when he was so clearly the cause of her misery? And, because she hadn't cried, he'd been able to let her go. It had been the right thing to do.

"I hate tears," he said. He couldn't bear to see her cry.

"I know that," she sobbed into his shoulder. "I'm sorry. I can't seem to ... help it. I'm a drama ... queen, *na?*" She pushed away from him, rubbing her runny nose with the back of her hand. "*Ugh.* Sorry for being all disgusting and melodramatic. I'm PMSing. I'll be fine in a couple of days. But don't worry. It's not your problem. Besides, I've done what Daddy asked. I can leave now. So, I think I'll catch the first flight out tomorrow. Get out of your hair."

She was making excuses for him, letting him off the hook —again. It shamed him. And it maddened him that she thought of him as such a cad, such a coward that he'd allow her to shoulder the blame for him.

He tunneled his hands into her glorious mane of silky-soft hair, but instead of shaking her like he'd intended to do, he slanted his mouth over hers and kissed her—again.

There! Now, she couldn't apologize for him or his inadequacies or spout silly ideas about leaving him. Not ever again.

He swallowed her, "Urk!" and taking full advantage of her open mouth, he took the kiss deeper, tasting her shock, her anger, her tears, and most of all, her desire.

He slid his tongue into her mouth when she tried to shift away, to talk. He sucked on her lips, her tongue. He wasn't gentle; he didn't know how to be right then. Not that she was complaining about it from the sounds she was making. Within minutes, her arms crept up to lock around his neck while she tried to suck his tongue into her mouth. He squeezed her closer.

"Krish, wait," she gasped against his mouth, twisted a hand around the front of his shirt. "Just wait."

He didn't want to wait. He didn't want to talk. Didn't want to hear any more confessions that might send shock waves through his body. He wanted her as off-balance as he felt. So, he scooped her up into his arms and stood up—carefully, as he didn't want to throw his back or drop her—making her giggle in delight.

"Such a Rhett Butler move. You're not playing fair," she purred, giving him a Scarlett-like pout.

Luckily, he didn't have to carry her far or up a grand staircase—that would've tested his resolve. Four quick steps, and he set her down on the edge of the bed and slowly got to his feet.

She seemed a little stunned then, a little dazed, as if she could not believe what was happening. Tenderness pooled inside the cavern of his heart, and he smoothed her hair off her face, tucking it behind her ears. He wanted to assure her of—he frowned, he had no clue what. Yet she seemed to understand what he was asking.

With a quick nod, she began to peel her clothes off. Leather jacket went first, then shoes, and then belt. He should help her, but her slow striptease had robbed him of breath.

God, she was stunning.

Condoms. Condoms. Condoms. The word puffed out like smoke signals in his brain.

Were they really doing this? Zero to a hundred in one evening?

Fuck. It seemed like they were.

It was his turn to rein in caution. "Wait! Are you sure about this?" He needed a verbal agreement.

Her mouth kicked up in a saucy siren's smile. Hooking her fingers in the loops of his jeans, she pulled him close. "I want this. I want you."

Krish let out a deep, shuddering breath he hadn't known he'd been holding. He cupped her heart-shaped face in his hands and simply looked at her. Diya's bone structure was so fine and yet so strong. Beautiful. He would never tire of looking at her.

Her face had been his obsession once. An obsession he'd thought he'd cured himself of.

He dropped to his knees in the V of her legs, and unable to resist, he took her mouth again. She let out a moan that had him nearly crossing his eyes. And it got rough fast. Teeth gnashed and nipped; lips teased and appeased. He kissed his way to her collarbone and sucked hard. A sudden, unholy urge came over him to mark her creamy-white skin with a tattoo. His brand. God, he wanted to mark her everywhere. He was greedy. Selfish. Possessive. He was a beast, but she knew that already. She made a sound deep in her throat and threw her head back, giving him unfettered access to the spot joining her neck to her shoulder.

She pulled on his T-shirt, tugging, stretching. He didn't know if she wanted the shirt off or him closer.

He was half out of his mind already. Maybe she was, too.

He moved, his hips pushing into hers, and he groaned into her neck. Heaven. It resided there, right then, right between them. Mewling, she pulled his head up for another scorching kiss. Fused from mouth to crotch, he began to press forward until she was lying flat on the bed. Spread like a feast for him —only him. So, he set about to gorge himself on every bedroom fantasy he'd ever had of Diya Mathur.

With shaking hands, he uncovered her layer by layer until all that remained on her were two scraps of black lace.

"Damn." He raked his eyes over miles of delicious skin. He'd seen it countless times in magazines, in photos, on beaches, at home. But not like this. Never like this. And it was his to do with as he pleased for tonight.

Forever.

No! Just tonight.

She went pink wherever his gaze landed, and her skin was fire beneath his hands. She began to unbutton his polo. Her fingers were clumsy, shaking. He held his glasses in place with a finger as she tugged his polo over his head.

It was strange, being half-naked in front of her. It didn't matter that they'd seen each other in bathing suits before or that they'd walked in on each other while the other was changing clothes or preparing for bed. He knew every square inch of her body—he'd studied it for years—and yet it felt as if he were seeing her for the very first time.

"Not my jeans," he said gruffly when she skimmed her hands down his chest and tugged on the zipper on his jeans. He took her hands in each of his, linked them palm-to-palm, and pressed them flat on either side of her head. "Not yet." Not when the condoms were in the other room.

Diya didn't use any oral or insertable birth control because the hormones didn't suit her. They'd have to be careful.

Then, out of the blue, an image of Diya pregnant and

round with his child flashed into his head, and a different kind of fire began to rage in his veins.

One thing at a time, man. One night at a time.

He rolled them until they were both stretched out in the middle of the bed. He was still on top, and she felt amazing beneath him, surrounding him with her arms and legs and giggles. He'd been a goddamn fool to deny them this for all these years.

He pulled the black lacy cups of her bra down with his teeth and nuzzled her perfect mouthfuls until she was squirming. Not enough. He covered one breast with his mouth and began to suck, softly first then hard.

Her back bowed off the bed, her hands slapping against the headboard. "Oh God, Krish!"

Soon, she was panting, gasping, thrashing beneath him. They were both burning up, mindless to everything but feeling.

"Please, Krish. I need … I need …"

He cupped a hand over the triangle of lace that covered the apex of her legs, squeezing, rubbing, while his mouth continued its assault.

"No, no. Harder." Her thighs clamped together, trapping his hand there.

So, he gave her harder, and within seconds, she began to climax in a series of shivers and sobs. He wanted to prolong her pleasure with teeth, tongue, the curl of his fingers, but he also wanted to watch her come apart. He freed her breast from his mouth with a pop and pushed up on one forearm.

She was magnificent as she claimed her pleasure with the same abandon that she did everything else. Head thrashing, hair exploding all around it. Body shuddering. Her mouth was twisted as if in pain, but the sounds coming out of it, the delirious sounds she made as she curved her body into his, splintered the last of his control. He ground himself against the side of her hips again and again, and like an overeager teenager who was granted permission to go to third base at last, he shot off inside his jeans.

Jesus, God!

Spent, Krish rolled onto his back, breathing hard, wondering when was the last time—if ever—he'd lost his mind like that. He'd almost had an out-of-body experience.

"So, you *do* desire me?" Diya asked after a while. After their souls had crept back into their bodies and their chests were no longer heaving.

Krish snorted without opening his eyes. "What do you think?"

"I don't know what to think. I can't read your mind." A pause and then, "Do you love me, Krish?"

Even through the drowsiness that was claiming his satiated senses, her voice sounded wobbly, fearful, like she wasn't sure he'd answer. Like she was afraid of his answer.

He pulled her into his arms and kissed the top of her head. Then, he admitted a truth he'd never planned on voicing out loud ever. "Yes, Diya. I do."

She started sobbing again.

DIYA WOKE up the next morning to a familiar feeling of heaviness in her womb and pinpricks of pain across her abdomen and lower back. She rolled into a ball on the bed and moaned. *Gah!* The only bright spot about getting her period was no more weepiness, bloating, and headaches for a while. But no more hanky-panky for a week.

She stilled as her memory returned in one fell swoop, and suddenly, her cramps were relegated to the backstage.

She pried an eye halfway open and looked about for signs of alien life in her bed. No alien life was present in the room —human or feline.

Dread swelled in her heart. Krish had bailed, just as she'd predicted.

She sat up. Maybe she'd dreamed the whole thing up, as usual.

Nope, she hadn't. Her body felt weird and tingled in strange places. She looked down and took stock. Love bites. Beard burns. She was naked, but for the panties—which were ruined now because of her period. Crap. The sheets needed to be washed.

Diya scooted out of bed. Well, first things first. She cleaned up in the bathroom and got dressed in comfy, warm clothes. She went back into the bedroom to take care of the bedsheets, but when she stripped them off, out bounced a baby bootie from under the pillow.

For several seconds, she simply stood there, blinking at the bootie, wondering how it had gotten on the bed.

That's right. She smacked her forehead. She'd tucked it under her pillow yesterday and wished on it, if she remembered correctly. Wished for a baby daddy, and last night had happened. *Whoa!* The bootie had turned out to be a pretty powerful talisman.

Gingerly, she picked it up and stashed it back into the bottom of the trunk.

O-M-jeez! What had she done? What had they done? And why had Krish slunk out of bed like that without waking her? More importantly, why had he been *in* her bed in the first place?

Diya pressed a hand to her stomach that seemed to have an army of fire ants doing drills inside it. She needed breakfast and her pain meds, pronto. But, for that, she needed to leave the room.

Gah! How was she supposed to face Krish with any kind of sangfroid after last night? She'd screamed at him, then blubbered all over him, and then fallen asleep on top of him

… after experiencing the most amazing, incredible, glorious orgasm of her life.

Several orgasms, she now recalled in shock. They'd all burst out of her, one after the other without stopping. And all he'd done was touch her through her panties and suck her boobs. *Wow.* She wanted to crawl back in bed and demand that he repeat the performance. But she could only do that if she got over the bajillion gallons of embarrassment she was feeling.

She also feared his morning-after reaction. He was going to pretend like it had never happened. Or he'd say something horrible like it had been a mistake and he'd been drunk. If he tried to get out of what had happened or apologized to her, she would kill him for real today.

Point to be considered was, nothing had happened. They hadn't made love—not fully. She would've remembered the pain—lust haze or not. And she'd be sore. And he would've surely brought the house down, bellowing about false advertising, once her untouched state was revealed. No, nothing crazy had happened last night. No irreparable or irrevocable damage done to her heart or her hymen.

Bolstered by the thought, Diya marched out of the room. She'd sworn to be bold, and that was what she'd be today. She'd sworn to get over him … and she would as soon as he told her why he'd done what he'd done and then run off while she slept.

She strutted into the kitchen and found it empty.

Great. She would be bold after breakfast.

Fortified by a cup of hot oatmeal and a mug full of chamomile tea, she was popping her painkillers into her mouth when Krish wandered into the kitchen. He was rambling into his cell phone in Malayalam, which meant he was chatting with his mother or Vallima. Possibly even some elderly aunt or uncle from Kerala.

"Amma says hi," he said, solving the mystery of the mystery caller. He slipped his phone into his pants pocket and poured himself a mug of black coffee before looking at her.

Diya temporarily forgot to be mortified and full of dread and went straight for bold.

"Where are you going?" she demanded, taking in his stylish form lounging by the coffee machine. He wore a light-gray office suit, a striped blue shirt, and no tie. "Knaves are not allowed to leave the castle without their lady's express permission."

She slid off the barstool and placed her hands on her hips. Assuming Aya Ahuja had been telling the truth, Krish was still in negotiations with Wisco. He hadn't yet agreed to work for them. So, where was he off to? It was on the tip of her tongue to ask him if he was going to accept the deal or not and whether he was moving to Wisconsin. But, if she asked him about his work—and they ended up arguing again—she'd never be able to ask him about last night.

Her cheeks warmed as she thought about the feel of his hands on her. His mouth—God, his mouth had done such wicked things to her.

"Do you love me, Krish?" she had asked him last night.

"Yes, Diya. I do," he had replied.

But what kind of love was he talking about? Romantic or familial?

"I like you flushed." Krish's beastly eyes gleamed with —*was it laughter?*—over the rim of his coffee mug.

Diya was sure her whole face was scarlet in color. In fact, her whole body felt feverish. Goodness gracious. She wanted to fan herself. Was she menopausal already? Why was it so freaking hot in the kitchen?

Krish prowled forward until he backed her up against the

countertop. Without her heels, she was three inches shorter than him, and she had to tilt her head up to glare at him.

"Good morning," he said and tenderly kissed her on her nose. "Cramps are bad?"

There really was no room left for embarrassment when a man knew her intimately enough to know how terribly she suffered on the first day of her menstrual cycle. For couture's sake, this was Krish! She could order him to go out and buy her a box of tampons if needed. That wasn't necessary anymore since Pree had made her and Leesha switch to using doctor-approved organic tampons, and Diya always carried a supply with her.

And would wonders never cease? Krish wasn't avoiding her like the plague this morning or making ugly excuses about last night. The tight wad of tension in her belly loosened a bit.

She nodded into the crook of his shoulder, breathing him in. He smelled of aftershave and coffee and Krish—her favorite scent.

"It's bad, but I just took my meds, so I should be better soon." She peeked at him from beneath her eyelashes. "How did you know?"

"The sheets when I woke up this morning," he disclosed and eradicated another fear. He'd stayed with her the whole night.

"Why didn't you wake me?" She tangled her fingers in his hair and felt her heart burst open and happiness waltz around the kitchen. She'd never dreamed she would stand with Krish like this, talk to him like this.

"I thought you'd want to sleep in." His mouth slanted up in a wolfish grin, and he winked at her. "And, bonus for me, I got to skip boot camp."

Diya dropped one hand to his belly and patted it. "Cheating is not the way to get an eight-pack."

"Eight-pack? Isn't it a six-pack?" He caught her roving hand before it reached the naughty bits and pressed it over his heart, which had a nice, happy rhythm going.

"Not any longer. Guys can develop an eight-pack now." She imagined Krish with an eight-pack and razor-sharp hip bones and felt her knees wobble. O-M-jeez. How many super-gorgeous male models had she seen naked? Hundreds. Where was her backbone? "Evening session will be two hours long. I want an eight-pack on you."

He lightly bit her nose. "Don't be shallow. Looks aren't everything."

"True. But they are the first impression, which counts for a whole helluva lot. You think so, too. Have you ever met a woman and thought, *Oh, gross, but I'll chat her up anyway?*"

Not that the term applied to the Beast with his tall and dark looks that he grossly underplayed. On second thought, since his rugged personality and sexy smarts were enough to turn her brains to mush, it was a good thing he wasn't classically handsome as well.

Diya unearthed her backbone. "Exercise is not just about looking great; it is about health and vigor. You do want to remain vigorous in your old age, don't you, Krishu *aann?*"

"Any more vigorous, and you would've passed out last night," he said dryly and moved away to set his mug in the sink.

"Ha! Only because Neil had primed me up already. You hardly had to put any effort into the seduction; I was so ready to explode." She tut-tutted, sauntering over to the fridge. "Poor Neil. He worked so hard all evening, and you stole his reward."

Everything had changed between them. And yet, everything felt the same.

"You're just begging for it, aren't you?" he growled from behind her, his hand curving around her hip. Squeezing.

Diya's butt cheek tingled at the threat, but she stuck it up in the air even more while she drew the essentials for a mud mask out of the fridge.

She wasn't going to overthink Krish's inexplicable change of heart; it probably had something to do with his early midlife crisis. Instead, she was going to be thankful for her many outstanding blessings and enjoy his attention while she had it. She wasn't that big of a fool to think that their bonhomie was going to last forever.

She swung about, puckering her lips. "I've been begging for it for a long, long time, Beast. At the rate you're going, I think we'll both have osteoporosis by the time you give me what I deserve."

Krish snorted, his eyes dropping to her pouty mouth. "Oh, you're going to get your wish, Diya. You're going to get exactly what you've been begging for. And, this time, you're not allowed to change your mind."

He kissed her then, another slow, thorough invasion of her orifice that had her atoms exploding like fireworks. Finally, after an eternity, he released her and walked out the back door without looking back.

"Oh, honey, will you come home for lunch?" she sang out like she used to while playing house as a child.

Her imaginary husband didn't bother to answer. Typical.

Glazed with happiness, Diya sat down on the barstool and gave it a whirl until Krish's last, ominous words came back to haunt her. She stopped spinning, abruptly queasy.

What had they started exactly?

CHAPTER 12

Once Krish had decided marriage was the only sensible option, he saw no reason to procrastinate in garnering the family's approval. His mother and Kamal Uncle had been overjoyed by the news and given their wholehearted blessings to the match. Krish had asked them to keep it a secret though until he formally proposed to Diya. He wasn't going to make the same mistakes he'd made the last time.

As he drove to the office, Krish considered the various milestones he would cross today. Both his private and professional lives were about to take a sharp turn whether he was ready or not. All he could do was hope for the best.

He called his mother again. He would control what he could.

"Did you find it, Amma?" he asked as soon as she picked up and then berated himself for his impatience. But he wanted it settled. Done. No loose ends.

But it wasn't his mother who had answered the phone.

"Amma can scarcely contain her joy, Krishu *aann*. Or her astonishment. Neither can I, my boy. Oh, you have made two old ladies very happy, and the almighty *bhagwaan* will bless you for it," Vallima said. Though he couldn't see her, he knew Vallima was smiling; he could hear it in her voice.

"I'm happy to oblige, Vallima," he answered in his mother tongue.

"Imagine! Your good news has caused Principal Savitri Menon to stay up late, on a school night no less, to search her room for your *jathakam*. I am telling you it is in the desk, Amma," she said that last bit to his mother.

The desk in question ran along one wall of his mother's bedroom in the cozy little cottage in Pune, its pigeonhole hutch stuffed with books and papers, random stationery and photographs. Krish imagined his no-nonsense mother rifling through her closet and workspace to find his horoscope.

"I praise the Lord he's finally bestowed our Krishu *aann* and Diya *kutty* with sense. If only you both had listened to our sage advice all those years ago, I would be busy raising your children right now," Vallima prattled on. "What are you doing there, Amma? *Tche-tche.* Here, let me help. You have made such a mess."

Krish smiled, listening to the small, white-haired Vallima —who was only a dozen years older than his mother—call her employer Amma out of respect and at the same time scold her as if she were her daughter.

Amma came on the phone, obviously banished from the search. "I spoke to the *poojari*, as you'd asked, Krishu. He said today is an auspicious day for new ventures, and he'll make a list of possible wedding dates as soon as I send the *jathakam*. We are trying to find yours—oh, Vallima found it." Her voice grew faint as she thanked Vallima, and then she came back on the phone. "What a relief. Now, I'll speak to Lubna and ask her to send me Diya's *jathakam*. Okay?"

Krish grunted his thanks.

"I had no idea you were superstitious, Krishu," his mother said hesitantly.

He wasn't. But Diya was. As he'd stipulated, he wasn't taking any chances. She wasn't going to find fault in him or his motives this time around.

He didn't say that to his mother, of course. Not that he needed to with Vallima freely opining in the background.

"Everyone is superstitious about things that matter most to them, Amma. And about the things they are not too sure about but would like a divine validation for. Maybe we shouldn't get too excited. Ask him what he'll do if the priest says the *jathakams* don't match? Will he break it off again? Go on, ask him!"

"Hush, Vallima," said his mother. Then, she must've covered the phone with her hand because all Krish heard through the speakers was a muffled debate.

"Amma," he said, thinking Vallima had made a valid point, "please, make sure the *jathakams* match. Bribe the *poojari* if you have to. And, for God's sake, don't tell Alisha or the Mathurs if it comes to that. Diya mustn't know."

"Krish," his mother gasped in abject disapproval of such dishonesty.

They debated it for a few minutes, but Krish got his way in the end.

One hurdle cleared, he thought with satisfaction as he said good-bye.

Now, on to the next item on his Monday agenda.

AROUND MID-MORNING, the housekeeper arrived at the house.

A short, rotund woman who spoke "very leetal Eenglish," Maria managed to converse with Diya just fine and without breaking the rhythm of her duties. Diya, always happy to exchange gossip and information about the world at large, sat in the wingback armchair in the master bedroom, waiting for the oil she'd massaged into her scalp to seep into her hair roots as Maria spot-cleaned the room.

From Maria, Diya learned that the Peters were super-busy people, and like Mr. Menon, they were "always working." They were absentminded-professor types and quiet as turtles. The only thing going against them, according to Maria, was that they had no children and claimed they wanted none.

"Who not want to have leetal *chicos*?" Maria asked. It was obviously a rhetorical question.

She painted a slightly more intimate picture of the story-book homeowners, offering Diya more than the bare facts Krish had. Not only did Maria unveil the Peters, but she also dished some juice about *Meester* Menon. She said Krish's name like she was addressing God himself.

"Mr. Menon teach my son, miss." Maria smiled shyly at the revelation. "Alejandro is senior in high school. He go to college next year." Maria pronounced son as *sohn* and her son's name as *Alehandro*.

"Did he come here for math lessons yesterday?" Diya asked. She didn't remember any of the kids by name, having been too amused and thrilled by the Sunday school setup as a whole. Next time, she'd pay more attention.

Crap. There won't be a next time, she realized. She wouldn't be there next Sunday.

"Yes. Mr. Menon say Alejandro is smart." Maria beamed with pride while fluffing and arranging the multicolored pillows on the quilted bed. "I tell my son what good this"—she paused the fluffing and pointed to her head—"when you so lazy? When you no work hard?"

Diya nodded sagely, having debated many such questions with her mother all through her childhood.

"Allah only helps those who help themselves," Lubna Mathur had drilled into her children's heads. Especially into Diya's, who'd abhorred schoolwork. "The Almighty works very hard to make our lives better. We must follow his example."

Diya wondered if she should postpone her travel plans for another week or so. What Krish and she had started last night would need some major work on her part for it to thrive. If she left him alone to brood too soon, they'd tumble back to square one.

Thrive? She rolled her eyes. She should be grateful if they survived two days without fighting, let alone a week.

Diya silently vowed not to get her hopes up. In fact, she wasn't going to hope at all. She was going to enjoy a week of flirtation and snogging—as Aryan had put it—hopefully some shagging, and then leave because her life no longer revolved around Krish.

"I'm sure Krish won't allow any of his students to be lazy, Maria."

"I no worried now, miss. Mr. Menon is good teacher for Alejandro. He is good man. He not take any money for the lesson. He say no to money. He make them work instead." Maria swished a duster over the dresser.

Diya blinked. "He makes them work? Where? At his office?"

Maria shook her head. "No. At the community center. He teach big kids. They teach leetal kids. They have to keep place clean. Like that. The center very popular place now. Busy all the time. Alejandro all the time there, working with his friends."

Just like Krish to find a brilliant way to teach the kids not only math, but also about responsibility. And keep them out of trouble, from what Maria was indicating. If Krish had been in the room, Diya would've leaped into his arms and smooched him.

Maria brandished the duster over the dresser. "Every day, I count blessing that Mr. Menon come into my son's life. My husband … he no good influence, miss. He has problem."

Diya took a wild guess at Maria's husband's "problem" and understood completely why Krish had taken Alejandro under his wing. Her heart squeezed in sympathy for both Alejandro and Krish and even for Maria.

"Mr. Menon is good man," Maria repeated. "First, he help Alejandro. Then, he help my husband. Then, me. He recommend me for many house job."

Diya was unsurprised by it all. Krish had always been a kind and helpful man. Although his philanthropy used to be geared toward saving animals before, working with kids had to be as rewarding.

It was only after Maria left and Diya was alone again that a wild thought struck her. Her knave had ditched her despite his promise to do otherwise. He'd tucked tail and run away in a suit.

And he still hadn't mentioned a word about Wisconsin.

WHAT HAD THEY STARTED?

Diya ruminated over the million-dollar question while she soaked in a bubble bath. When she couldn't take all the thinking and mental sleuthing anymore, she pulled the drain plug and stood up, water sluicing down her body. She took a quick shower before stepping out of the tub, dabbing herself dry with a fluffy white towel, and spraying cocoa butter moisturizer all over her body.

She was dying to talk to Leesha about these new developments, but she couldn't put her BFF in the delicate position of gossiping about her brother. Anyway, Diya could guess what Leesha would say—or what she would have said had it been any other man but Krish.

Step away, Dee. The man is toxic for you. You're too emotional about him to think objectively.

All of it was true. Yet Diya didn't want to walk away, even when her gut was warning her to run far and fast.

Since her gut was hormonal at the moment, she would take it under advisement.

Squeezing drops of a BB cream and sunscreen into her hand, she mixed it up and dabbed it over her face. She paused to stare at herself in the vanity mirror.

She looked unchanged. None the worse for wear this morning, except for the three lovely hickeys on her neck, shoulder, and breast. She probably had more, but these were all she could see. She ran her fingers over them until they tingled again. They were badges of love, of possession. She used to dream about Krish marking her like this, of her showing the world they belonged to each other.

Was her dream coming true? Were her wishes being granted finally?

She didn't know.

Krish wasn't an impulsive man, and last night had been nothing but impulse, a jealous reaction. Why had he kissed her? Why after all these years? What was going on in his head, his heart? How could she be sure of anything unless he talked to her? Would he expose his heart?

And what about her own heart and mind?

Her mirror image shrank as her old fears rose inside her like ghosts in a graveyard.

There was one thing Diya did know. Where Krish was concerned, her heart and her mind were unreliable.

CHAPTER 13

*D*anny "Dillo" Jones scrawled his signature across the last of the documents, and Armadillo Farms and Foods ceased to exist. Wisco's takeover was complete.

Krish watched the consortium of lawyers and accountants representing both companies congratulate each other and begin to gather their things from the conference room table. Somewhere in all the paperwork being stuffed inside assorted briefcases was his letter of resignation, effective immediately.

When the suits finally left after exchanging a bit of small talk and some jokes laced with good-byes and good lucks for the future, Krish sank back into his chair and let out a heartfelt groan.

"I reckoned you would take their offer," Dillo said and took a swig of his beer. "You're too young to retire, boy."

A Texan down to his marrow, Dillo exuded an aura of rock-solid strength, even at seventy. Dressed in jeans, a suede jacket, and his ubiquitous Stetson, Dillo always looked as if he were about to climb on a horse and ride off into the sunset with a blade of grass sticking out of his mouth.

It was the last time Krish would see the old man lean back in his squeaky conference room chair, a smile creasing his shrewd, wrinkled face. It was the last time they'd both be in this conference room together—this room where they'd planned and debated on everything from the price of fruits to world domination.

"I said the same when you announced your retirement last year," Krish reiterated, grinning.

"Touché!" Dillo raised his beer bottle high, the creases in his suntanned cheeks deepening. "To retirement."

Krish clinked his glass of chilled water to the bottle. "To retirement from corporations and boardrooms."

Dillo was right. Neither one of them was ready to retire in the truest sense of the word. Not yet.

"So, what should we do now?" Dillo asked, already sounding bored.

Krish's mouth kicked up on one side. "Now, you go to Florida and get your health back in line while I begin a new phase in my life."

"Nothing wrong with my health, boy. When am I seeing you in Florida? We need to discuss those investments you had me look at." Clearly, the man had zero plans to relax.

"Soon," Krish promised. "As soon as I've settled things here."

He, too, was looking for a new home, embarking on a new career, taking on a new wife. The newness in his life felt good, exciting. He felt in sync with it.

While Dillo finished his beer, Krish savored one last look around the conference room that he'd lorded over for the past several years. It was a bittersweet moment, sure, but he didn't feel a single pang of regret that he'd never see it again.

"What now?" Dillo asked again. He'd finished his beer and stood up, adjusting his Stetson.

Standing up, too, Krish grinned at the man who was his

boss, his mentor, his partner, and friend, rolled into one. "Now, Mr. Jones, you may accompany me to the jeweler you swear by and help me choose an engagement ring."

"You're getting *married*?"

The question, the voice of the speaker, wiped the smile off Krish's face. *Fuck.* He briefly closed his eyes before turning to face Aya, who stood framed within the open doors of the conference room. She looked composed, as always, despite the shock inflected in her voice.

"I believe I'll say my adieus to the rest of the staff," said Dillo and started walking toward the exit, stopping to shake hands with Aya. "It's been a pleasure working with you, young lady. I reckon the transitioning is going well for y'all?"

"It's been smooth, Dillo. The people at Wisco are great. No problems so far." Aya had been brought in as an external liaison in the human resources department a little over a year ago when the deal was finalized and both companies had begun integrating. With her neat and trim personality, Aya had managed to lump together, reshape, and whittle down a larger, more competent workforce for Wisco.

Krish hadn't expected to see her today. She was supposed to be in Wisconsin already, settling down at Wisco's head-quarters. They'd said their farewells on Thursday night at dinner—which he hadn't been able to reschedule because she'd said she was flying out over the weekend.

Why was she still in Dallas? Was there a problem? Then, it struck him that, whatever it was, it was no longer his problem. He'd resigned.

Dillo tipped his hat to her and walked away to say his good-byes to his old staff, leaving Krish and Aya alone.

Krish walked to her, kissing her on the cheek. The gesture was perfunctory and awkward. They'd been awkward ever since their breakup six months ago.

"So, are you getting engaged?" Her dark eyes cut to his.

Krish ran a hand through his hair. Was he? He hadn't asked Diya, and she hadn't said yes. He had no clue how to answer that question, so he said nothing.

Aya took that as an affirmative. "What about your aversion to commitments?"

She wanted marriage and children on top of her thriving career. When she'd made her wishes known, he'd told her he wasn't interested in marriage or even long-term commitments. He'd assured her he'd make a terrible family man. He'd explained why.

None of it had been a lie. Yet here he was, about to propose marriage to Diya, making him a liar in Aya's eyes.

How could he make Aya understand about Diya? How could he tell her that he'd loved Diya all of his life in one way or another? That not a day went by without him thinking of her or worrying about her. There was nothing he didn't know about Diya Mathur. And she knew him, all of him—the good, the bad, and his ugly side.

"Never mind," she said when he took a minute too long to answer. "It doesn't matter. Anyway, it's not why I need to speak to you."

She smoothed an imaginary wrinkle from the sleeve of her navy-blue pantsuit even though her clothes were never creased. Even her hair wouldn't dare to come loose from the tight French knot she twisted it into for work. During office hours, Aya was all business, but she also knew how to let her hair down. Krish admired her ability to separate the personal from the professional. They had that in common.

"Is there a problem?" He slipped his hands into the pockets of his trousers. He hoped she wasn't going to rehash the discussion about Wisco. His resignation was a done deal.

That had been another point of contention between them. At first, Aya had tried to dissuade him from accepting Wisco's offer, insisting it would be career suicide to tie himself down for five years in the middle of nowhere. She hadn't been wrong exactly, but her motive against it might have been. Ironically, once Wisco had made her an offer she couldn't refuse and she'd begun working for them, she'd changed her tune.

"Rayna told me of your new project. Have you lost your mind?" she asked, surprising him.

Although why he was surprised, he had no clue. Aya and Rayna Peters were good friends, after all. In fact, Aya and he had quite a number of common acquaintances through work and from university even though they'd never connected in school. Therefore, awkward or not, they both had to maintain a veneer of friendly equanimity, no matter what had happened or not happened between them.

"I don't believe so," he said coolly. "But you're welcome to your opinion."

"Don't get annoyed with Rayna for telling me. She is worried that you and Darren are in over your heads."

"We're not. You can assure Rayna of that when you speak to her next," Krish replied with more confidence than he felt about his new venture.

Darren and he, along with a couple of other investors, had decided to pool in their collective resources and buy a cyber school. More than simply invest, Krish wanted to get involved in running the enterprise. But, whether he did or not or it worked out or not, it was none of Aya Ahuja's business. It was Rayna's though, but knowing Darren, he hadn't explained anything to his wife.

That reminded him that he should talk to Diya about it once the proposal was out of the way.

"Is that all?" he asked, impatient to get on with his day.

Aya was taken aback by his brusqueness. *Shit.* None of this was her fault. Not her concern, true, but not her fault.

He took her hand and squeezed it, both in apology and

good-bye. "I'm sorry, Aya. About … everything. I know you mean well, but …"

"It is not my business," she finished for him with a shrug. This was what he liked about her—this ability to leave the drama out. "I'll see you at the hoedown?"

He hadn't expected to see her at the office farewell party either.

"I won't be alone," he warned. He'd never lied to her. Not about his limits. Not about his affections or expectations. Some things were just not meant to be.

Aya nodded stiffly and walked away without another word.

Around noon, Diya received a message from Krish that he wouldn't make it home for lunch, and since it was no fun cooking for one, she simply reheated the breakfast oatmeal she'd prepared in unsweetened almond milk to soothe her stomach. She ate at the kitchen counter while getting some work done on her tablet.

She responded to e-mails, CCing Rocky on all of them. She checked her schedule and rearranged some of it. Then, she started fiddling around on Scheherazade's designing app. Her cell phone buzzed as she tried to create her own bespoke version of a strapless sheath. It was her mother.

Diya wondered why her mother was calling her again. She'd spoken to her parents not two hours ago. "Mummy, mummy, mummy," she sang. "Play some Rummy … in a rich man's world. That makes no sense, does it?"

"No, it doesn't." Her mother's voice sounded oddly tense. Lubna Mathur was never tense.

Diya's stomach dropped. Had the trolls started up again? When would it stop? Had something happened to Daddy?

"What's happened, Mummy?"

"Diya, sweetie, are you absolutely sure about this? What is the rush? Tell me you have thought this through sensibly, baby."

Okay, that was ... weird.

"Um, what are you talking about? Thought what through?"

There was no way her mother had guessed what had happened—or not exactly happened—last night. No mother was that attuned to her child, even a favorite child.

"Enough, Diya. Stop joking about something so serious. Yes, I dearly want to see you married. But only if you want it, too. Tell me the truth, baby. Did you get engaged because Daddy pressured you?"

The world tilted sideways until gravity was a joke.

Engaged? To whom?

Was it Hasaan's doing? Had he leaked rumors of a phantom engagement across the internet while she slept? But he would've warned her before making any such announcements. Texted her. E-mailed! She'd spoken to him the day before, and he'd not said anything. In fact, he'd been a ball of nerves about meeting Saira for the first time.

"Who in heaven's name am I supposed to be engaged to?" she shouted. "Don't tell me Daddy thinks I'm interested in Neil just because I said he was cute. I find all men on motorbikes with doctorates cute. Is this some roundabout way your husband is trying to get me to say yes? I swear, I'm this close to committing patricide, Mummy."

"Diya, what is going on?" her mother asked.

"You tell me because I have no idea." Diya jumped to her feet and nearly fell. Her legs were as wobbly as a runway neophyte's on her first pair of platform heels.

O-M-jeez! The Shakespearean comedy of her life had just taken a very non-comedic turn. The Beast was going to blow up like Mount Doom over the new rumor, which would spell the end of their two-second, unconsummated affair. And, to think, she'd wasted a whole morning dithering over whether to heart or not to heart him again.

She was torn between the desperate desire to call the Beast and reassure him or to catch the next flight home, so she could strangle her meddlesome father to death.

"You're not engaged?" Now, Lubna Mathur sounded as confused as Diya.

"No!" *Who the hell had spread those rumors?*

"Then, why did Krish call us and his mother and ask for our blessings?"

Whaaat?

The fashion neophyte who'd been teetering about on polka-dotted Lady Gaga platforms keeled over and fell off the runway with a splat.

Apparently, she was mad at the wrong man.

To keep her wrath at the Beast's high-handedness from exploding in an altogether unhealthy fashion, Diya distracted herself by going window-shopping. Oh, all right! She window-shopped only for herself, but for her near and dear ones, she managed to accrue some quality purchases.

Like the stuffed ski bear for her nephew, Sidikins; the latest Apple watch for Daddy; perfumes, body lotions, and pashmina scarves for the women in her life; a set of makeup brushes for Millie, who was a makeup artist; a smartphone skin for her agent, Rocky; et cetera, et cetera. Up and down the mall she marched until her crampy womb hurt less than her biceps and fingers did from carrying all the shopping bags. She only stopped at a Starbucks for a chai latte and another dose of meds.

Another benefit of shopping therapy was that it helped her work out why the Beast had done what he'd done.

Control-freak Menon did not do emotion well. She'd forced him to confront his feelings, asking him point-blank if he loved and/or desired her. The admission must have scared the bejesus out of him. It must be making his belly curdle. *Gah!* It was making her belly throb—but in a good way. The engagement was Krish's way of taking control of his out-of-control pheromones.

Fine. She got it. And she wasn't exactly averse to the idea of an engagement. So what if he'd told the family before he'd actually proposed to her? Of course he wanted their approval first. His actions were time-honored and his intentions noble.

Dadima used to say that a person's values were interwoven with their family traditions. Of course, Dadima had meant it as a taunt to Kamal and Lubna Mathur who'd broken every stringent family tradition possible—they'd fallen in love, two people of different faiths, eloped in a penniless state, and against all odds, survived. It grated on Dadima's nerves that her daughter-in-law never relinquished Islam and that her own Hindu son never insisted his wife do so.

Unlike Dadima, neither her parents nor Savitri Aunty were inflexible or narrow-minded people. They wouldn't be offended if Krish hadn't sought their blessings. But Diya was glad that he had. It was an auspicious beginning to a happy ending. She'd insist on a long engagement though since he'd deprived her of a long courtship with bouquets of snogging and wooing.

Her phone buzzed halfway through her chai break.

"Lovey! What's up, girl?" Diya said into the microphone.

Lovey's reply was a shrill screech. "Congratulations! Oh my God! I can't believe it! Oh my God!"

Diya had to hold the phone at arm's length to save her eardrum.

"Who told you?" Diya asked, gritting her teeth.

Krish is a dead man, she swore. She was going to be widowed before ever getting married. Asking their parents' permission was one thing, but how dare he tell Lovey that it was a done deal before he'd even proposed to her.

Apparently, someone in Krish's office had overheard the happy news from someone else who'd heard it from someone else and so on and so forth across DFW's American-Indian grapevine until it had reached Lovey's big-lobed ears. She'd called Krish first, but he hadn't answered, so she'd called Diya.

Diya didn't bother telling Lovey about the non-proposal and promised to meet up for a wild celebration soon.

She called Krish as soon as Lovey disconnected. The call went to voice mail. She left a pithy message, asking him to call her back.

He didn't. He didn't send a text either.

With her mood reverting back to PMS sour, Diya exited the mall in long, angry strides. She dumped the bags in the passenger seat of the Porsche and peeled out of the parking lot. She was so upset with the Beast that she forgot to switch on the GPS, and twenty minutes later, she was well and truly lost.

She pulled up alongside a shoulder on a highway—or was it a parkway?—and scrolled down past addresses on the GPS. As she did, she noticed a saffron-colored flag flapping in the breeze on top of the marble-white steeple of a Hindu temple across the road.

Not one to ignore omens, Diya took the next exit that would lead her to the temple.

It had been two months since she visited a temple or mosque or church. Two months since she placed the bootie at Lord Vishnu's feet and prayed over it. Today seemed like a good day to have one of her mental tiffs with God.

.   .   .

MEANWHILE, across town, Krish and Dillo were on a mission inside a boutique jewelry store.

Bodine Johnson—owner, head designer, and Dillo's personal jeweler—was giving the soon-to-be groom a master class on engagement rings in general and diamonds in particular. After an intense show-and-tell, Krish settled on a two carat, D flawless, ideal-cut diamond set in a platinum casting. The media often ascribed the "flawless" accolade to Diya, which made the stone perfect for her.

That morning, Krish had palmed one of Diya's fashion rings from her bauble pouch—an eminently ingenious move according to Bo and Dillo—which allowed Krish to walk out of Bodine's with the right-sized ring in his pocket.

Krish slipped a sweaty hand inside his pants pocket and curled it around the velvet box.

"That was the easy part," Dillo said, slanting an amused look at Krish.

Krish exhaled through his nose. "I know."

"Treat it like an arbitration, my boy. Wheeling and dealing, back and forth—you're already good at it. You'll be fine." Dillo climbed into his black Chevrolet Silverado parked at the curb. "Let's get together over dinner soon and celebrate. I'd like to meet her. The missus would, too," he said before driving off.

Krish mulled over Dillo's advice as he got into his own car. Kamal Uncle had said something similar nine years ago —about marriage being a kind of merger.

Krish somehow doubted any business-type arrangement would please Diya. It certainly did not appeal to him. It never had. If he were to marry, he wanted his marriage to be like the one the Mathurs shared and not what his parents had had.

He had no doubt Diya would be the perfect wife for him. But what kind of a husband would he make her?

Regardless, it was time to get the show on the road. He sent his intended a text.

Start primping as if it's your birthday. I'm taking you out to dinner.

It was too late for doubts. He'd crossed a line last night, and there was no going back now.

CHAPTER 14

The temple visit had done wonders for her mood.

Now, back home, Diya lounged about on the terrace, munching on apple slices and chair-dancing to her Bollywood party playlist. Call her insane, but the loud, fast-paced music relaxed her.

Not so much the cats. All three had scampered over the wall the second music blared out of the Bluetooth speakers. Nora had actually snarled at the boom box as if she were a dog in attack mode.

Her phone screen lit up with an incoming message in the middle of a particularly noisy number. From Krish.

She rolled her eyes at his incredibly provoking message and continued to twerk on the chair. Whatever happened to *please* and *thank you* and making smiley faces at the woman you supposedly loved and were about to abjectly beg to be your wife?

She texted back grumpily: First or last birthday?

THE BEAST: Is there a difference since you were swaddled in

pink both times? You can slip into your REAL BIRTHDAY SUIT once we're alone ;)

DIYA NARROWED her eyes at Krish's attempt at text flirting, then fired back.

HA-HA. You are hilarious—NOT!

BUT, he certainly was trying.

She let out a gargantuan sigh and switched off the music. Then, she went into the room and began to sift through her trunks. She knew what she wanted to wear for her proposal dinner. Last November, after she'd signed the contract with Scheherazade, she'd visited the headquarters in Turkey to get familiarized with the brand and outfitted for the PR tours. Marianna Jordan, the head designer, had encouraged Diya to describe and also design a couple of her ideal outfits. It had been as if she'd given Diya the keys to paradise.

Diya had gleefully experimented with stylized cuts and easy-maintenance fabrics and colors. She'd imagined wrinkle-free couture for a travel wardrobe. Of course, until today, she hadn't worried about wrinkly clothes because someone was always there to iron out those pesky details.

Diya found what she had been looking for. She'd worn the dress at a garden party in Milan, and it fit her like she'd been poured into it—the next best thing to a birthday suit.

She held up the dress by its beaded halter strap and wondered if it was a bit much. Then, she shrugged. He had said to dress up. After all, tonight was going to be the most important night of their lives.

She hung the dress on a hanger and hooked the hanger

behind the bathroom door. The steam would take care of any stray creases in the dress while she showered and washed the day from her skin along with the final vestiges of her peeve.

Life was too short to be pissed off at the people you loved.

She'd worked it all out in her heart-to-heart with the gods that afternoon. The awesome meet-cute with Sharda Patel had further cinched the deal.

At first glance, the old woman sitting on a bench outside the temple looked like a Dadima clone. But appearances were nothing if not deceptive. The book in Sharda's hands— Sharda Patel had asked Diya to dispense with the respectful honorific of Aunty that all Indian women of a certain age got saddled with; that was how cool she was—had obliterated any similarity between her and Diya's grandmother. Not that Dadima didn't read, but Diya would bet she'd never read what Sharda had been judiciously blushing over. It had been a Regency romance, the cover with the typical half-naked rake nearly smooching the half-naked damsel who was practically begging to be smooched.

Diya's snigger had made Sharda Patel look up from the book.

"That's something you don't see outside a temple," Diya said with a cheeky grin.

"Are you wondering why I'm reading a romance novel outside the temple?" Sharda said in perfect, accent-less English.

"Only a little," Diya replied.

"It's my husband's death anniversary, you see."

"Right. Totally makes sense then." Diya had been delighted by the old woman's offbeat humor.

"He used to tease me about my romance addiction. Called the novels my 'puppy-shame' books. They're my way of remembering him ... and to see if my lady parts still work as they are meant to," she said, her eyes dancing with unholy glee.

Diya had nearly fallen off the bench from laughing, and the two of them ended up exchanging phone numbers after a lovely, long chat.

Giggling at the memory, Diya got out of the shower and began to dry herself.

Puppy-shame books indeed! Diya had some puppy-shame stories herself. A precocious toddler, she'd routinely run around the house naked, flashing her plump butt for all to see. With an older sibling's clothed authority, Priya had mercilessly tormented Diya. Krish, too. They'd sung the puppy-shame song nonstop until Diya would burst into tears.

"Shame, shame, puppy shame, all the monkeys know Dee Dee's name."

Smiling as the past played peekaboo in her head, Diya paraded between the bathroom and the bedroom, naked as puppy shame, doing the glamour dance she did so well. She rubbed a bronze-tinted moisturizer on her epidermis. Applied only a bare minimum of makeup on her face—no need to detract from the dress—emphasizing her doe eyes and masking the bite marks. She air-dried her hair, pulling the long, straight length of it over her left shoulder. She secured her breasts with sticky gel cups and shimmied into the zipless dress before slipping her feet into a pair of golden stilettoes. Last, she slid a beaten gold armband over her right upper arm and adorned her ears with a pair of long diamond earrings.

"Et voila!" She blew a kiss at her reflection like she did before any major event. "You are magnificent, my love. Absolutely ready to be proposed to."

Then, a horrible thought struck her. What if Krish was in

jeans? Worse, what if he didn't change out of his office suit at all? *Eek!*

She ran toward his room to prevent disaster. His door was ajar, the room empty. She heard the shower running in the hall bath. Whew. Saved. Time enough to adjust his wardrobe to her approval.

She waltzed into his room and stopped short by the queen bed, gaping at the clothes laid out on it. A pair of dark trousers, the self-on-self dark blue Versace shirt she'd nagged his mother into buying for him in London last September, and a sport coat with reinforced suede elbows from Zara. A bit on the casual side, but she honestly hadn't expected him to go formal—no matter how important tonight was for them. Even this much was too much chic to take in.

The shower shut off, and Diya quickly crossed over to the armchair by the window. But, as she was about to sit down and adopt a nonchalant yet vogueish pose, her eyes fell on the small red velvet box sitting on the dresser.

Double eek! Her heartbeat tried to break all speed limits then. O-M-jeez! It was true. It was truly true. He was really going to propose. He hadn't gotten her an engagement ring the last time.

She stared at the box, her mind going blank with terror.

Terror? Yes, yes, abject terror.

The bathroom door opened and shut, and soft footfalls came closer and closer until Krish appeared in the doorway, a towel tucked around his hips. His aftershave smelled divine. She wanted to lap him up like ice cream.

A slow, rakish grin kicked up one side of his face as he simply stood by the door and looked at her from her head to her feet and back up. "Hey," he said when at long last their eyes met. Locked.

She seemed to have frozen into a statue. She could not move. She was a hot, clammy statue.

One thick eyebrow quirked up as he took in her terror-struck expression. He noticed what she was trying not to stare at but still what her eyes kept bouncing back to.

"That's yours, by the way. Go ahead. Open it." He walked to the dresser, and with a flick of his finger, he set the box of temptation spinning like a top.

That unfroze her right quickly. She lifted her chin. "No way, *hombre*. Not without you on bended knee, a red rose clamped between your teeth, and a lot of begging."

Their eyes clashed in the cherry-wood dresser's mirror. His wet hair had been combed off his face, and his glasses were a bit foggy from the shower. Like his mother and sister, Krish was lean all over. He was a shade darker than them, his skin water-chestnut brown. He had a small patch of hair in the center of his chest and a thin line of hair that ran from his navel downward and disappeared into his towel. His shoulders and arms were lightly muscled, his back straight and smooth, and his legs long and supple, like someone who walked daily or was semi-athletic. Really, except for the slight jut of his beer belly, he was in good shape.

"Babe?" His beastly smirk drew her attention to his mouth and the fleshy lower lip. "With your system currently down for monthly maintenance, guess who'll be on her knees tonight? Roses and begging optional."

Diya's jaw dropped open. She was so shocked—and impressed—by his perfectly pitched double entendre that she couldn't come up with a single witty comeback.

Then, another one of her lifelong dreams was fulfilled. Krish whipped off the towel and pulled on his boxers, giving her a brief flash of him—all of him.

Diya collapsed on the bed, blushing and giggling like a twit. "O-M-jeez, Krish. Who's the puppy shame now?"

· · ·

La Rouge was French dining at its finest.

Krish had chosen the restaurant for its seen-and-be-seen status—a fact Diya had more than appreciated and preened over when they arrived. He'd managed to reserve one of the private dining rooms. Rather, his assistant had managed it—one of the last duties Charlie had performed for him. Krish was going to miss the enterprising young man, who'd been an asset beyond compare through Krish's tenure at Armadillo. With his persuasive tongue, Ivy League connections, and boundless energy, Charlie was an asset to Wisco, and Krish had made sure the senior management knew it.

The private dining room was an homage to Renaissance France with its mahogany furniture, padded cream-colored walls, long mirrors, sconces with silk shades, and fussy drapes. Strains of classical music drifted out through discreetly fitted speakers within the decorative ceiling. They looked misplaced in the elegant room.

A burst of laughter had Krish turning his attention back to Diya. She was currently entertaining the head chef with her animated banter and endless tales.

Tales bordering on the ridiculous, he thought with a shake of his head. It figured she'd be the centerpiece of all things wacky.

The chef drawled out Diya's name into *Dee-yeah* and not *Dee-yah*, as it was meant to be pronounced. Just like he was Chris and not Krish in this country. I say tomato, you say to-mah-to, and never the twain shall mix. Not that accents or cultures or countries needed to mix or blend. *To each his own*, was Krish's philosophy.

"It wasn't that funny," Krish said as soon as the chef trotted away to prepare the next course in their nine-course feast. It was irritating, the way the man had hovered and fawned over *Dee-yeah*.

"Don't be such a sourpuss. The incident at the temple was

legend. Can you imagine a woman like Dadima—salt-and-pepper hair, bad knees, sweater over the sari? But that's where the similarities ended. Sharda Patel was unreal, Krish. We discussed whether the hero jerking out in front of the heroine was appropriate or not."

Krish blinked. "Sorry, don't you mean, jerking off?"

"Uh-huh." Diya took a long sip of her pink champagne. "And, no, we did not mix up any idioms or metaphors. We had a very nice discussion about why masturbation is called jerking off and not jerking out when clearly *out* is the pertinent action and not *off*."

"And you had this bizarre conversation right outside the Hindu temple?" Krish could only shake his head.

"And we weren't struck down by lightning either. Amazing, isn't it?" Diya beamed at him before she remembered that she was pissed at him.

She looked gorgeous in fuchsia, even scowling. He'd made the mistake of calling her dress pink and been reprimanded for his ignorance. The body-hugging outfit was layered in pink and gold tassels all over and had no back to speak of. He'd had no brain to speak of when she pirouetted to show it off.

"Why are the most expensive clothes made from the least amount of material?" he'd asked and gotten a withering stare as an answer. By then, he'd already fumbled the proposal.

In his defense, he'd been excited and eager to show her the ring, and she'd been staring at the box, so he'd just reacted. For God's sake, they were buddies—well, lovers now, but they were *familiar*.

"We don't need to stand on ceremony. We had a traditional Indian engagement before, and I see no reason to make a movie production of it this time when I already know your answer." His second mistake—saying that out loud.

"Do you know me at all?" she'd asked with large,

wounded eyes that had made him feel lower than the lowest cad. "I make a movie production out of everything. And a HELL NO to your crappy proposal."

The doors opened, and with all the pomp his proposal had lacked, La Rouge's head chef marched into the dining room, followed by two smartly dressed servers carrying white plates covered with silver domes. The production put a momentary pause in Krish's mental self-flagellation. As one, the servers took off the domes and placed course number four in front of them.

"Spicy sea urchin sushi in lettuce cups," the chef announced and apprised Diya of the nutritional value and calorie count of the dish, as she'd requested.

Then, the trio trotted out, leaving them to enjoy the meal.

They ate in silence that was bursting with flavors. While Krish enjoyed peace and quiet in all its essence, this wasn't how he'd envisioned their re-engagement would unfold. He nudged Diya's foot under the table in silent apology. She moved her leg away.

"What do you want, Dee?" he asked, exasperated now. "You want me to go down on my knee? You want me to grovel? Fine. I'll grovel once we're home."

"That's what you think going down on one knee is? Groveling?" she asked hotly. "I don't want you to grovel. I want you to mean it." She flapped a hand in the air. "Just forget it. Forget the whole thing. I won't marry a man who keeps secrets from me and who lies to my face."

"What the hell are you talking about now?" Krish dropped his fork and knife on the plate, completely baffled.

"Do you deny that you pretended to go to work today? Your girlfriend—ex-GF told me everything. I know about Wisconsin and Wisco. I know you're negotiating with Wisco about something." Diya's eyes shot daggers at him.

Now, he got it. Krish leaned back in his chair in relief.

The elephant in the room hadn't been his lack of romance at all.

"I CAN'T BELIEVE you kept all that from me," Diya said on the drive home.

She'd held her tongue all through the exquisite dinner, all through his statement about his resignation and the cyber-school investment. But, she didn't want to play nice anymore.

Why had she built her hopes up? A leopard never changed his spots.

"What else are you hiding?"

"Nothing."

"I don't believe you." She crossed her arms across her chest. "Why do you keep things from me?"

The Beast was unperturbed by her anger, hiding his thoughts behind his fancy, rimless, non-reflective-glass spectacles. "Calm down. It wasn't personal."

She took a deep breath, counted to twenty, and exhaled. "Shall I *personally* corkscrew the heel of my shoe into your brain?"

He flicked her a glance. "Amma and Alisha don't know about it, either."

She didn't care that he hadn't told his family. She was here in Dallas, not them. He should've told her. If they were to marry, she wanted them to share their lives, not compartmentalize parts of it.

"I always work it out in my mind before I tell anyone; you know that," he said.

"So, you've worked it all out? You've decided you're going to run a school?" She tried not to sound incredulous. This decision from a man who'd blamed his mother's teaching job for ruining his life.

"Yes." He gave her a longer glance. The shiny surface of his face was again hiding something deeper. He wasn't sure of his decision, was he?

Just then, he reminded her of a brash fifteen-year-old Krish, trying to appear angsty to compensate for the lost, hurt, bewildered boy he actually was.

Her anger depleted instantly. *Gah!* What was she going to do with this man? He made her blood boil one minute, and the next, all she wanted to do was pet him.

"Tell me the rest, Krish. And please, don't leave anything out."

He did better than tell her. He showed her. He'd already given her a brief outline of what Darren Peters and he expected to gain from their investment. When they reached home, Krish grabbed her hand and dragged her straight into the office.

It was a spacious, hexagonal room tucked away in the back of the house, between the living room and the bedroom floors. Built-in shelves lined three of the walls, bursting with books. A fourth wall was a large picture window, showcasing the woodland, and had a long, padded bench underscoring it. A cozy place where one could stretch out with a book and a mug of tea. Two cats crawled out from under the bench to stare at Diya in unblinking curiosity. She bent down to say a quick hello and then took a slow turn about the room to resume her inspection.

A tall grandfather clock stood in a corner by the door, and the entire floor was covered in gray industrial carpet. A large birdcage stood in one of the nooks, nesting four colorful parakeets around a fake tree. They'd started twittering as soon as Krish switched on the lights.

Two desks faced each other in the middle of the room with enough space between for four people to form an arm-length circle. Both workspaces were junkyards of paper and work paraphernalia. Krish handed her a thick file with a transparent plastic cover. There were two more of the same on one desk.

"*Outreach School Project*," she read off the front of it. Then, hefting the file between her hands like a weight brick, she raised her eyebrows at Krish. "You don't expect me to read this, do you?"

"I'm not delusional. You wouldn't understand the technical jargon anyway, as it's mostly analytical mathematics." He kissed her nose, even as he grinned pompously.

She stuck her tongue out at him. His focus shifted to her tongue, her mouth. The tingling started up again, raising the fine hairs all over her body. He leaned in to give her a hot, openmouthed kiss. She couldn't help herself either. She touched her tongue to his and shivered. He stripped off his coat and draped it over her shoulders without breaking their lip-lock.

"So, about OSP," he murmured against her cheek when they finally came up for air.

"Huh?" She blinked at him. What were they talking about? Oh, right. Full disclosure that she'd insisted on. "Tell me," she said, sliding her arms through the sleeves of his jacket and wrapping herself in his scent, his warmth.

"It's a start-up. A privately funded cyber school offering comprehensive subject classes to grades one through twelve. It's already affiliated to a number of public schools in the US, and students have the option to sit in for physical examinations at those schools. Eventually, we want tie-ups with schools all around the world. Cyber schools are the future. Their potential is limitless. They can reach millions of students at once, in any corner of the world. Anyone with access to a computer and the internet will be able to get a certified education. Children, or even adults, who can't go to school because of geography, money, a disability will be able to get home-schooled at their own pace, in their own environment, for their own interest and development. Eventually, we hope to have physical classrooms in places where affiliate schools are scarce and the internet is still something out of science fiction. Education is key; it's sacred, Dee. Humanity cannot evolve without knowledge, learning, progress, growth."

He took her hand—the one his ring would be winking on had he proposed to her correctly instead of bowling the box at her like a cricket ball.

O-M-jeez! She couldn't believe he'd just thrown the ring at her, yelled, "Catch!" and expected her to gleefully put it on. She'd been so stunned that she didn't even lift her hands to catch the damn box, and it had bounced off her chest to the floor.

Anyway, letting bygones go, Diya tangled her fingers with Krish's and pulled him down to sit on the padded bench by the window. A gray-black cat wove from windowsill to windowsill and jumped onto his lap as if his sitting down had been an invitation. Krish stroked the cat, making it purr and Diya shiver in envy, as he talked about his new enterprise.

His words *were* full of technical jargon about how OSP worked and where he expected it to go and what role he wanted to play. He didn't only want to be an investor and business advisor; he also wanted to teach. He gained steam as he gave her numbers and statistics—his forte after all. He asked her to open the file and showed her pie charts and graph lines that looked like her father's EKG report. He told her everything, except the most important thing.

"Why, Krish?" she asked finally.

This job was the complete opposite of what he'd been doing for the past fifteen years.

"What do you mean?" He stood up, freeing his hands of fur and her.

The kitty cat did not like it one bit. Neither did she.

"Why this? Why now? Why not Wisco?"

His eyes slashed to hers, cutting sharp like diamonds. He didn't want to answer the questions. But they were the only answers she was interested in.

Also, "Why me? Why us? Why now, Krish?"

What had changed? Why had he changed?

Had he changed?

They stared at each other, their breaths rising and falling in opposite beats.

His Adam's apple bobbed as he swallowed. "You don't trust me. You think I've jumped off a cliff without a safety net to catch me. You think I'm acting out of character because I'm … what? Bored? Having a midlife crisis? Going senile?" He'd read her mind, as usual.

He cupped her cheek. Then, he slid his hand around to the nape of her neck and applied a light pressure. "Don't worry, Diya Mathur. I know what I'm doing with this project … and with you. I'm committed to both."

Not exactly the declaration of all-consuming love she wanted. But it was a start.

That night, they slept together again without actually *sleeping together.*

Like the previous night, they wound up in the master bedroom. It had the bigger bed, hence more room for monkey business. And, goodness, Krish was an absolute monkey about bedroom business.

He was innovative; he had to be, considering she was partly off-limits due to the "monthly oil change." He was funny and uninhibited and completely thorough. His thoroughness was no surprise. Krish was a meticulous man and more than invested in proving his *Homo erectus* status.

They minutely studied each other's bodies and learned how best to pleasure each other despite limitations. In one way, Diya was glad she had her period. She wasn't quite ready to go all the way. She wasn't quite ready to give Krish that final bit of control over her. It was too important a step to be taken lightly, and she didn't want to jump off the cliff until she had a few safety nets of her own spread below her.

Near dawn, after a third round of mattress mayhem, she lay on her stomach, gasping for breath, when she felt Krish grope for her hand. She tried to tug it back but only succeeded in flapping it about on the mattress.

"Stop. No more *lovin' feelin'*. Please, let me live," she groaned. Her insides were mush.

Romance novels had it right. It *was* possible to die from pleasure. A less conditioned heart would have given up pumping by now.

"I need your hand for a second, babe." He tugged insistently on her left ring finger.

Diya's eyes flew open. Rather, her left popped open, and her right eye remained pressed against the mattress. She rolled her eyeball toward Krish through the wreckage of her hair. He was stretched out on his side next to her, the race-car-red velvet box in his hand.

"No," she shot out succinctly. *Oh no. No way!* She tightly fisted her hand.

"In some countries, the custom is to wear the engagement ring on the right hand. It's left mainly for the US and UK." He tried to pry her right hand open.

She gathered her strength and rolled over, scooting back until her butt hit the headboard, and crossed her arms, burying both her hands into her armpits. There. Now, none of them were accessible.

The Beast was not at all discouraged. He sat up and pushed his glasses up on his nose, fire and determination sparking his dark brown eyes. "Don't be childish, Diya. Give. Me. Your. Hand."

"You sound like a dictator, not a delirious suitor," she said, her own resolve hardening. If she gave in now, she would never gain her footing with him. "I explicitly told you the kind of proposal I'd be willing to accept."

"Babe, you know you're going to marry me. I know you're going to marry me. Hell, the whole world knows it by now. Give me your hand."

"Babe," she echoed, hoping the sarcasm would blitz him good and nasty where the sun didn't shine. "I know no such thing. As for the 'whole world' knowing, whose fault is that, you blabbermouth?"

Krish pulled his glasses off and pinched his nose. "Be reasonable. Going down on one knee in a tuxedo with a rose shoved between my teeth is stupid. It's not our custom."

Neither was the engagement ring, but he seemed adamant to put one on her.

She shrugged. "The tuxedo is optional."

He hopped off the bed, and for a second, she thought he was going to kneel before her, that he was going to give her the fairy tale. Her heart lifted, only to come crashing down when he stalked off into the bathroom and slammed the door in his wake. The shower came on a second later. He was going to brood in there and think up methods to bully her. Beastly control freak.

Diya flounced down on the bed and pouted until she got the heebie-jeebies again. She pulled the quilt over her head and tried to sleep.

What was she doing, saying no to Krish? And what was he doing, saying yes to her?

Why was her life all topsy-turvy all of a sudden?

KRISH FOUND the entire rigmarole of deciphering and communicating emotions a complete waste of time. Once he decided on a goal, he went after it. The *why* didn't matter, only the *how* did.

If a negotiation wasn't going as expected, he pressed down on an opponent's jugular—not hard and not to harm, only to warn—until it did. If that failed—and it rarely did— he felt no qualms about using underhanded tactics to come out on top. With Diya, he'd learned to use the latter.

He spent a long time in the shower, and by the time he came out of the bathroom, she was sound asleep, surrounded by her guardian cats. Europa lay, curled around her head, like a strange, animated hairband. Sam slept between her quilt-covered feet, and black-pelted Nora lolled alertly by her hip, tail swishing in slow motion.

Krish stood by the bed, looking down at his sleeping Beauty, trying to get the myriad of emotions she triggered in him under control. His mind took him back years to another night he'd been roiling mad and guilt-ridden like this.

He'd stolen into his sister's room, armed with a penlight and permanent marker, where both girls were sleeping side by side on Alisha's bed where he'd drawn impressive Mahabharata hero-type mustaches on their faces—thick black handlebars ending in circles on their cheeks. He'd done it in retaliation for them ratting him out.

Diya had found out that he'd forced Priya to smoke a Marlboro and have a beer with his gang of rowdy friends. He'd thought it was such a dashing, grown-up thing to do and not realized that his sister and Diya were spying on him. Both girls had run straight to Diya's father and reported him. Priya had been grounded for a month while Krish had been lambasted for a good three hours and then put to work at the dental clinic after school hours and on weekends. He'd thought he'd gotten off lightly at the time. He'd soon learned better.

"It's the devil's job to tempt," Kamal Uncle had said, comparing Krish to a devil, "but to give in to temptation is a far worse crime in my eyes, especially for my daughter." He'd gone on to say he would've grounded Krish, too, had he thought the action would have any positive effect on the misguided young man.

Priya hadn't spoken to any of them for the whole month she'd been grounded. And Krish had silently nursed his anger until the night Alisha and Diya had a sleepover and he had the perfect opportunity for retribution.

The permanent marker hadn't washed off their faces for weeks. Diya had refused to be seen in public until it did and hadn't gone to school for two whole weeks, missing tests and a throwball tournament she'd been training for.

Krish had been in gargantuan trouble for the stunt. More so when his mother had realized he'd been under the influence that night and disclosed the ugly truth to the Mathurs. There had been other repercussions to his actions. His mother and sister had moved to Pune that summer, leaving him behind with the Mathurs because he'd been adamant not to change schools in his final two years of high school. He hadn't expected his mother to leave him behind. He'd thought, if he put his foot down, she'd change her mind and stay in Mumbai.

Krish had lost both his parents—his whole family—in one year. He'd been festering his aloneness ever since. That year had taught him self-reliance; you could only depend on yourself.

Diya had forgiven him the minute the ink washed off her face—she wasn't one to let things fester. The sparkly, stuffed pink poodle he'd bought her as a peace offering had also helped. Un-bribable Alisha still held a grudge against him and probably would until the end of days.

Krish opened his fist, and the diamond ring on his palm caught fire as it refracted light spilling from the night lamp. He went to his knees by the bed and groped under the blanket for Diya's left hand. Her palm was soft and warm and dainty; her long, shapely fingers were topped with a glittery pink-gold nail polish.

He slid his ring on her ring finger and kissed her hand to seal the deal.

Diya slept on, undisturbed. But Nora watched him with

cat-eyed disapproval. It was a sneaky move on his part—one for the gallows, for sure. But he also knew Diya would never take the ring off. She believed in omens. To remove her engagement ring, except to shower, would not bode well in her heart or mind.

So, that was that. The deal was done. It had never been a negotiation, not on his part. They were engaged, and there was no need to pretend otherwise. Now, he could only hope she'd forgive this stunt as easily as she'd forgiven the mustache one. He'd take her shopping tomorrow, just in case.

With a sigh, Krish gathered up his clothes and left the room. They both needed their beauty sleep.

DIYA WOULD NEVER, ever, ever talk to the rat bastard again.

She did seek him out for boot camp late in the morning though and put him through the mother of all workouts that sorely tested even her awesome stamina. But she did not speak to him. She didn't so much as even breathe in his direction. Kudos to him, he didn't try to make excuses for his rat-bastard behavior.

She wasn't angry he'd taken the coward's way out of expressing his feelings. Honestly, she'd known he'd do something like this—oh, all right! She had NOT expected him to shove his ring up her finger in the middle of the night like some kind of thief in reverse. But she should have.

In lieu of a chewable breakfast that she was too irritated to cook or consume, Diya whipped up a whey protein, yogurt, berry, and banana smoothie and poured it into two glasses. She picked her glass and slurped it down while trying to voodoo summon the Beast, so she wouldn't have to break her vow of silence and call him into the kitchen and throw his smoothie in his face.

He didn't appear. The cowardly beast was hiding in the office.

Well, she was not going to allow him to cower in peace. She was going to confront him … nonverbally. She would smite him with her mute displeasure.

Smoothie in hand, she stomped into the office and stopped short with a gasp when she saw that he was video-chatting with the parents. All three of them. Apparently, his mother was in Mumbai and at Diya's house. O-M-jeez!

Okay. Be cool. You can handle this.

She sashayed around the desk, making sure to keep out of the laptop's camera range while setting his smoothie down on top of the plastic-protected OSP file since there weren't any coasters handy. Then, she strolled over to the window and took a seat, smoothing a hand down her butt as she did so to preserve the wrinkle-freeness of her diaphanous, hand-kerchief-hem dress that Maria had ironed for her. She casually crossed her legs and pinned a hostile glare on the Beast as he spoke to the parental trio.

"The date at the end of March is fine. I'll wind up work as soon as possible, and we can be there in the next couple of weeks," he said without looking at her.

Diya's entire body clenched in horror. *What date?*

"There are several auspicious dates throughout the year, Krishu. Isn't next month a little too soon?" *What's the hurry?* was implied but not expressed out loud.

"We don't want to wait, Amma. We've waited long enough," Krish said.

Diya sprang up then and ran to the laptop before he could do more damage.

"Hello, hello, you guys. Oh, I miss you so, so much." She blew kisses at all three parents, her heart melting as she saw their happy but confused faces. God, she really, really missed them. Missed home. Oh, she wanted to hug all three of them. But first things first. She had to repair the damage.

Adopting her most horrified expression—she didn't have to reach far—she placed a hand on her chest. "Goodness me, Aunty. I don't know how to tell you this, but your son is stark raving mad! He belongs in a mental institution. We are NOT engaged. He is making it up. And I'm so sorry for putting you all through this again."

The parents froze inside the laptop. The mothers looked at each other, and her father went beetroot red in the face. *Uh-oh.* He was about to blow a gasket. Maybe she shouldn't have blurted it out like that.

Krish tried to shove her out of the conversation. Diya didn't budge.

"What's on your finger then?" He pried her left hand off her hip and shoved it at the camera. It filled the tiny picture-in-picture window on the top right corner of the screen. "We are engaged, people. This is not a discussion."

"See? I told you he's mad. Krishu *aann*, please remember, this is not an engagement ring. It's my birthday present. A very generous one, I admit, but appropriate since you've forgotten so many of my birthdays," Diya lied and elbowed Krish in the oblique when he pinched her butt in warning. "I know; I know," she re-addressed the parents. "A thirty-thousand-dollar birthday ring is a bit much. It's like … wow! I'm so touched. Actually, he's touched in the head, but he's super generous, so I'll overlook that." She'd taken a wild guess at the price tag, but it sounded like a reasonable amount for a two carat diamond. Gosh, it was so pretty.

God, Diya. Focus!

Krish muttered behind her in Malayalam. She wanted to step on his bare feet in her house slippers, but she refrained. The mothers no longer looked stunned, just resigned. They'd witnessed enough spats among the M Brigade to understand what this was. It was about supremacy. In the dog-eat-dog world, only the kitty cat could survive.

"Call me on the landline now," Daddy bellowed and moved out of camera range.

"I'll speak to him," Krish said. But, before he left the room for the oh-so-private man-to-man, he threw down an order. "The first date on the list, Amma. Don't listen to this fool. We *are* getting married."

Neither of the mothers looked pleased by his attitude. Yay for understated matriarchy! *Err* ... not that the matriarchs were especially pleased with her either.

"Kindly explain what's going on," her mother ordered, and Savitri Aunty gave a terse nod of agreement.

Diya sat down on the office chair, suddenly tired of fighting. She gave the moms a brief, censored version of what had happened in Dallas so far. "I'm sorry we got your hopes up, but this won't work if he won't relent even a little. I'm dearly hoping he does. But do you understand why I can't give in?"

The crazy thing was that, when her mother asked, "Give in to what, baby?" Diya had no answer. Just that her gut felt un-joyous and queasy, and to her, it was indication enough that something was majorly wrong.

CHAPTER 16

"It's not about the stupid proposal ... or not only. But he doesn't get it," Diya spoke into the wireless ether while she rolled the grocery cart down the canned goods aisle.

She'd slipped out of the house as soon as the phone call with the mothers ended. Avoiding the Beast had been the primary reason, but they also needed fresh groceries that would carry them over for the next few days. The most pertinent reason for leaving the house had been to clear her head. As soon as she'd roared down the driveway in Krish's Porsche, she'd called her voice of reason.

"He can't keep bullying me into doing things his way. We're not children anymore. Marriage is supposed to be a partnership. He needs to understand that," Diya went on.

"And yet, both of you are behaving exactly like children," Leesha said, brutally. "Besides, we both know that Krish has never truly succeeded in bullying any of us into anything. So, stop with the *I'm such a doormat* act. Did you talk to him, Dee? Have you expressed your concerns, your feelings in clear words?"

Diya felt only marginally bad for putting Leesha on the spot against her brother. "No."

"Dee, you're the one who told me that, unless women spell things out loudly and clearly, men will never get it. Quote, 'Men are not equipped to deal with life's vicissitudes.' Unquote."

Diya remembered the quote from a self-help book. She'd cited it last May when Leesha and Aryan were on the verge of breaking up. "I know exactly what kind of vicissitudes Krish is equipped to handle. Zilch. I know he won't be comfortable unless he's controlling the whole relationship by himself. Gah! He's you in the masculine. You know that as well as I do. I know him and how he thinks."

"Then, what's the problem? If you know him, you know he would never take advantage of your ... *ahem* ... doormat nature. You also know he wouldn't have taken this step unless he was one hundred percent committed to it."

Diya stopped at the fruit section, wondering if her anxieties were baseless. Here, she'd been offered the one thing she'd spent her whole life wanting, and yet she was hesitating to accept the goodies. But how could she not be suspicious? She'd bitten the apple once before and been poisoned in the heart and soul in return. The Beast did not have a great track record in the relationship department.

"The problem is, I know him too well," Diya confessed.

The past would always be present between them, the good and the bad—his sweetness and his rejection. She didn't know if she could get past it. Truly forgive him.

"Rubbish," Leesha scoffed. "You're being just as stubborn as him. How much can anyone truly know another person? How well do you know me? You know I'm not the type of woman to go on a blind date with a stranger I'd met online. Yet I did. You know I didn't believe in love and marriage and babies. Yet here I am, in love and married and trying to get pregnant. People can change, Dee. That's the beauty of us. We change constantly. You've changed. I certainly have. Krish has changed, too, especially in the last couple of years. You just don't want to see it."

Leesha's words rang a very loud bell in Diya's head. Oh, she'd noticed the changes. His temper had mellowed. He'd become less impatient with his mother, with all of them. He spoke to his mother and Leesha and Vallima nearly every day now when, a few years ago, he hadn't called even once a week. And then there was the midlife-crisis thing.

Diya sighed. She knew Krish had changed. It was only that she wasn't sure she approved of the change. She'd loved Krish from afar for most of her life. Could she love him close-up? And what about him? He'd never approved of her or her lifestyle. He'd never desired her before, and suddenly, he did? Could a person change that much?

After promising Leesha she'd think long and hard about it, Diya hung up the phone and called Hasaan. It was a relief to talk about something other than the Beast. She made Hasaan tell her all about Saira.

He gleefully admitted that they'd met thrice already and had plans to meet again. Apparently, Saira was a riot to talk to and had intrigued him with her radical views on extremism and how it related to existentialism. Hasaan hadn't yet met her privately and without her veil. Saira's father had very strict rules about courtship and customs, and no one was allowed to violate them. Not knowing what Saira looked like did seem to aggravate Hasaan but not enough for him to walk away like he'd planned. Hasaan was wooing Saira in earnest. *So sweet.*

And, so totally unlike her courtship.

Diya huffed out a breath. *What courtship?* Wham, no bam, and yet she was engaged.

She began to select fruits at random—apples, oranges,

pears, bananas, and a bag of seedless red grapes.

"Gina will get in touch with you on Friday with a new itinerary," Hasaan said as their conversation wound toward work.

Gina was Hasaan's assistant, and until Diya hired one of her own, she managed Diya's scheduling and travel arrangements when it pertained to Scheherazade business. Her agent, Rocky, handled everything else.

"The jet will pick you up on Sunday, *chérie*. It should be sometime in the morning."

Sunday. She'd be gone in five days. She didn't want to go without hashing it all out with Krish, but she had commitments that couldn't be postponed any longer. It had been hard enough juggling and rearranging her existing engagements because she'd taken these unexpected ten days off.

That reminded her, she really needed to look for an assistant before either Gina or Rocky threw a tantrum and quit on her. Rocky had started signing his emails like so: *Yours truly, Overworked Agent/Undercompensated Manager/Handmaiden-in-Waiting.*

While she was at it, Diya also needed to look into hiring a financial manager now that her finances had exploded into the megastar range. She would've asked Krish for references had she been on speaking terms with him. She needed a new lawyer, too, one familiar with international business law, as Hasaan and Leesha had advised. Several interviews and meetings had been lined up to that end and postponed, but Diya would have to sink her teeth into all of the above once she got home. And she had to make a decision about the apartment in Istanbul.

Gah! There was so much stuff she needed to get off her plate, not the least of which was her non-engagement to the Beast.

Hasaan yawned. It was after midnight for him. "Right.

That's my cue. *Khuda hafiz* until I see you, Diya *jaan*."

As her friend and boss had never before called her *jaan* or darling—though the literal translation of the word was *life*—and it was something Saira did, Diya burst out laughing. "Someone's getting awfully smitten and influenced by his lady. That's so cute, Hasaan *jaan*."

On that teasing note, Diya said good-bye and disconnected the phone. She was happy for Hasaan and Saira, truly. It pleased her that they'd managed to get past their reservations.

Diya pushed the cart into the deli section where a ridiculous variety of cheeses were on offer. *Jeez.* Why did life have to be so complicated and so full with hard choices? Cheese should just be cheese, but no, she had to pick between Gouda and cheddar and feta and Muenster. She selected three fresh cheeses from the smorgasbord when her phone buzzed again.

"Hi, Lovey. What's up?" Diya answered, pushing the cart toward the cold dairy section. Good thing she'd shrugged on a sweater over her short summer dress.

"You forgot, didn't you?" Lovey accused.

"Forgot wha—oh crap!" She'd scheduled a massage with Lovey for ... *right now*, she realized, checking the clock on her phone. "Give me half an hour. Shit ... the groceries. What do I do with the groceries? Should I drop them home first or get them to the spa? There's fresh cheese and dairy in here."

"Leave them in the car. It's cold enough today. And hurry. I have another appointment right after you. I'm going to try to push her back an hour," Lovey said.

"You're a doll! See you in a bit." Diya disconnected the phone and ran toward checkout.

Two hours and a Swedish massage later, Diya dumped the

grocery bags on the kitchen counter and ran up to her room to use the bathroom and change into a pair of denim shorts and a T-shirt. Twisting her hair into a bun at the nape of her neck, she walked back into the kitchen to begin preparing a late lunch, only to find her personal knave unloading the groceries and putting them away.

He knew he'd goofed up and was on guard. She could tell from the tense set of his shoulders and the fact that he wasn't meeting her eyes. Good old Daddy must have yelled at him for upsetting his favorite child.

"What are we having for lunch?" he asked gruffly.

Huh. It seemed he was going to ignore everything, including the fact that he owed her an apology.

Diya picked up a medium-sized cast-iron pan from the drying rack and placed it on the burner, which she ignited and twisted on low. While the pan heated, she tackled the prep work for a couple of omelets.

Krish hovered by her elbow as if awaiting instructions from her or for the sky to fall on his head—whichever came first. Sideways, his belly looked a little tighter. Definitely a little less round. His white shirt with the rolled-up sleeves contrasted his dark skin well. Actually, the man-of-leisure look suited him really well.

Focus, Dee.

She selected half a dozen eggs from the carton and cracked them open in a bowl, wrinkling her nose at the eggy odor. She scooped out most of the yellows and threw them in the trash. As her hands moved, the heart of her diamond fractured into a thousand colors, drawing her eyes. It was too delicious a stone to give back really.

"Here's how it's going to go down, Beast. I'm keeping the ring," she said, shooting him a dark look when he tried to hug her.

He lazily stepped back and gestured for her to keep going,

looking amused but also wary. Amused and/or wary was fine. If he had looked smug, she would have smacked his head with the cast-iron pan.

"For all concerned parties, we're engaged. But, between you and me, we're together on a strictly probationary basis." She sprayed the pan with Pam and decided her year in law school hadn't been a complete waste of time if she could instinctively spout useless legalese. "We'll take each day as it comes, get to know the lay of each other's land. And then we will decide together whether we should continue the relationship or not. *Together* is the word of the millennium. You will not make unilateral decisions from now until forever more. Is that understood?"

She whisked fresh cheese and eggs into a batter and added chopped tomatoes, dill, chilies, and cilantro to it before stirring once more. She looked at Krish when he didn't answer. He was leaning against the counter, arms crossed, his brow furrowed.

"You have five days to woo me and convince me this can be our world *together* and not your world alone," she finished. It was a good plan.

Some weird emotion flickered behind his eyes, through the rimless glasses. "Why five?"

"I'm leaving for Istanbul on Sunday morning." Diya turned to the hot pan and poured in two-thirds of the batter.

"No." With a giant step, he closed the distance between them, his hands reaching for her. But he stopped as soon as she held up a hand. Not a drop of amusement remained on his face.

"I have to leave on Sunday." She made small circles with the spatula in her hand, indicating the kitchen and the two of them. "This little domestic cocoon we have going here is not real, Krish. It's not my life. It's not yours either. This isn't even your house." Oh, but how she wished it were. She so desperately wanted all of it to be real. But she had to be sensible about this. She could not afford to have her heart trampled on again.

He gave a harsh laugh, a sure indication of the coming hailstorm. "Isn't it ironic that you're talking about what's real and what's not when you are the one who lives inside a castle in the clouds?"

No, he doesn't know me at all now, she thought sadly. "And that's why we have to do this. And we have to be completely honest with each other. Agreed?"

He shook his head, frowning harder. Diya gave him some space to think. She pulled out six slices of bread from the breadbox and slid them into the toaster while keeping an eye on the omelet.

"What don't you agree with?" she asked.

"All of the above." He smiled faintly, as if he couldn't help it.

The omelet was done. As she was copiously scent sensitive, omelets were her least favorite food. But they were also full of protein, so she'd eat them because it was good for her body. She tossed the extra-fluffy omelet onto a plate and set it on the placemat on the counter. Krish grabbed a plate out of the crockery cupboard and piled it with toasts.

"We have a problem then. But, first, let's finish lunch. Maybe you'll understand the equal rights movement a bit better on a full stomach."

WHILE DIYA MADE her own omelet, Krish made himself a three-toast double-decker sandwich.

She wanted honesty, did she? But how much honesty could she bear before she looked at him in disgust? And how much honesty could he bear from her before he did the same?

He was torn between wanting to shake Diya for putting them through this and applauding the ballbuster behind the pretty face.

"Ask me whatever you wish to know, and I'll give you an honest answer," he said, swallowing a mouthful of the egg sandwich.

She took the barstool next to him and started eating her omelet with dainty little forkfuls. He got up to pour them water. While he was up, he filled up the coffeepot and switched on the coffee machine. Then, he sat back down to polish off the rest of his lunch while the coffee brewed.

"Why now?" she asked, picking up her glass of water. "I asked you before, and you didn't answer. Why do we make sense as a couple now and not then?"

"You're the one who broke our engagement. Not me," he pointed out, the lie twisting his gut.

Diya sighed. "Krish, I'm asking for honesty. I only did what you pushed me to do. You refused to touch me. You refused to kiss me. You were refusing me, Krish. How can you deny that?"

She wanted honesty? Fine, he'd give her honesty.

"Just to be clear, I wanted you then as much as I want you now. I want you in my arms, in my house, in my bed. I might not have wanted marriage, Diya, but I wanted you. And I won't have sex with you without marriage. If you think it's old-fashioned, so be it."

"You want to marry me to sleep with me? Get serious, Krish." She rolled her eyes at him. The cheek of her.

"I'm dead serious, babe." He grabbed her hand and pressed it against his crotch. He got instantly hard. "Feel that? That's what you do to me without even trying. I've been all kinds of hard since you got off that plane. Hell! You want the truth? I've had a hard-on for you since you were freaking fourteen years old and suddenly grew boobs."

"Krish!"

Aghast, she snatched her hand back and set her glass down on the counter so hard that water sloshed in all directions, some of it spilling on his unfinished plate. He pushed it back; he wasn't hungry anymore.

"I'm being completely honest." And he loved the fact that, for all her brazen insolence, his crude gesture had put a fiery blush on her cheeks. Christ, he was a dinosaur in a business suit.

She snatched up a paper towel and began to mop up the mess.

The coffeepot began to bubble, and Krish stood up and poured himself a steaming mug. "Want some?"

She glared at him again—or not again since she hadn't stopped glaring at him.

"Do you seriously think we can have an affair without the benefit of marriage and not suffer any consequences?" he asked seriously this time.

"Just what do you mean by 'suffer the consequences'? How dare you imply that being with me will make you suffer. I'll be the one suffering, believe me. Shackled to a prehistoric beast. Oh, what joy—*not*!"

He started laughing at her melodrama. "I didn't mean it like that." He groaned, rubbing a hand over his face, his rough stubble prickling his palm. He hadn't shaved today. "Look, Diya. Jokes aside. I won't have some frivolous flirtation with you. That's where I draw my line."

"What rubbish is this? You've had plenty of affairs before, and I don't see a string of ex-wives behind you. You've never once thought of marriage with any of them. You told me yourself that you would never marry because of your fath—" She broke off, her stricken eyes flying to meet his. "I mean …"

"I know what you mean," he said, tightening his hold on

his coffee mug. He watched the dark liquid swirl as it cooled. Yes, they needed to hash this out but not in the kitchen. "Come on. Let's go sit on the sofa."

He held his hand out to her, but she looked at it as if he were pointing a gun at her.

"Why?"

"Because, if we're going to talk about all of that, then it's going to take a while, and I want to be comfortable."

She narrowed her eyes, searching his face, and decided he meant it. "Fine," she said ungraciously. "Give me ten minutes." She began to clear up the remnants of their lunch.

"Leave it, Dee," he said when she started washing the damn dishes. "I'll do it later."

"Fine. Fine." She dried her hands and swept past him into the living room.

He followed her with a shake of his head. But, before she could sit down, he grabbed her around the waist and sank down into the armchair with her on his lap.

"Krish, let me go," she said without struggling. She either wanted to sit on his lap or was mindful of the steaming mug of coffee he was holding.

He took a hot sip and set the mug down on the side table. She immediately tried to get up, but he held fast. "Please, sit. If we're going to talk about my defects, I might need your shoulder to cry on."

"Oh brother." She rolled her eyes but didn't try to get up again.

He dared to kiss her cheek. "Thank you."

"Okay, okay. None of that," she said, crossing her arms across her chest. Clearly, there would be no cuddling.

"Ready to hash this out?" he asked.

"Finally!"

He dared another quick peck on her nose. "What was your question? Ah, yes. Why do I want to marry you?"

CHAPTER 17

"Do you know that, before Sunday, I'd never seen you with a man?" And he hadn't liked it one bit. Krish still felt a sick rage whenever he recalled Diya kissing that ass, Neil Upadhyay.

Diya tensed in his lap. "What do you mean?"

He twirled a lock of her hair that had escaped her bun around his finger. "I've never seen you dress for a date, go on a date, get excited about a date. I haven't met any of your boyfriends. You've never introduced me to any of them. Except for Hasaan."

"Surely, you're mistaken," she began, frowning. "Hasaan is not my boyfriend. He's my boss. We wouldn't cross that line. Bad for business."

Krish nodded. "Good to know. But, yeah. I'm not mistaken. I've heard of your legions, of course. And seen pictures. And let's not forget the media harping about your sensational escapades every other day. But I've never actually, in real life, seen you with a man—a potential mate."

He worked her bun loose, letting her hair spill over her delicate shoulders and down her back. He drew his fingers across her collarbone, the curve of one shoulder, down her left arm, to her hand where his ring adorned her fourth finger. She purred and arched like a cat at his touch, and it made him want to growl like a tiger and bite her.

What was he doing? She wanted to talk.

"I hadn't seen a man hold your hand, wrap you in his arms. Hadn't watched him kiss you," he choked out. His hands were on her knees, and he spread them apart. The shorts allowed him to smooth his hands over her skin like silk, glide upward without hindrance.

"Krish, please stop," she mewled. Paradoxically, her legs widened, and her hips thrust forward as his fingers tested out the seam of her denim shorts at the juncture of her thighs.

But he took his hands away. "Shall I stop? Stop what? Speaking? Or touching?"

He was hard as a rock already, and they'd barely started making out. He wanted to touch her, taste her. He wanted to gorge himself on her.

"I hated seeing you with Neil. I hated seeing your arms go around him. And I wanted to kill you both when you kissed."

Goose bumps sprang up on her arms, and when she tilted her face up to kiss him, he leaned away. She wanted to discuss their relationship. He would discuss it.

"You see, Diya, I've always thought of you as mine, even when I pretended otherwise. It's easy to fool my mind that I feel nothing for you when I live here and you live in Mumbai."

"So, what you feel is jealousy. Possession." Her chest was rising and falling, as if she'd skipped rope for a half an hour.

"Protectiveness. Desire," he corrected, his hands busy on her body.

"Lust," she argued, quivering in his arms. "God, Krish. Stop that! You said you only want to sleep with me."

"I said, to begin with, I want that."

Abruptly, he turned her, so she faced away from him. Her hands clutched the arms of the chair for balance while he adjusted her legs, so she sat astride him. Reverse cowgirl. The diamond on her finger gave him permission to feel every sentiment she forced him to.

"Shall I stop?" he whispered in her ear.

She shook her head, so he cupped a hand between her legs, another around her breast. She wore a padded bra beneath her T-shirt.

"Unhook your bra," he said, his voice guttural. The second she did, his hand slipped inside and took possession of her breast.

That damn tabloid had been right. It was a perfect handful. She moaned as he played her body like a guitar. He rubbed and tweaked; he pulled her hard against him, and his hips twitched. Her head fell back against his shoulder as she arched higher. Her nails dug into his thighs.

"Krish ... we can't," she panted. "We *can't* ... I'm on my..."

He remembered and slowed. He dipped his head to feast on her earlobe, and she moaned. So quickly, he'd become obsessed with the taste of her, the smell of her, the weight of her, the warmth of her.

Her breath was coming in puffs. She responded to him like a dream, wild for his touch.

Already, she was on the brink of climax. He could feel it shuddering through her. Through him. His heart pounded furiously inside his chest, his hands relentless on her succulent body.

"You asked me why. It's because I love you, Diya. I honestly love you."

She shattered in his arms. "I love you, too, Krish."

He knew that. He'd always known.

· · ·

THEY SPENT the day in bed, getting up only to use the bathroom and to eat. It was like they were marooned on a lost island, and until a rescue boat found them and the world invaded, they could live as they pleased.

It was Diya's fairy tale come to life on a budget.

The unlimited budget fantasy had allowed for a more extensive star cast made up of serving elves and knaves, magnificent and ever-changing sets, unlimited glittery clothes, and animals that meowed and chirped and whinnied but did not poop.

However, this version was also fine. Or was actually better because, in this one, Krish did not gallop about on a horse, brandishing a sword, or brood in solitary confinement under a tree. Rather, he talked to her.

He gave a broader overview about how and why he'd become involved with OSP. He confessed to feeling dissatisfied with the monotony and general quality of his life—personal and professional—for a couple of years now.

"Burnout?" she asked, pressing on the pressure points on Krish's toes that relieved tension, neck aches, and hypertension. "With the hours you keep and the projects you take on, no wonder. And why haven't you told me … any of us … about these doubts you've had for so long?"

She sat, cross-legged, at the bottom of the bed with his right foot in her lap while he reposed against several fluffy pillows like a rajah, his hands linked behind his head and a blanket thrown over his puppy-shame region. She itched to pull off the blanket, but it wasn't time to play Emperor's New Clothes yet.

They'd both decided complete nudity went very well with complete honesty. Only she couldn't be completely nude because of her period, so she had a pair of miniscule gym shorts on.

"Yeah, like anyone in busy, self-absorbed Mumbai has time to hear my woes," he said with a snort.

"What? How dare you say such a thing." She ran a knuckle along the center of his foot to punish him. Krish was ticklish there.

He jerked his foot away. "Stop that. It's a fact that Mumbaiites are a selfish lot—like the citizens of any fast-paced city. Anyway, what would I have said when I didn't know exactly what was wrong myself? That, despite an upwardly mobile lifestyle and a career that I was damn good at, I wasn't happy? Do you know how stupid and ungrateful that sounds when millions of people around the world don't have jobs—good or bad? I've surpassed my own goals for success—or what I considered was success. I am—was on the freaking board of a major food company. I've made a ton of money over the last decade. Stowed some of it away in solid investments—the flat in Mumbai, stocks, fixed deposits. If I don't work for a couple of years, it won't make a goddamn difference in my lifestyle. The thing is, I can't *not* work. But I want to love what I do, Diya. I don't want to do it just because I'm good at it. I don't need to anymore."

She massaged his foot in soothing circles. "Relax. Don't get defensive. We're just updating our bios here."

"I am relaxed," he growled. Then, he sighed. "Do you understand what I'm saying?"

She nodded. "I think so. You've become very Amreekan in your thinking. A materialistic fatalist. Wait! Is that a paradox? Whatever. You know what I mean."

He sat up, frowning. She let go of his foot and crawled up the bed and into his lap.

"I do get it." She kissed his jaw, his chin. "A lot of people feel the same, Krish, even in India. Most just have to suck it up and keep doing their jobs because they have to provide for their families. But some have the luxury to make the change. And, out of those few, fewer still have the guts to take the leap. You do, and you have. And it's great that you have. I'm not sitting here to judge you."

He pressed his forehead against hers, careful of his spectacles, and exhaled noisily, as if releasing some invisible tension.

He'd been worried about her reaction, she realized with a start. Worried that she'd see it as quitting. Or downgrading his lifestyle.

A few years ago, she would have. But not now. She truly got what he meant by wanting to improve the quality of his life. And, by that, Krish didn't mean material wealth and success—or not only that. He didn't mean living in a swanky apartment and buying a fast car and having a flush bank balance—all of which he did have. He wanted success on a more evolved scale, a humanitarian scale. He wanted to boost his moral worth in life.

It was a good ideology. It was hers, too. Only she went about achieving it in an entirely different fashion.

"So, you decided to *Embrace the Change* and invest in children's education," she said, letting him know she truly understood what he wanted out of life. That, in this respect, they weren't so different.

"Remember the kids you met here on Sunday? Usually, the lessons take place at the local community center, but last week, I had them come over here. I didn't want to leave you alone to think up more mischief," he said, smirking.

She bit his shoulder. He tasted salty and slightly bitter. He needed a shower.

He didn't even wince and leaned back against the pillows again, taking her with him. She settled against him, her ear listening to his heart.

"I got involved with the center two years ago as a tennis coach. Somehow, one thing led to another, and I ended up tutoring the kids as well. It was because of Alejandro … ah, he's Maria's son. The housekeeper," he explained in fits and bursts, his heart doing the same against her ear.

Diya planted a kiss on his chest. "I know who Alejandro is. What's the matter? Why is your heart racing?"

He started flapping a hand in dismissal and then paused. "Remind me to tell you about Alejandro later, okay?"

Diya nodded, her eyes suddenly stinging with happy tears. He'd listened. He was doing what she'd asked. He was being honest.

"Where was I? Ah, yes, I was tutoring at the center for a few months when, suddenly, an avalanche of kids began to pour in. Pretty soon, I had to rope in friends and colleagues to help out with the classes. Right now, there are close to a dozen volunteers—professors, bankers, lawyers, stay-at-home moms, anyone willing to part with their time really—who are on a weekly teaching schedule."

"How amazing." Diya was suitably impressed.

Krish beamed with pride. "Six months ago, two gentlemen by the names of Ricky Cruz and Jacob Marsden strolled in and asked if the center wanted to be a part of the Outreach School Project. They'd started it two years prior to that, and they were looking for partners. They wanted to expand their operations beyond the few schools they were affiliated with—both mainstream and alternate." He tilted his head down, checking to see if she was paying attention or daydreaming.

"I'm listening," she murmured. "Go on."

"OSP needed an influx of capital to expand it to the next level where it could become a viable industry. They asked if we were interested. I was. I didn't even have to think about it. Darren has been on board from the beginning, too. Rayna has some issues … but that's between them." He pursed his lips but went on, "With the right investments and endowments and nurturing, OSP can reach—should reach its potential. Imagine millions of kids from all over the world, logging in to take classes. With those numbers, it'll make a tidy profit on application fees alone and pretty soon will start paying for itself."

"Again, amazing!" Diya wondered if it had struck him how like his mother he was, even while discussing numbers like his father.

Krish kissed her cheek and then pushed her off him to sit up. "I want to go back to school, too. Get a master's in education, just to solidify the teaching platform."

"You want to go back to school?" Diya scrunched up her nose. She hadn't been able to stomach her first round of schooling. To do it a second smacked of masochism.

"Not your glam, hmm?" He chuckled. Oh, he knew her too well in some ways. "I'm going to practice what I will be preaching and get my degree online."

"Cool," Diya said while her mind flew in another direction. That would mean they could live anywhere in the world, right? *Gah!* They needed to discuss so many things in five days. "Where are you going?" she asked when he climbed out of bed.

"To piss, if my lady permits."

He gave her a naked bow when she gave her permission. How did he not look foolish doing that? Sigh. She had it bad, didn't she?

Momentarily alone, she went over everything he'd revealed about himself and fell a little more in awe of him. He wasn't claiming this was a purely altruistic venture— which would have been fine, too, if that were his goal. No, he was treating it like a business venture. One he hoped would flourish under his hand in more ways than one.

More and more in this overgrown, overachieving world, humanity's future was becoming a question mark. Education was one way to improve the human fate. Leading a conscientious life was another. Too many people disregarded one or the other, and too few adopted both. It was easier to live selfishly and in the present, get on with one's life without any foresight into the future. *Let the ones in the future deal with their problems, for we have plenty of our own.* Insular thinking like that had brought the world to the mess it was in today.

When she spoke of such things to her friends and colleagues, many took it the wrong way. She tried to explain that, to lead a life of moral quality, one didn't need to become the Buddha or a Gandhi. Small bits and pieces of sagacity per individual were enough to freeze the Arctic back to a safer ice mass or feed the orphans of the world.

"Now, there's a sight I don't see often. Beauty brooding," Krish teased, coming out of the bathroom.

Speaking of bits and pieces, she eyed Krish's bits as he got into bed. "Oh, look! Your puppy shame has come out of hiding again." *Enough jabber and disclosures for the day,* she thought, flipping her mood switch to sexy.

"That's no puppy shame, babe. It's the Beast." He roared with laughter at his own joke.

Diya rolled her eyes. "Whatever it is, tell it that it's time."

"Time for what?" Krish wheezed, wiping tears from his eyes.

"Time to rise and shine." She suggestively wiggled her eyebrows. They only had four and a half days left. She wanted to make the most of it.

That set him off again. "We're on a timetable now?"

"Well, more like a contest. We have to beat Leesha and Aryan's record of seven orgasms in twelve hours."

Krish's laughter sputtered to a stop. His puppy shame went back into hiding again.

He collapsed on the bed and covered his face with his

hands. "Christ, Jesus. You can't mention my sister and orgasms in the same sentence, Dee-Dumbs. You just can't."

He blathered on about her triggering his nightmares and being scarred for life and needing to see a shrink and other bullshit until Diya took the Beast firmly in hand. After that, Krish forgot that he even had a sister.

CHAPTER 18

It was time for a reality check.

Yes, there was a diamond ring on her finger, but Diya still couldn't shake the feeling that the engagement was fake. Oh, outwardly, it seemed real enough. It had all the trappings of a valid engagement, like the congratulatory messages from family and friends. Complete strangers tweeting and posting about the happy event and direct-messaging her with their good wishes. Her fan pages looked like an Instagram account of a florist. And their home in Mumbai, her mother informed her, appeared and smelled like the Valley of Flowers. Then, there were the voice mails and the phone calls and the e-mails and ... *everything*.

The electronic world had infiltrated their little Adam and Eve paradise.

Diya found she did not like it one bit. The media still harped about her pregnancy. Although, this time, they weren't snide but more congratulatory toward the expectant, happily engaged couple, wishing them all the very best for their threesome—as in, engagement, marriage, and bundle of joy, all in one year. O-M-jeez! Talk about blinkered journalism.

By Wednesday afternoon, Diya was ready to commit mass genocide on all technology. If there remained no electronic devices connecting the world, there would be no evil.

Krish, never a dummy about her cabin fever, studiously kept her away from sharp objects. He also pocketed her smartphone for safekeeping and then took her out for lunch.

After lunch, he took her shopping. Krish became Romeo to her Juliet—or no, not R and J because they died in the end. Diya didn't want anyone to die. Krish wooed her like Veer wooed Zara in *Veer Zara*; like Ranveer Singh had courted his co-actor Deepika Padukone in real life until she said, "Yes!"

Krish bought her bags full of sparkly things that didn't break any rules in her contract. Some of the presents were utterly ridiculous, like the pair of pink plastic shoe earrings studded with Swarovski. Even her eleven-year-old self would have been embarrassed to wear those. But they made her giggle, just like he'd intended when he wore them. He bought her badass biker boots. Again, they were something she'd never wear in public—ever—limitations in her contract notwithstanding.

"They're not for a public screening anyway," he said with a straight face, his eyes fiery with lust. "Wear them only for me and only with your tattoo."

He was charming her with his teasing and touching and smooching.

He fed her tiny pieces of chocolate and cooked her low-fat meals—and rather well, Diya was shocked to admit. But then he'd been cooking for himself for a good long time. They watched a Bollywood flick or three on the Apple TV, and he sat through all the songs without fast-forwarding them or fidgeting or falling asleep or checking his e-mails.

On two separate nights, they rocked two different nightclubs. They met up with Lovey and her sister, Shayna, and Miguel and a bunch of other friends. He introduced her as his fiancée to everyone. She had to bite her tongue to not contradict him.

Thursday morning, they brunched with the Joneses at their ranch house, where Diya ended up cooking most of the meal with her personal knave acting as the sous chef.

Throughout this courtship, Krish never lost his temper once. No matter what she said or how she dressed or how snappily she behaved. And, instead of soothing her reservations about their relationship, his easy commitment to it only increased the flutters in her stomach.

"It's like you've swallowed a Zen meditation kit and now only ooze out cosmic calmness," she remarked, sipping on a Prosecco and feasting on the fruit, cheese, and bread spread before her.

For heaven's sake, Krish had planned a picnic for them. If that wasn't alien behavior, she didn't know what was.

They hiked through the woods behind the house on Friday afternoon until they found a sunlit clearing for the picnic. The spot was something out of *Snow White and the Seven Dwarfs*. A brook gushed close by, birds chirped and danced, and raccoons skittered over exposed tree trunks, disappearing into their holey homes.

"It's part of my twelve-step program," Krish said, watching her closely.

He'd been trying to steer the conversation toward a serious note the whole morning, but she'd avoided it by flitting from task to task like a bumble bee. They'd poured their hearts out to each other over the last few days. He clearly thought it was time to bare their souls.

Diya kept her expression neutral, but inside, she was properly scandalized by his confession. What did it mean that he was in a program? Was he a recovering alcoholic? She couldn't believe it, wouldn't believe control-freak Menon would ever lose control of himself like that.

"Let me tell you where I met Alejandro." Krish flicked an ant off his backpack, which was still half-full of yummy picnic food. The ant fell on the red-checkered picnic blanket and scrambled off to join its brethren, who were mounting a siege on the half grape that Krish had set aside for them.

She'd forgotten to ask him about the kid. He'd asked her to remind him.

"I met him at an AA meeting. Outside it," he said.

Alejandro had come to fetch his father, who'd lost his license in a DUI. There had been a scene between father and son. Krish didn't give her specifics, but she could guess. There had been lots of scenes between Krish and Chandra Menon, too.

Diya's heart went out to the boys, both of them, Alejandro and Krish, as she listened to the story. Krish had been going to random AA meetings for a couple of years and believed it helped him come to terms with his fears.

"What fears, Krish?" she interrupted. She'd known he was tormented about the past. She'd known he had issues, but she'd never thought he was afraid.

"I'm not an alcoholic," he said. "Not yet. But I could become one. I have the potential for it, the prerequisites, but I'd rather avoid it at all costs."

So would she. And there was her sensible, cautious, and caustic Beast. Frankly, the un-beastly version of Krish freaked her out. She wanted her Beast back. "So, you attend as a measure of prevention and not treatment?"

He gave a slow nod.

"You should stop drinking if it bothers you this much." She'd never understood why he drank every day. She'd asked him a million times.

"It's a test," was his perpetual reply.

His control-freak disorder, she thought. Maybe he needed to be in a twelve-step program for that.

"It is about control, Diya," he said. Of course it was. "About setting limits and living within those limits."

"What happens when you cross the limit?" Why did he test himself this way? What did he want to prove and to whom?

"You were right. I manipulated you to break our engagement nine years ago. I pushed you away because I felt out of control around you. I didn't want you to love me. I didn't think I deserved you. I don't deserve you even now. A good man would stay away from you. Stay the hell away. Clearly, I'm not that good or that strong." His lips twisted in self-loathing. "You have to promise me you'll walk away, if I ever cross that limit. Promise me, Diya." His eyes pinned her in place. They wouldn't let her look away, brush it off. "I won't have you look at me the way my mother looked at my father in the end. I will not be able to bear it."

And there, she had her answers. Why Krish had hurt her, rejected her. Why he wanted her now and on what terms.

He didn't stop there. He didn't just bare his soul; he slashed it open and forced her to examine it.

Chandra Uncle's disease and death had twisted Krish from a laughing prankster to a sullen, humorless boy. He'd loved his father and hated him at the same time. He'd turned the hurt into anger and the fear into recklessness. He'd been hell to reason with and impossible to handle. When his mother had accepted a permanent teacher's position at the school in Pune and decided to put their Mumbai apartment up for sale, he'd said monstrous things to her. He'd flatly refused to leave Mumbai. Savitri Aunty had put aside all her misgivings and her own broken heart and had asked Diya's parents to take Krish in. So, Krish had stayed with them and finished his schooling, and then he'd left India for further studies at her father's prodding. Patiently but firmly, Daddy had coerced the old Krish back.

Not completely though. The carefree boy Diya remembered had had dreams. Larger-than-life dreams of owning a safari in Africa, of becoming a veterinarian and saving the world's animals, and of marrying a pretty girl he could order around and having an offspring or two to spoil rotten.

The man Krish had become, while good, doubted his own goodness. That man kept secrets. He broke promises. He'd promised to come back to India after college. He hadn't. He'd left their home. He'd left them. He'd left her. And never looked back.

Diya reached out a hand and cupped Krish's cheek, forcing him to look into her eyes this time. "I won't make any such promise. I don't need to because I know you. You are a good man, Krish. And you are strong. What you are not is a shadow of someone else's DNA." She sat back and picked up a piece of Gruyere. "If that was all that was bothering you, then *pfft*, it's over. Done. Let's finish this yummy cheese before the ants attack it."

Krish gave a half-perplexed, half-resigned groan. "You amaze me, *desi* girl. You're the strong one."

"Aw, shucks!" she said in a very un-*desi* Texas twang, and they both laughed a little.

But it wasn't so simple.

Diya mulled over his revelations in her head on the hike back home. Krish was silent, too, shooting her nervous glances every so often. Once home, they saw that Maria had come and gone, waving her cleaning wand about, and now the house sparkled like a Sanjay Leela Bhansali movie.

They both went into their respective rooms and ran through their individual bedtime rituals. When she came out of her bathroom, he was waiting by her bed in just his pajama bottoms.

Neither of them smiled. Somehow, another line had been crossed, and all Diya wanted to do was leap back.

She walked forward. He helped her out of her nightshirt but left her panties on at her request. She pushed his pajamas down over his hips, and he kicked them off.

He asked if they could go all the way. He wanted an irrevocable, physical consummation.

"I can't," she lied to him.

"It's been five days. Shouldn't your period be over by now?" he asked, circling her navel over and over with a featherlight touch.

She shivered. "Not yet. I'm still spotting."

"I don't mind," he said quietly.

"I don't think so."

"Tomorrow?" he pushed for an answer, a promise. A commitment.

"Maybe," she lied again, a chill settling over her heart.

Tomorrow was her last day in Dallas, and she was no closer to believing their fairy tale than she'd been on Monday. It felt like a fantastic dream, one she'd wake up from any minute. The situation was scary enough without adding the pressure of her virginity into the mix.

She simply wasn't ready to give Krish full and absolute power over her.

SATURDAY DAWNED, sun-soaked but cold, over the Dallas–Fort Worth metroplex. Despite the chill in the air, Armadillo's farewell hoedown was a honking success.

Krish strode through the packed barnyard, eager to get back to Diya. He'd left her on the dance floor, line-dancing with a throng of people in her biker boots and having a gala time. He'd coaxed her to wear the boots, arguing that what she did in Dallas would stay in Dallas and not make its way into the Turkish *Pomp Adore*. Also, the boots were more fitting for a dusty horse barn than practically any shoe from her wardrobe. She'd agreed, only because she wasn't stupid even if she was *shoepid*.

"Shoepidity," she'd educated him, "is the act of wearing utterly ridiculous shoes because—*come on*—they are incredible."

Apparently, fashion magazines not only showcased fashions and fashionistas; they also fashioned trendy words.

Krish tapped Diya on her brand-new Stetson. In a checkered pink-and-blue shirt and jeans, she blended well into Texas. She spun toward him, fun and laughter dancing in her eyes, and his heart broke a little as he watched her joy. He would never again be the reason she stopped laughing.

Yanking her close, he tilted his head to one side to avoid clashing their hats and kissed her as if his life depended on it. And kept on kissing her. He didn't stop through the wolf-whistles, wisecracks, and applause springing up around them.

Her arms slipped around his waist, and she pressed herself against him. He tasted corn and mustard on her tongue and wondered if she could taste the hot dog he'd just scarfed down. And her scent—sweet and tart with a hint of jasmine—made him shiver. He knew her scent. He was never *not* going to know her scent. Even with the country air saturated with the smells of food and horse, his nose had honed in on her scent.

The song changed to a slow-paced number, and she swayed to the beat. And, still, he kissed her. Softly now.

Last night, he'd thought he'd made a huge mistake, confessing his fears. She'd been too quiet on the hike back. But, no, she'd been quiet most of yesterday and this morning, too. She was having doubts like before. He would erase all of her doubts until all he saw were hearts in her eyes.

Only when it became absolutely necessary to draw breath did he lift his mouth from hers.

She dazzled him with her smile. "What was that for?"

"Stay." It came out like an order, so he softened it. "Don't go. Stay here with me. For two more weeks, and then we can travel to Mumbai together and get married in March."

"Krish." Not just her voice, but her eyes also rebuked him. She removed her hands from his waist and readjusted the angle of her Stetson from askew to jaunty. "I have to be in Istanbul by Monday and then in Mumbai by Friday. The following weekend, I have a show in Dubai, and … I'm sure there's something after that, too."

No, he hadn't imagined it. She'd grown cold feet since yesterday.

"So, you have no time for us? No time to get married? Is that what you're saying?" His heart squeezed with hurt. He wanted to howl in rage.

"We are having a trial engagement, Krish. What's the rush to the altar?"

"You said five days. I've given you five days, Diya. Make up your fucking mind."

They were back to glaring at each other in the middle of the dance floor while waves of people twirled merrily around them. Abruptly, she spun on her boot heel and dodged through the foot-stomping crowd.

He closed his eyes, counted to ten, and went after her.

He'd had it up to his nose with her attitude. Why didn't she just tell him what was wrong? She'd demanded honesty, and he'd given her that. He was trying to be less of a brute, but the more chivalrous he got, the more impossible she got.

Halfway between the line-dancing and the food stalls, he got waylaid by a group of old colleagues and teammates and had to stop and chat as they offered their congratulations and good-byes. He excused himself as soon as he could. He wanted to go home with Diya. But he couldn't yet. There were speeches to be given, toasts to be made, farewells to be said. Krish would give the final speech in honor of Dillo.

He could have sworn, had anyone asked, that he'd be able to spot Diya anywhere, no matter the density of the crowd. The fashion world claimed Beauty Mathur was incomparable, even among her peers, so she should stand out in a crowd, right?

Wrong. He couldn't see her anywhere. His temper frayed at the edges as he searched for her across the barn. Stupid woman couldn't stay put in one place, could she? Always had to hop from place to place, job to job. Man to man.

He kicked up his pace, making a circuit around the dance floor, strung with colorful fairy lights, and the live country band again. He discounted the barbeque and food pavilions because Diya had already eaten and sprinted flat-out toward the family area where there was a little country fair going on. He hopped inside the Moonwalk; Diya was more than capable of bouncing about in there like a toddler. She wasn't in there or on the Ferris wheel. Or at the hair-braiding station. He covered every inch of the hoedown without any luck.

Krish halted by the barn where the women's restrooms were. It was the only place he hadn't searched. But, if he went in there, there'd be a riot.

And then he heard her laugh. The giggly, throaty, musical sound that only Diya made.

Blindly, he moved in its direction. He found her by the paddocks that were separated from the festivities by a line of magnificent live oaks. She was chatting with Jenny, Dillo's wife. Her youngest grandson, eight-year-old Jimmy, and a bunch of other children were riding ponies in the paddock.

Jenny warmly hugged him when he walked up. She'd given him plenty of those today. He kissed her cheek, feeling lost and bereft all over again. He was going to miss the Joneses.

Diya had turned away from him and was watching the young riders. She'd zipped her fleece vest up to her chin. The wind had picked up in the past hour, and it had grown chilly. But he was oblivious to the weather as his blood was running hot because of her.

"Hey, y'all." Dillo's middle son, Jackson, joined them at the paddocks to watch his son, Jimmy, ride the pony. "Hey, Krish," Jackson said after he hooted and praised his son. "Ms. Aya's looking for ya. She's by the stage."

At last, Diya deigned to meet his eyes, but he wished she hadn't bothered. Her glacial expression tried to burn a hole right through his gut.

Krish sighed and accepted that it was just not his day.

IT WAS six in the evening by the time the hoedown wound down.

Despite everything, Diya had had a great time. Dillo and Jenny had been absolutely overwhelmed by the speeches and toasts and tokens of love and admiration everyone had shown them.

"She knows Dillo well, has worked for Armadillo. She had to be there," Krish said as he drove them home.

Once again, they were in the Porsche, pissed off at each other.

"Of course," she said. "Did I imply otherwise?"

"I should have told you she would be there," he went on as if she hadn't spoken. Like he was feeling guilty that he hadn't warned her. "It slipped my mind."

"It's fine." She really didn't want to discuss Aya Ahuja now.

But that didn't stop Diya's brain from envisioning her. Aya was a pretty little thing. "Little" only in height, as she was voluptuous everywhere else. Diya recalled another one of Krish's girlfriends from way back; she'd been short, cute, and busty, too. His type was becoming pretty evident to her. Another reason for the golf-ball-sized knot of panic lodged in her throat.

She was not short, not cute, not top or bottom heavy. She was not his type at all. Not physically, not spiritually, not practically. She believed in God. He was an atheist. She lived in the east, he in the west. She was a good-time girl. He was a sober numbers man. Why did he love her?

"Diya, why are we fighting?" he asked softly.

"Are we fighting?" She was finding it difficult to breathe.

"Why are you behaving this way? What did I do wrong?" He flicked on the indicator, glanced in the rearview mirror, and changed lanes. "Look, it was supposed to be a surprise, but since you're pissed off about it … I plan to propose to you at our engagement party in Mumbai. I'll go down on my knee with roses and tuxedo and anything else you want and beg you to marry me in full view of our families and friends. Okay?"

He thought this was about that? Yes, of course he did. To him, she was a superficial bubblehead, wasn't she? A drama queen. The whole world thought it.

But he should know better. He should know her by now.

She kept her silence. If she spoke, she'd start to cry.

"For God's sake, don't pout."

His temper was fraying. She could tell by the way his fingers tapped against the steering wheel. She got ready for a nasty yelling match, but he said nothing else for the rest of the drive.

She went straight to her room once they got home. Two of her trunks were loaded, locked, and upright. Krish had a huge, roaring fight with her when she started packing the third one.

"I'm asking you to stay for two lousy weeks." He flung his Stetson on the bed, and then he rolled up the sleeves of his cowboy shirt. He fisted his hands by his thighs like a gunslinger, minus the guns.

"I cannot. I have a job, too." She ripped off her cowgirl hat and flung it on the bed right on top of his.

"The world won't collapse if you don't show up to shoot some hair-dryer commercial or attend a designer party," he hurled the hateful words in her face.

"Don't you dare belittle my career," she raged, so she wouldn't cry. "Yes, it panders to the pretentious desires of life, but believe me, you have to be smart and lucky and bloody gorgeous to climb to the top." Oh, she had a lifetime of venom to get out of her system on this one. "I'm insanely good at what I do. I'm at the top of the food chain in my profession, so why the hell would I jeopardize that for two lousy weeks? Do you know … do you have any idea what my hair-dryer and designer-underwear commercials pay me?" She tossed the number out to the numbers man and had the satisfaction of seeing his face go white in shock. She told him what she expected to make from Scheherazade. "That makes me exponentially more successful than you, Krish. More successful than Leesha, Priya, my parents, and probably Aryan combined." She paused, breathing hard. "Or maybe on par with Aryan because he's filthy, stinking rich, too."

She felt sick, talking to Krish about money, so she snatched a dress off the hanger and began to fold it. "It's not about the money anyway. It's about my reputation."

"What reputation?" he asked hoarsely, still shell-shocked by her financial disclosures.

"My reputation as a model, you jackass. I never bow out of my commitments. Never! Not unless I'm dying. Everyone in the industry knows that, once I give my word, that is it."

He went rigid then. "And you haven't given your word to me. You won't commit to me."

Diya balled up the dress she'd folded between her hands. "Krish …"

"You really don't want to marry me," he said starkly, as if it had only just dawned on him. His eyes were huge behind his glasses. Hurt. Angry. Fearful.

She wanted to fling herself into his arms and scream, *Yes, yes, yes, I want to marry you!* She'd done exactly that nine years ago.

"It's not a no," she whispered, her anger fizzing out.

"Okay. Okay, that's good." He took a deep breath and blew it out, his relief blatant. He sat on the bed and patted the spot next to him. "What is this about then?"

She sat down beside him, utterly miserable. "You have this hold on me, Krish. You've had it since I was born, I think. I can't deny you anything. Even when I don't want to do something, if you ask it of me, I always end up doing it. And then I start resenting you for it."

"I don't mean to force you."

She took his hand in hers, palms kissing. "You have never forced me. It's just that I have no backbone where you're concerned. That's one thing. Another is …" She turned to squarely face him. "Where do you see us living together?" She still couldn't say marriage. It still seemed an impossible dream. "Here, right? In Dallas?"

He nodded slowly, wariness still reflected in his beautiful brown eyes.

"I can't live here. What would I do here? I'm moving to Istanbul. Hasaan wants me there two weeks out of every month for the next two years. More, if we decide to renew my contract, which seems highly likely at this point. I've even put in a deposit on a flat there."

Krish removed his hand from hers and stood up.

"Then, there's all the traveling I do—not just for Scheherazade, but also for the other brands I'm in contract with or for fashion shows and ..." She shuddered out a sigh as if she'd just finished an atrocious crying jag. "I have a lot of commitments, Krish."

"What else?" he asked and began pacing up and down the room.

She felt relieved he was listening, actually listening, and not shooting her down. "There will be parties, lots of them. You'll have to escort me to at least some of the major industry events."

She didn't add that he would need to upgrade his lifestyle to match hers. Krish was no dummy. He knew what she meant. Yes, he had money, but he'd already pledged it to the Outreach School Project. He had enough to maintain his current lifestyle, even after that, but if something went wrong, he was prepared to live frugally until his investment paid off, he'd told her. As his wife, he would expect her to live as he did.

Well, Beauty Mathur did not do frugal. As her husband, Krish would have to learn how to live as she did. He would essentially have to live with her, let her foot at least the fashion bills. Would proud, self-sufficient Krish agree to that? She had her doubts.

"I will decide when we have children. Not for two years definitely." She got to the part he would find the most difficult to swallow. "My public image or the lack of it that titillates the world will not magically vanish when we marry. I will still be bitched about, slandered, dissected ... and so will you. There will be rumors and fake news. Can you handle that?"

"I thought—" He choked off the rest of his words and cursed a blue streak.

But she had been ready for that, too. She knew exactly what he'd thought. "You expected me to give up my job, move to Dallas, and merge my life with yours." Her heart wept for him, for herself, for what their choices had done to them. "I would have happily done that nine years ago, Krish. I can't now. I will not now."

"Is this because you think I rejected you?"

Was it payback?

She shrugged. "I don't know."

The girl she'd been loved her Beast to the point of madness. That girl still lurked beneath the strong, shiny shell of the woman she'd become. It was up to him to soften the veneer and get to her core.

It had always been up to Krish to prove his love for her.

a week later, Diya stormed into her Mumbai flat, heading straight for her parents' bedroom on a pair of shoepidly high platforms. When she found the room locked, she banged on the door as if the house were on fire.

"Come out! You interfering, nosy, stubborn old man," Diya yelled at the top of her lungs. She was going to rip Kamal Mathur limb from limb and feed him to the tigers at the Mumbai Zoo.

The door opened, and an older, plumper, sari-clad but no less flawless version of herself walked out. "Oh, you're back. How did the interview go, baby?"

Lubna Mathur was referring to Diya's interview with *Cosmo* earlier in the day—the very interview in which she'd found out just how diabolical her father was. Her mother caught sight of her distraught face, and instantly, sleep vanished from her eyes.

"What's happened? What's wrong?" she asked, feeling Diya's forehead for a fever. "Are you ill? Your face is red."

"I'm going to kill him, and you won't stop me today. How

dare he! How dare he interfere in my business!" She slipped past her mother and into her parents' bedroom.

By then, Kamal Mathur had woken up from his afternoon nap and was sitting up in bed, blinking sleep from his eyes like a wise, old owl. A handsome one at that.

Diya loved her father very much. But he had to die.

"What's this about an engagement party?"

"What about it?" her father asked, yawning noisily. "I've booked the Grand Hyatt for the ninth of March. Krish will be here by the seventh." Her father stood up and stretched. His at-home attire, a cream-colored *kurta-pajama*, was utterly creased.

Diya poked her father hard in his belly.

He jerked in shock and finally noticed her livid face. "Are you okay, baby?"

"No! You have ruined my life," she wailed and flounced away.

"What have you done? Why do you never listen, Kamal?" her mother railed at her husband.

Her father actually had the audacity to look wounded.

"Don't you dare pretend we're the evil ones. You're not even sorry for what you've done," Diya said, clutching her head with both hands. "Daddy, please. Stay out of this. I know what I'm doing with Krish. Don't force me to run away and never speak to you again because I *will* do that if you continue to manage my life. Let me handle this."

"Pray tell me, how are you handling it when Krish says you will decide when the official engagement ceremony will take place, and you say, 'Not now'?"

"It means that the decision is in my hands, and I have decided *now* is *not* the time," Diya bit out through clenched teeth.

"What the hell do you mean by that? If not now, then when?" her father bellowed. "You are thirty years old!"

Diya looked up at the rotating ceiling fan and groaned. It was crazy hot in Mumbai, and she felt the heat and humidity even more after Dallas and Istanbul. The cotton day dress she wore had wilted as soon as she put it on. Thank heavens she'd taken a change of clothes for the interview. She should stick with shorts and tanks for a few days. To hell with fashion in this heat.

"I don't want him at all if you force an engagement on us. Got it, Daddy? You have already messed up everything by your drama. Now, stay out of it."

She pecked her father on his cheek to soothe the sting of her harsh words while he sputtered nonsense about the family name getting dragged through the mud because of her shenanigans. She hugged her mother and sailed out of the room as her father continued to holler threats at her back. The threats, she noticed, were vaguely similar to the ones she'd just issued against him.

"She's mad!" he yelled, his voice stiff with injured, do-gooder pride. "I am helping the idiots."

"They don't need your help," her mother responded with utter unflappability.

"Ha! Without my help, they would never have …"

Diya paused in the doorway of her own room, which lay directly across from theirs. She made a U-turn and stormed back inside.

"Never have what, Daddy? What do Krish and I have between us besides a broken engagement and some family connections? And, now, you've ruined everything by your interference. How will I ever know whether he wants to marry me because he truly loves me or because of the pressure your pathetic blubbering put on him? I won't be anyone's obligation. I won't."

Diya wouldn't put it past Krish to have done just that. To save her reputation, to salvage her family's honor were reasons enough to explain Krish's sudden change of heart. He felt obligated to her father. Each man held the other in the highest respect. Each man filled a space in the other's life that was missing. Daddy had sponsored Krish's education. Yes, Krish had paid Daddy back in full, possibly with interest, but it didn't mean he felt any less indebted.

"Stay out of my life, please." Diya had said those words to her father many times before. This time though, he knew she meant them.

"Didn't you get knocked up by some Arab?"

Diya burped and shot an extremely malevolent look at Shankara Munshi, the utterer of those awful words, before she turned to Leesha in bafflement. "Why is she here?"

"Because, until our mutual client gets a rousing victory in court, Alisha and I are inseparable," Shanky answered in Leesha's stead.

Shanky, a social activist for women's issues and a regular migraine inspirer, had butted into Leesha's home uninvited, like she'd butted into the conversation.

The three of them made a lopsided triangle around the granite coffee table in Leesha and Aryan's eco-friendly apartment that Aryan had designed, sharing *vada pavs* bought from the food vendor below the building. Sprawled on a shaggy white-and-espresso-toned carpet, Diya had gorged on two whole *vada pavs* already and three glasses of prime vino. She was probably going to get zits on her face and a bad stomach because of the fried food, and she'd gleefully lay the tragedy at the Beast's doorstep, too. Diya hadn't spilled her tragic tale yet, not wanting Shanky to bear witness to her patheticness.

"You're exactly his type." Diya examined voluptuous

Shanky up close. The woman was wearing baggy jeans and a jaundice-yellow top. *Ugh.*

Shanky looked oh-so condescendingly down at Diya—only because she was sitting on the sofa and Diya was on the floor. "I'm going to assume you're not talking about my blood type here."

Leesha sniggered but stopped when both Diya and Shanky glared at her.

Shanky was a big-time blood donor, apparently. And a social crusader fighting against sex trafficking. And she raised money for breast cancer through fundraisers.

Now, hold on tight! There was no need to start playing a harpsichord and crowning Shanky's head with a halo. She was no saint. But Diya had to admit, Shanky had balls.

"He totally goes for big boobs, big butt, short women. Your disgusting color coordination in apparel is another tick mark in your favor. Plus, you're kind of pretty. Shave your arms and your mustache, darling. Thread your eyebrows. Get a facial, woman."

Diya blinked, imagining Shanky all well groomed and chic. It was an amazing before-and-after transformation taking place inside her head—a different beast turning into a hairless beauty. Go figure!

"Come to think of it, if you got all spruced up, I'd go for you too. And I'm not even semi-gay," she added.

Leesha burst into guffaws this time and laughed long enough that she started hiccuping. Leesha hiccuped when she laughed too much. *See?* Everyone had problems—big or hiccup-sized or beastly.

"What a vain and senseless thing to say. Can't say I expected any better from the brainless Beauty," Shanky jeered.

She wasn't tipsy at all. And, as Leesha was mostly a teetotaler, she wasn't either.

So unfair, Diya grumbled to herself.

"Let's get back to what I said before your unasked for *tipani* on my body hair. If you're preggers by some man who won't marry you, why not marry Alisha's brother since he's offered to save your ass?" Shanky gazed at Diya as if she were a lab experiment gone haywire.

"If you don't want my two *tipani*'s worth of advice, I don't need yours either. I only take advice from my BFF," declared Diya and looked pleadingly at her best friend. "I'm right, right?"

"About what exactly?" Leesha mumbled, her hand hovering over her laptop.

"Wait," Shanky butted in again. She really had abysmal manners. "Are you pregnant or not?"

Before Diya could fabricate another miscarriage—her eighth one, last count of the media—Leesha enlightened Shanky. "She's not, and she never has been. Let me clue you in on one of the best-kept secrets or best-played charades of the century—Diya is a virgin. Apparently, if a guy cannot make her shiver, then he's not worth sleeping with, and no guy has made her shiver besides my idiot brother, but she won't sleep with him until he morphs into Prince Charming."

In a nutshell and then some.

"What?" Shanky's thick, wormy eyebrows came together in the middle of her forehead. Concentrating on them made Diya's eyes cross.

"Dee's got scruples. Amazing, isn't it?" Leesha grinned like the cat that had swallowed a canary.

Diya burped again, too woebegone to bother shushing Leesha's runaway mouth. "I'll only sleep with him if he really, truly loves me and cannot live without me and not because of some obligation he feels for my father."

"Wait. Your father wants him to sleep with you? That's disgusting."

Leesha shushed Shanky for being stupid and then said, "I don't think Krish feels any such obligation, Dee."

"You're wrong." It was pathetic to be an obligation and not the love of someone's life.

"Is that why you broke it off last time?" Leesha's eyes were like the Beast's—big and brown and just lovely. She didn't have specs though.

"He didn't want me. He wouldn't kiss me," Diya whined, ignoring Shanky's horse-like snort. "And he has … issues."

"Who doesn't?" This from Shanky.

"It's guilt, too." The admission sent a rush of pain through her heart. "I told him I loved him. I told him that I would never marry anyone else because of him. How else was he supposed to react? I practically trapped him into an affair … and I'm not even his type!" Then, she divulged just how far she'd fallen. She told them about the bootie. "I got one for myself, too. And, that Sunday in Dallas, I performed voodoo with it."

Leesha blinked in astonishment. "Come again?"

"Remember the tantric we met in Pune years and years ago? He taught us a chant to make our wishes come true. We had to choose an object of desire, put the talisman at Lord Vishnu's feet, and pray over it. I did all that, and it all came true. Leesha, I've lured your brother into my clutches with a love spell," she wailed, nearly in tears.

For a moment, there was total silence in the room. Then, Shanky started laughing like a hyena, and Leesha hiccuped her heart out. Diya was too heartbroken and distressed to get angry with them. Leesha smacked Diya on her head, calling her an idiot. It was a mean, mean world when even your BFF turned on you.

The hyena gasped, "Oh, please, let me handle this." She grabbed hold of Diya's shoulders and shook her hard. "Idiot woman, are you so desperate to battle some fantasy dragon that you're inventing problems for yourself? Just accept it, Diya. You're a ridiculously lucky individual whose every wish in life has come true. Accept it. Enjoy it. Appreciate it. Be grateful for it. And maybe the world will resent you a little less."

"She's right, Dee. Grab it all and enjoy it while you can. You never know when your luck will change." There was a doom in Leesha's voice that had been missing for more than a year. The pre-Aryan Leesha had been a doomsday predictor, not the post-Aryan one.

Diya stared at her BFF. "What's wrong? What's happened?"

Something was definitely off with Leesha now that she thought about it. Aryan had been moody, too, earlier this evening when Diya barged in on them, all mad because of her father. When Shanky had arrived, Aryan had excused himself to go to the gym, and from there, he'd visit his grandmother and uncle who lived a few streets away. He'd laughingly said that he was happy to make himself scarce, so the ladies could have their little bitch-fest in peace. But his laugh had sounded forced. False.

"Nothing is wrong exactly." Leesha darted a hesitant look in Shanky's direction.

For once, Shanky took the hint. "I see we won't be doing any work tonight, so I'll head home and feed the rats and the cockroaches their dinner. Poor things must be starving." She made to get up, but Leesha caught her arm.

"No, Shankara, stay. It's okay, really."

Diya stared. Since when did Leesha consider Shanky a confidant? Diya's heart burned, but she immediately felt awful for feeling jealous, so she drank more vino.

"We had a consultation with Priya last week," Leesha began.

Diya interrupted her with a whoop. "You're pregnant! I

knew it! I knew the bootie would work." Diya crawled around the table and hugged Leesha hard.

"Actually, it didn't. We went to see Priya because I'm not getting pregnant. She wants us to do some tests. Just some routine tests to see if everything is as it should be. Aryan has freaked out. He's jumped to the conclusion that we're going to have issues conceiving like his parents did after his birth … and what came after."

"Why didn't you tell me?"

Oh, she was a bad person, such a terrible friend. She'd been ranting about her life for the past how many weeks and never once asked Leesha what was going on in hers. And poor Aryan. His mother's fertility problems and manic depression had led to one of the most traumatic events in his life. No wonder he was upset.

"There was nothing to tell, Dee. I have my hands full with Aryan right now. He's not handling it well."

Diya hugged Leesha again. "What can I do? Tell me. What should I do?"

Shanky had sat quietly through Leesha's revelation. But, now, she looked at Diya in approval.

"I don't think I need your womb just yet," Leesha joked despite the tension radiating out of her. "Make him laugh. Distract him, Dee, because I can't seem to be able to. Not even in bed because he's automatically thinking … we both are … whether we're making a baby or not."

"Done. What else?" She vowed to call Aryan up every other hour and harass him. She'd help him shop from Scheherazade's fall collection for men on the tablet. That would cheer him up. He was a clotheshorse, just like her.

Leesha wiggled their joined hands. "The *else* is, don't waste time second-guessing my brother. Trust him to know his own mind. If he says he loves you, then he loves you."

But it wasn't Krish's mind she didn't trust. It was her own heart Diya couldn't trust.

248

*T*hree weeks later, Krish Menon arrived in his birth city against the express wishes of his reluctant fiancée.

Ex-fiancée. She'd ditched him. Again.

He stood for a brief moment outside the Arrivals terminal, basking in the hot, humid, strangely pungent air and the waves of humanity surging in and out of the airport like the tide on Chowpatty Beach.

Usually, his welcome committee was comprised of Amma, Alisha, Vallima, and Diya. This time, only his *aaliyan* —brother-in-law—had come to fetch him, and Krish had to make do with a hearty handshake and manly hug. He found he missed the prodigal-son-returns welcome where two of the four women—usually Vallima and Diya—would fall, weeping, into his arms and berate him for taking far too long between visits.

"Are they all mad at me?" he asked once they were ensconced in Aryan's BMW and the chauffeur—a turbaned sardar named Singh—steered the car out of the airport.

Aryan grinned. "In varying degrees. You should have kept

your mouth shut over the photo, old chap. Not cool. No matter how angry she made you."

Krish closed his eyes as irritation and embarrassment stabbed at his insides. That was the problem in a mostly female household—nothing remained secret for long. And when you brought Beauty Mathur into the picture…

Three days ago, a photo of Diya lip-locked with a mystery man on a yacht had hit the global newsstands, and like any normal jilted fiancé, he'd lost his head.

"Exactly what kind of fashion move prompted you to allow the man to stick his tongue so deep inside your throat that he was licking your navel from the inside?" he'd snarled over the phone.

Diya had responded in kind, and then the fight, the accusations, the need to destroy each other with words had overridden all civility. He'd called her an unfaithful, promiscuous bitch. She'd called him an invidious, lily-livered bastard.

Aryan was right. He should have kept his mouth shut.

Diya's stubbornness to not commit to him was frustrating them both. Didn't she see that?

Krish looked out the window, where vehicle upon vehicle pooled around the Beemer, hampering their progress into town. It was one in the morning, and yet there was traffic on the Mumbai roads, the city that never slept.

Maybe Diya was right. Maybe they were just too different to make it work. She'd warned him what her world would be like. It was his mistake that he hadn't taken her seriously.

Kissing another man had been a test—he knew that now —a test he'd failed.

"What do women want?" he asked aloud.

It was a rhetorical question, the kind a man might throw into the wind, preferably over a glass of whiskey in the dead of night, but Aryan answered anyway, "They want your body first. Then, your mind, your heart, your soul, and finally, your sperm in a cup."

Krish thanked God his sense of humor hadn't left him. "Tiff with Alisha?" he asked, chuckling.

Aryan sighed. Shrugged. "Just one of those married-couple conflicts."

"Unmarried ones get into conflict, too," Krish pointed out with a huge yawn.

He hadn't slept in three days and had traveled eight thousand miles to get there. It was a good thing Diya wasn't in town. He hadn't the energy for a boxing match tonight. She was in Dubai, then Paris after two days, and then she flew to Riyadh for Hasaan's wedding next week.

Krish fell asleep for the rest of the drive and woke up when they reached home. Alisha and he co-owned a flat in a building in South Mumbai. It lay empty now since she'd married and moved into Aryan's Bandra flat.

He followed Aryan into the building, leaving the chauffeur and the liftman to tackle his luggage and bring it up to the flat. It amazed him that, within moments of standing on his home soil, he could readily relinquish the autonomy he proudly exercised in Dallas.

The door to the flat opened as soon as he stepped off the elevator, and the women—*his* women—spilled out.

"Welcome home, big, ugly *sahodharan*." Alisha walked into his arms. She was dressed in a sari and had *sindoor* coloring her forehead and bangles clinking on her wrists—the marks of a married woman.

He took his baby sister's face between his hands and kissed her forehead. "Marriage seems to agree with you, *sahodhari*. You look domesticated," he teased and laughed when she punched his arm.

"I went to the temple with Aryan's grandmother for a *puja*, you atheist," she retorted.

Krish hugged his mother next. "Amma."

He'd blamed her for his father's decline. He'd hated her for a long time, but like Diya, his mother was quick to forgive his transgressions.

Last, he turned to Vallima, and when she fell, weeping, into his arms, his sense of entitlement and homecoming was complete.

Aryan and Alisha left soon, as they both had early starts in the morning. His mother, too, had an early start, driving back to Pune. She'd come to Mumbai only to welcome him home. So, they stayed up, talking for a while.

Krish told his mother everything—about his work, the AA meetings, his fears, and Diya. Amma had plenty to say, too, not the least of which that she was proud of him, thrilled for him, and had complete faith in him. Then, she told him to stop being a fool and go get his girl.

With a load off his chest, Krish slept for twenty-four hours straight. When he surfaced, Vallima pampered him with food and more food, garnished by a bolstering conversation.

"In my eyes, you've never been anything but a prince," she stated.

He visited the Mathurs that very day and told them pretty much what he'd told his mother. He assured them he'd fix things. But, as the days passed, he began to doubt his own story. He grew despondent as Diya sorely tested his mettle. And, finally, a week from the night of his arrival in Mumbai, he cracked.

"What the hell does she want from me?" he asked his sister, charging into the Chawla residence. "I've agreed to every demand she's made so far, so what's the problem?"

Alisha gave him a look only a sister could give a brother—a blend of derision and pity. "I guess she wants you to suffer, my foolish *sahodharan*."

Following Alisha into the living room, he was taken aback by the total lack of chaos on the dining table. No papers, no law tomes, no files, and no laptops, such as he'd seen over the past week. Best of all, no Shankara Munshi with the weird laugh and creepy stare.

"Suffer what? A nervous breakdown? Her idiocies? Believe me, I'm suffering." He shoved his hands into his hair.

"Oh, grow up!" Alisha plopped down on the sofa with a heavy sigh.

There were bags under her eyes, and her cheeks were bloodless from fatigue. It was late. She was in pajamas, and Aryan was in bed already. He felt awful for keeping her up past her bedtime, but he needed answers. If anyone understood Diya's mind, it was his sister.

"Dee is right. You're treating this whole thing like some childish game. You tag her. She tags you. You catch her. She runs off."

"That's not true. I have made every effort to show her I'm serious. And why the hell wouldn't I be serious? Do I look like the kind of man who goes around buying rings for women he doesn't plan to marry?" He paced in circles. He couldn't seem to sit still. His Zen had been shot to hell.

"Don't ask me. I believe you. And, in her heart of hearts, she believes you, too. But, Krish, it's more the why you want to marry her that bothers her."

"But she knows why." He loved her. He told her that every single day—or had until she stopped taking his calls and reading his texts or e-mails.

"I don't think she's convinced of the quality of your emotions."

He sat down and slanted a look at his sister. "A trip to Disney World?"

Alisha ruffled his hair in commiseration. "Afraid not, big, ugly *sahodharan*. She's not six. You will have to battle the imaginary dragon, climb that mountain, leap over oceans, just like any normal prince. Don't look so aghast. Aryan will help you. He's really good with overly romantic gestures."

Krish scowled at his sister but remembered something his mother had told him the other night.

"When I left your father, I fully expected him to come after me and beg me to come back. But he didn't because he had his pride. And I couldn't return because I had mine."

Was that what this was all about? Diya wanted him to prove that he loved her more than his pride, more than his reason, more than love itself?

Krish stood up, reenergized at last. Could it really be as simple as not waiting for her but going after her?

"Go wake your husband, *sahodhari*. I need his assistance."

CHAPTER 21

*I*t'd been theorized that beauty and brains were mutually exclusive charms, and Diya Mathur had just proven it conclusively.

She wasn't just shoepid; she was stupid. Also, her feet were sore from dancing all night in Lady Gaga shoes.

O-M-jeez! If anyone had told her how wild and fun a traditional Saudi wedding could be, she wouldn't have believed it.

Hasaan and Saira's *nikaah* had been solemnized that afternoon, and right after, the parties had started. The men were with Hasaan in a palace a few kilometers away, and the women were with Saira in this breathtakingly beautiful desert oasis in the middle of Ash Sharqiyah, the oil-rich Eastern Province of Saudi Arabia.

Diya bounced about the glitzy ballroom she'd dubbed as Scheherazade's Party Cave and regretted abjectly that she'd been such a bitch and not asked Krish to be her plus-one for the wedding. Not that he would have been allowed in here with her. He would have been with the men elsewhere. But close.

"Diya *jaan*, taking a break?" Saira shimmied up to the wet bar that served only the best champagnes and liquors. She was radiant in an exclusive Scheherazade creation, a beautifully cut, one-shoulder gown in moonbeam white.

"My feet are calling me stupid," said Diya. And so was her head.

Had she really run away from the love of her life because of some stupid fantasy checklist and a little bit of fear? Leesha was right. *Gah!* Shanky was right. Everyone in the whole damn world was right. What did it matter how or why Krish loved her as long as he did?

She had to go to him now. She had to leap into his arms and be his doormat for the rest of her life. She scanned the room where twelve hundred fabulously dressed women partied away as if there were no tomorrow. Not a single one was wearing an *abaya* or a *niqaab*. They didn't need to be veiled; there were no men at the party. But they would all be veiled tomorrow, for their men.

"I have to go, Saira *jaan*," Diya shouted over Bedouin D'Araba's crooning.

Saira grinned and blew her a kiss of complete understanding. Hasaan must have filled her in about the tale of Diya and the Beast.

Diya grabbed a handful of her baby-pink sequined showstopper, hitched it off the floor, and made for the exit. It took her a while to navigate the labyrinth of tables decorated in rose red and gold, where dinner had been served earlier, and the sheer number of women boogying away, but she made it out before midnight. The merriment would go on until tomorrow night. Talk about a never-ending rave.

She ran up the grand staircase to the second floor, too revved to wait for the elevators, and down the corridor of the palace hotel toward her suite at the other end. There was a gang of hotel personnel standing in front of her room; some were giggling while others argued in Arabic. The entire staff at the hotel was female, so the wedding guests could roam about as they wished and not get hampered by custom.

"What's going on?" Diya asked the two women who'd been allotted to her as her personal staff for the wedding.

"Ma'am, there is a man inside your room," Lelah, the older of the two, informed her.

"What?" Was she being robbed? Her things. All her lovely, totally replaceable things were in danger? "Why are you standing here and giggling? Call security."

Diya opened the door a sliver and peeked in. The marble floors, gilded ceiling and fixtures, lush carpets—it all seemed as pristine as when she'd left them. Not ransacked at all. No sign of a robber robbing her things either.

She slipped inside, looked about, and screamed when she finally caught sight of the robber in her balcony.

Not a robber. A gargoyle. The ugly, misshapen creature was hunched over the balustrade with his chin on his fist as if he was thinking. And he was whistling? What kind of gargoyle whistled?

She screamed for help. "Call security, Lelah!"

The gargoyle looked straight at her. Moonlight spilled over his face, and it changed, turning even more hideous as he smiled. Then, he jumped to his feet and walked toward her.

"Babe!" Krish said, opening his arms wide.

Diya yelled even louder. "O-M-jeez! What are you doing here, Krish?"

She ran to him, grabbed his arm, and pulled him inside her room. Quickly, she shut the ornate balcony doors and yelled for Krish to draw the curtains as she ran back to the main doors and locked them tight. They were shut already.

Thank you, Lelah!

She spun around to look at him, her heart prancing like a victorious racehorse. "What the hell do you think you're doing? And what in heaven's name are you wearing?"

He was outfitted in an embroidered suit with a matching headdress like an Arab. He looked ridiculous.

He came. For me!!!

"I was at Hasaan's wedding celebration. Apparently, jeans are taboo at such a shindig." He removed the headdress and threw it in the general direction of an oak wood armchair inlaid with pearl. He didn't stop there. He started removing all of his clothes.

"Damn thing itches," he grumbled. He smelled weird, like rosy-sweet *akhtar.*

Diya was mesmerized by the Beast's striptease. She'd missed him so much.

The banging on the door brought her back to her senses.

"We are in so much trouble by this stunt of yours. You can't be here. This is a female-only palace. If they find you here, they will turn you into a eunuch." She gathered up his clothes and tried to shove them in his hands. "Put them back on. We have to figure out how to smuggle you out of here before they castrate you."

"Don't exaggerate, drama queen," he said, grinning at her in a pair of black boxers with glowing neon-pink lips.

"I'm not exaggerating. There are strict rules of behavior in this country and severe punishments for the infidels."

He dismissed her words with a flick of his hand.

"You are going to be of no use to me as a eunuch. Put your clothes back on!" Diya moaned.

He laughed.

The idiot!

The banging finally stopped. But she still went to check what was happening outside. They were going to hang him for a robber or castrate him as a molester. She was never going to lose her virginity now. Life was so unfair.

Lelah stood guard at the door, but most of the other guards and personnel had dispersed. One other security officer remained. She was talking on the phone. Was she calling the police? Panic was making Diya delirious. Or was it Krish? She was finding it hard to breathe, to think.

Krish tugged her inside and locked the door. "It's okay. Hasaan fixed it, so we won't be disturbed tonight. I can't leave this room until the hotel empties of guests tomorrow evening."

Diya looked at Krish in shock. She couldn't understand what he was saying. What was he doing here?

He drew her to the center of the room. Right above them was an enormous chandelier with a thousand crystal drops bursting with light. The walls and panels around them were carved in intricate frescoes of doves and peacocks and veils of jasmine. Without the clothes, he no longer smelled of incense. He smelled like himself.

Krish raised both her hands to his lips and kissed them one by one. His eyes glittered behind his glasses, love pulsing out of them.

She felt undone. Completely, utterly undone.

She also felt very tall. Her feet throbbed in her Lady Gaga shoes. She kicked them off without taking her eyes off him. The broad planes of his face were relaxed, happy. A thick stubble had erupted across the lower half of his face.

She licked her lips and shivered when his eyes dropped to her mouth.

"So, you were never in any danger? You didn't battle any dragons for me?" she asked because her stomach was bloated even though she hadn't eaten anything all evening—a sure sign of PMS. They didn't have much time.

His eyes gleamed with laughter, but his face grew solemn.

"I will battle dragons for you every day for the rest of my life. I will cherish you, all of you, every day for the rest of my life. I will love every pink inch of you every day for the rest of my life."

The whole world knew she was a big crybaby. She should be wailing by now. But, tonight, she could not cry, did not want to. She wanted to remain clear-eyed to see her Krish, to memorize every expression on his beloved face as he spoke his vows to her.

"I don't care where we live as long as we're together. I will care for my body and my health. Yours, too. I will wear tuxedos and skintight leather pants if you want me to. I will wax my eyebrows and my chest for you ... but I draw the line at a Brazilian. I want babies, lots of them, whenever you are ready. If I falter, I expect you to steady me. If you falter ..." He paused there, his eyes darkening into hard rocks. "If you falter—and by that, I mean, if you ever ... *ever* kiss another man again—I will spank your ass until it is permanently tattooed red," he growled.

He had completely, utterly bewitched her.

He took hold of her left hand and caressed the diamond ring she hadn't taken off since he hustled it on her. On the stroke of midnight, he went down on one knee, wearing only pink-lipstick boxers and his spectacles. He should have looked moronic. He looked simply perfect.

"Princess Diya Kamal Mathur," Krish said loudly and clearly, "will you grant me the honor of becoming my wife?"

"Yes, Krish Chandra Menon, my Beast, I will."

She did not cry even then.

HE TOLD her how their personal fairy tale had come about when they retired to the suite's ginormous bed. They couldn't stop touching, kissing, talking, and cherishing each other.

Naturally, they were naked and beyond ready for the glass-slipper final act. She still hadn't told him she was as chaste as the fabled Snow White. She didn't want him to feel performance pressure or worry about causing her pain. Maybe there wouldn't be any pain. Maybe, by now, her hymen had dried up and dissolved on its own.

"What do you mean, I didn't battle any dragons for you?" He came up on an elbow to frown at her. "I faced the formidable Sheikh Al-Hanna for you. I climbed that flimsy trellis outside and nearly fell off four times before I reached the safety of your balcony. If I'd fallen, I would have broken many bones. Look!" He held up his hand. It had angry red welts on it. "I scraped these raw. And look at my chin where I banged it against the balustrade."

"Aw! Poor baby." She dutifully kissed his chin. "So, you were just going to wait for me to come back to my room? What if I hadn't come until tomorrow?"

He waved a hand at the door. "Hasaan is there with Saira. Apparently, the groom is allowed inside the haloed feminine halls for the reception. He was going to send you to your room under some pretext."

"Clever," she said, impressed by the convoluted planning. A couple more adventures like this, and he'd overtake Romeo and Rapunzel's prince in romance.

"Thanks." Krish buffed his nails on his naked chest.

"Do you know Hasaan has never seen Saira unveiled? He has no clue what she looks like. She told him, if he wanted to see her face, he had to marry her. And Hasaan agreed because he was completely in love with her by then." Diya sighed at the unbelievably romantic story. She'd always known brains could be as attractive as beauty, and now, Hasaan knew it, too.

"It's a good thing she's pretty, or we'd be attending a divorce tomorrow," Krish said in his usual unromantic way.

"Love is blind, you beastly man." Diya poked him on his firmer stomach. He'd kept up his core exercises.

"Of course it is. If it wasn't, I certainly wouldn't have fallen for you," he teased. "You're too tall, too skinny, too beautiful." He squeezed the firm globes of her butt. "Too much of a handful."

"In other words, I'm not your type." Oddly, the thought didn't bother her anymore.

Krish didn't deny her statement. He just smiled like the wicked beast he was.

"I might not be your type. I might be a super bitch. And I've been promiscuous in the past. But, Krish, I have never been unfaithful to you." It was time for the truth, the whole truth, and nothing but the truth.

His smile disappeared. "Diya, I didn't mean—"

"Shush!" She leaned in close and at long last confessed the truth to him.

"What?" He stretched back and peered at her in confusion.

She rolled onto her back and gave him a smoldering smile. "I've been saving all my shivers for you."

"You've never ..." he croaked. His shock gave way to hilarity instead of amorous intent, and he howled with laughter.

"It's not funny, you beast. I tried very hard to get rid of it. It's just that no one—" She broke off as the enormity of what she felt for him hit her again. "There has never been anyone but you, Krish. There can never be anyone but you."

He cupped her face in his hands, and he made her look at him. Their eyes met through the see-through barrier of his glasses.

Then, the Beast said the most romantic thing Beauty had ever heard or read or imagined in her life, "Our fairy tale won't end with true love's kiss, my heart. It will begin with one."

And then he kissed her.

THE LEGEND OF BEAUTY MATHUR
BY M. DIXIE
POMP ADORE

*I*t has been a decade of unmitigated success, both personal and professional, for the former Indian supermodel and brand ambassador for the House of Scheherazade, Diya Mathur-Menon, known popularly and nostalgically as Beauty Mathur.

She was the first Scheherazade, and through her, Sheikh Hasaan Jabbir launched and shot his fashion house straight to the top of its turf, where it has remained ever since. She announced her retirement from modeling the day her two-year contract elapsed, stating personal reasons for her decision.

Fortunately for us, Beauty Mathur did not fade into the night. She transitioned from the front of the runway to its underbelly by heading Scheherazade's design division, once again proving the Mathur-Jabbir combination is a win-win for the world of haute couture. As renowned as she is for her grace, beauty, and winsome nature, her eclectic designs and fashion acumen have made her an international legend to be compared with the likes of Coco Chanel.

"There is simply nothing about fashion I do not understand," she said confidently. And, when asked to comment on her very unusual lifestyle, she did so with a twinkle in her eyes. "My husband and I are like Hades and Persephone. We each get to be doormats for half the year."

Diya Mathur-Menon and her professor husband, Krish Menon, divide their time equally between their castle in Istanbul and their mansion in Dallas with their two cyber-schooled boys, two widowed mothers, a retired nanny, half a dozen dogs and cats, and an Arabian pony. The ex-supermodel will turn forty this year, looks twenty, and is expecting her third child soon.

Those are some impossible glass shoes to fill, but Beauty Mathur fills them effortlessly. Speaking of shoes, she says to watch out for this year's Scheherazade Baby collection. The booties will bewitch you.

The End

ABOUT THE AUTHOR

Falguni Kothari is a *USA Today* bestselling author of "messy love stories" and kick-ass fantasy tales that are a "good choice for women's fiction book groups." Her novels are all flavored by her South Asian heritage and expat experiences, and delve into common, yet unconventional, themes of marriage, romance, friendship, family and parenthood. Her books have been reviewed and praised in a number of podcasts and publications, including *The New York Times Book Review*, starred reviews in *Booklist* and *Shelf Awareness*, *Popsugar*, *Woman's World* magazine and *The Times of India*. Her essays and short stories have been published in *Femina* (India), *Better Homes and Gardens*, *Book Riot* and *Writer's Digest*.

She is also an award-winning Indian Classical, Latin and Ballroom dancer, practices karaoke in her downtime, is an empty-nester, and loathes flying and deadlines.

Find her online at www.FalguniKothari.com where you can sign up for her newsletter for the latest updates and two free short stories.

ACKNOWLEDGMENTS

Being a writer is a tedious, lonely thing sometimes. At other times, my life is full of wonderful, helpful people and it's those people I want to that.

Thank you to Jovana Shirley, who helped me edit and proof and polish this book.

Thanks to Kate Tilton, my assistant, for her hands-on availability and ability to find me any and all answers that I need.

To some amazing authors and friends, who give me their ears and eyes whenever I wish. Shilpa Suraj, Aarti Raman, Sudesna Ghosh, you are my morning chai.

To my mind, body and soul consultants, Komal, Pallavi and Trupti, my day doesn't work without you.

To my family, my endless gratitude for taking care of the home front so I can hibernate in my writing cave at any and all odd moments of our life.

Lastly, and always, a huge thank you to my readers. This is all for you.

Love,

Falguni

www.ingramcontent.com/pod-product-compliance
Lightning Source LLC
Chambersburg PA
CBHW050830190726
48286CB00007B/2031